ALSO BY ALAN LIGHTMAN

Origins

Ancient Light

Time for the Stars

Great Ideas in Physics

Einstein's Dreams

Good Benito

Dance for Two: Selected Essays

The Diagnosis

Reunion

A Sense of the Mysterious

The Discoveries

GHOST

GHOST

ALAN LIGHTMAN

Pantheon Books, New York

Copyright © 2007 by Alan Lightman

All rights reserved. Published in the United States by Pantheon Books, a division of Random House, Inc., New York, and in Canada by Random House of Canada Limited, Toronto.

Pantheon Books and colophon are registered trademarks of Random House, Inc.

Library of Congress Cataloging-in-Publication Data

Lightman, Alan P., [date]
p.   cm.
ISBN 978-0-375-42169-3
1. Psychological fiction.   I. Title.
PS3562I45397G48 2007   813'.54—dc22   2007005298

www.pantheonbooks.com

Printed in the United States of America
First Edition

2   4   6   8   9   7   5   3   1

This book is dedicated to
Vanna, Phally, and the young women residing in the
Harpswell Foundation Dormitory for University Women
in Phnom Penh

GHOST

I SAW SOMETHING.

I saw something out of the corner of my eye.

It's been a week, but I still have that awful image in my mind. It burns. I close my eyes, and I see it. I open my eyes, and I see it.

But . . . where are the words to describe it?

I feel nauseated. I stare at the glass of water on my desk, wanting to drink. I stare at the glass of water. The flat top of the liquid looks so strange to me now, a silver ellipse, quivering like my stomach, trembling with each tiny vibration—my nervous foot tapping on the wood floor, a voice in the next apartment, my breath.

I need to settle myself. I haven't slept well for a week. In bed, I lie awake and think. My hands are shaking. I can barely write. Now I'm looking at my hands, wrinkled yellow skin, veins crossing and branching. I feel dizzy. I can't look at my hands anymore. Where can I rest my eyes? I see a pencil, stubby and blunt like a dull knife.

How can something happen that isn't possible? I don't know. Black is white. White is black. Up is down, down is up. Perhaps I imagined it.

I think that I saw something impossible. Am I crazy? I'm not crazy. Let me calm myself and figure out how to say this. I'll pick up the dull knife of a pencil and write.

For breakfast this morning, I had a fried egg and two slices of dry toast, like anyone else, what little of it I could keep down. Before that, I shaved. I dressed. What else can I say? Just at this moment, I'm sitting at my desk by the window. I can look outside and see the street in front of my apartment building, children kicking a red ball back and forth, houses, mailboxes, garbage cans, a glass bottle in the grass, a laundry line with damp clothes draped over it. Isn't that just normal life? Or I could turn around in my chair and look at my room. I'll do that. I see a bookshelf and books, some wedged in sideways. I see my bed, half covered with the quilt my ex-wife gave me. I see a standing brass lamp with a crooked linen lampshade. A box of crackers on the table, cracker crumbs. A glass of water on my desk, this pencil, this pad of paper.

The Pythagorean theorem, I still know: The square of the hypotenuse equals the sum of something or other. It has to do with the sides of triangles. Would a crazy person at age forty-two be able to remember anything about the Pythagorean theorem?

I'm beginning to feel dizzy again. The nausea comes in heaving cartwheels. My hands. I can't write. I should just breathe slowly. Breathe. Breathe.

Let me read what I've written. Okay. My eyesight is good. I mention eyesight because I think I should list all the relevant factors. You see something weird, and, of course, the first thing you question is your eyesight. Or your mind. I want to put down in writing what I can. I've tried to tell a few people, but I can't find the words. Even now, I can't find the words. Ellen suggested I write it down. I'm not sure what she thinks, whether she really believes me. We were having dinner at her favorite Indian restaurant, she flirting with the waiter as she always does, half trying to make me jealous and half just being herself, and she held my hand after I told her and said I should write it down.

Where was I? My eyesight. When I go to the optometrist for my biannual examination, I can read the bottom row of letters on the chart. As a child, I was always the first one to spot the school bus coming. I could see the tiny yellow speck in the distance, just the smallest glint of yellow. My friends thought that I was cheating, that what I really saw was the cloud of dust trailing the bus, but I saw the tiny yellow dot. I'll admit that I've never needed such good eyesight for any practical purpose. My books have regular-size type. When I worked in the bank, the numbers were never so small, but I could have read them if they had been.

My hearing is also good. When I saw what I saw, I didn't hear anything unusual. I have no recollection of any sound at all, aside from the ticking of the clock in Martin's office.

And I don't think I'm at all . . . how should I put it . . . *suggestible.* I believe that's the word. Never in my life have I been suggestible. At a party years ago, a hypnotist tried to put me under and failed. He said I was not "suggestible," and then he looked at me as if I were a man unable to fall in love. If I could travel back to that party years ago—I think I was in my mid-twenties—I would tell that guy and everyone else that I am happy not being suggestible. I prefer seeing the world as it is.

I feel slightly better. I managed a sip, and I am holding it down. Breathe.

Now my head is beginning to boil. And the cartwheels are flying again. I wish I hadn't seen what I saw. I want the world to go back to where it was a week ago. The thing lasted only a few seconds. A few seconds. Why can't those five seconds be smudged out and erased? What is five seconds in the space of a year, or even a day? I must have imagined it. I caught it only out of the corner of my eye. Just a brief hovering thing in the corner of my eye. What was it? Where are the words to say what it was? The thing looked so real, as real as my handwriting at this moment. Could I imagine something so real and so bizarre at the same time? I was feeling fine that day. I wasn't having headaches or eye problems or strange thoughts. My mind was clear. That morning, I arrived at the mortuary at nine, as usual. I made some phone calls to locate a death certificate, I met with Martin, I helped a family pick out a casket. And then, in the late afternoon, in the slumber room, that's when it happened.

I don't believe in supernatural phenomena. I don't believe in magic or hyperkinesis or spirits. When I was a child, my aunt told me that the seasons are needed for plants to grow, and that the sacred Spirit of All Living Things re-creates the seasons each year. With all due respect to my aunt, the seasons are caused by the tilt of the Earth. The Earth is just a big ball of dirt out there in space, and it happens to have a tilt to its axis. It's a proven fact. Eons ago, some meteor hit the Earth by accident and cocked it over at an angle. In summer, the Earth's axis points toward the sun, making us hotter. In winter, it points away from the sun, making us colder. What could be more logical? Cause and effect. No tilt, no seasons. It's physics, or whatever. It's like the Pythagorean theorem.

I'm exhausted.

What? What? How long did I nod off in my chair? I should look at my watch on the bureau, but what does it matter. Time has passed. The shadows have moved through the room. I'm just writing down everything that comes into my head. It's something to do. I should go out for a walk, call Ellen, anything. Somewhere in my apartment there's a novel I would finish if I could bring myself to read. It's a novel by a Japanese writer about an umemployed man who sits at home all day and gets pornographic phone calls from strange women. It rained Friday. I came home from work, walked next door to the diner, and asked Marie to bring me some hot tea. Then I just sat at the window of my apartment and watched the sheets of rain falling outside. I didn't go out for supper. It was raining too hard, considering that my galoshes have holes in them. Some of the tenants ventured out and returned laughing and sneezing and dripping pools of water by the front door. Marie, bless her heart, stayed late to make sandwiches for us housebound tenants. She personally brought over the food and delivered it to each person's apartment, humming some show tune.

Marie often stays late at the diner or here in the apartments, even though she has her own family to take care of—a bedridden husband with multiple sclerosis and a grown son who gambles away all his money and lives at home. Occasionally, her son comes here, knocking on doors and asking for a loan. Just a one-week loan, he says. He has a sad face, and he always tells a heartbreaking story. Then Marie chases him off, he begins screaming at her, she screams back at him. From time to time, I do give him a little money.

Voices trickle in from the hall. Henry. George. Raymond. Someone else I can't place, a new tenant. Most are middle-aged men like myself, single, living on moderate incomes. A few younger guys, trying to save. A few women and married couples. Although I've been here for several years, I still don't know any of the other tenants well, certainly not as friends. We see one another at breakfast. We pass in the hall, or at the laundry in the basement. I've come to realize that I don't want any friends here. I've had friends in other places and at other times of my life. To be honest, I don't mind being alone. I read. Something changed after Bethany left me. I wanted to be alone. I hate living alone, but I want it at the same time.

I'm just writing. It's something to do. I don't even know if everything I write is true.

I've got to hold my burning head very still. Or I should lie down. Perhaps Marie can get me an icepack for my head. But I shouldn't burden her with another task on her day off. Today she should be home with her family, or at church. Early this morning, she came into the lobby downstairs wearing a beautiful dress and pink high-heeled shoes and said that she was on her way to church but just wanted to stop by and "tidy a bit." That was hours ago, and she hasn't left. I can hear her singing in the hall. Marie truly seems to enjoy the place, all the more so because it used to be a rambling old house, with a sitting room downstairs, and she says it has a "coziness" to it.

Marie believes in the supernatural. When I told her what I saw, she replied that she wasn't surprised, with my working in a mortuary. She said that spirits remain in the body for three days after mortal death. And she spoke the word *mortal* with an emphasis. Marie believes that she has received certain signals from her dead mother, such as odd chirpings of birds and doors suddenly opening by themselves. She reads the astrologer's report in the newspaper.

Logic, I should say to Marie. But I don't want to upset her. Marie has been extremely kind to me, and she earns very little for her long hours. But I want her to understand. Cause and effect. The tilt of the Earth. Am I repeating myself? I want to say to her: Logic is what holds it all together. Without logic, anything could happen. People could turn into frogs. The Moon could suddenly fly off into space. If one illogical thing happens, then a million illogical things can happen. The entire world might come apart piece by piece, like when you pull a stray thread on the sleeve of your jacket. The fabric starts to unravel. And once it starts to unravel, nothing can stop it. First the sleeve comes undone, then the shoulder, then the lapel.

Marie has been asking questions about what I saw at the mortuary. Yesterday morning at the diner, she came over and sat next to me and she said, "You've been chosen." I realize now that I shouldn't have told her anything. "I imagined it," I said to her. Maybe I did imagine it. "No, you didn't," she said quietly. Then she asked me to take her to the mortuary, to the slumber room. I shouldn't have told her anything.

I feel ill. I'm not sure anymore what I know and don't know. It's Sunday. Yesterday was Saturday. I should go out for my walk by the lake. I should visit Ellen, do something. But my hands are shaking. I'm going to lie down.

AS HE PRESSES THE BUZZER in front of the discreet two-story building, he realizes that he has never set foot in a mortuary in his life. Mortuaries repulse him. And now, at age forty-two, when most men have comfortably settled into their professions for the duration, he stands in front of this house of the dead, hoping for employment.

A tall woman opens the door. Despite her tailored wool suit, she is quite unattractive, with spidery red veins on her ears and an angular jaw. She seems annoyed, as if he has disturbed her from some urgent business. After a wordless examination, her gaze crawling over him, she tells him to follow her to the sitting parlor. He begins to explain his situation. "Oh no, don't talk to me," she says with a vague smirk. "I'm only the receptionist. The director will speak with you in a while."

He hesitates in the hallway. "I can come back at a more convenient time," he says. "I have other business I can attend to this morning." He has lied. He has no other business. And no other establishments in the area have job openings. In fact, there have been no openings for months. For months, he's done nothing but read. He's read all seventy-one chapters of Gibbons's *Decline and Fall of the Roman Empire.*

"Do as you like," replies the receptionist.

Uneasily, he lowers himself onto a beige-colored sofa. The sitting parlor is softly lit and pleasant-smelling, but without any windows.

The furniture shows considerable wear. The fabric of the sofa appears faded and tired, the arms of the embroidered wingback chair beginning to fray. The carpet is thin. On the antique coffee table is a vase containing a single white orchid, a box of Kleenex, and a volume of William Blake poems.

For a moment, the receptionist stands in the parlor, hands on her hips. Then she returns to her desk in the room across the hall, leaving her door open. While he waits, he can see her glancing over at him every so often. What an unlikable person, he thinks. Probably unmarried.

The parlor is silent. He listens for sounds, expecting to hear the director talking in another room or perhaps the rattle of some grim equipment in the bowels of the building, but the only sound he can hear is the faint tapping of keys from the receptionist in the next room.

Absently, he thumbs through a magazine about birds. Then, in the quiet and the low light, he leans his head back on the sofa. As he has done so many times in the preceding months, he reviews the preposterous event of losing his job. For nine years, he worked in a prominent bank. And for all of that time, he had surely been one of their most useful and loyal employees. Not that he ever achieved a high rank or salary. That was never his ambition. He was content, in fact more than content, with a job that offered him new things to learn. While employed at the bank, he studied economics and business. He read *The Wealth of Nations*. When new investment opportunities presented themselves to the bank, he would research the fledgling businesses, work up the figures, and present his recommendations with enthusiasm.

Most important, he was skilled at his job. Since grammar school, he had been very good with numbers. Other people had their own talents. His happened to be numbers. Several years ago, he had even received a commendation from the manager for his proposal of a new method to assess certain risks.

And then, three months ago, without warning, he received a notice that he was to be let go. No explanation offered, except that the bank was being "reorganized." What did that mean? It was doublespeak. He had lost his job for no reason at all. One day he was receiving commendations for his brilliant ideas, the next he was fired. And the nearest similar job to which he could apply was four counties away, even farther from his mother.

He opens his eyes and stares at the cream-colored ceiling. Most likely, his math skills will go wasted here. The small advertisement said only that there was an opening for an "apprentice." What would an apprentice at a mortuary do? he wonders. Would he ferry corpses on a trolley from A to B? Would he assist in the embalming? Would he drive a hearse? In his mind, he pictures himself weaving in and out of traffic behind the wheel of a large black car, a casket in the back sliding this way and that.

He vows to himself that he will remain here only long enough to find other employment. It is purely a practical matter, a matter of financial necessity. In fact, he will not even tell his mother about this temporary inconvenience. For years, he said to his mother that he was the manager of the bank. He sees no harm in this slight fabrication, since it makes her happy and proud. His mother never pries into his life. Not once has she asked to see his small rented apartment. She's never asked how he spends his evenings or weekends. When he and Bethany divorced years ago, his mother never asked a single question. She only smiled sadly and said that she wished he'd had children. He too regrets that he never had children. Twelve years he and Bethany were together.

Lately, he has begun to think a great deal about the path of his life, about his mortality, about the fragility of the world. It is all such a tenuous thread. Harry Milken, his best friend from school, has an attractive and clever wife, two children, a lucrative job as a law partner advising corporate transactions. Every year at Christmas he receives an inscribed photograph showing Harry and his family standing in front of their mansion with its winding graveled driveway and exquisite gardens. Many times Harry has invited him to visit, but he cannot bring himself to go. He doesn't know what he would say.

He was always as capable as Harry. Even more capable, in some respects. In school, he tutored Harry in mathematics, patiently going over Harry's uncomprehending mistakes. "Math is like broccoli," Harry said. Harry always compared things to vegetables without explanation. After athletic events, the two of them lay sweating on their backs, under a tree, and stared at the clouds drifting slowly overhead. On weekends, they went to the same parties and met the same girls. They were both considered good-looking and bright. It was so humid and close that evening in the cloakroom of a club, well after midnight, the two of them drunk and sprawled on the parquet floor, Harry trying to explain to his pretty date why he couldn't take her home, the girl's lipstick smeared, Harry apologizing to her and to David, and then, for some reason, tears suddenly in his eyes. That moment another thread. And then. Twenty-odd years slipped away. How had it happened? Surely, a critical decision must have been made at some point, sending their lives hurtling in different directions, but what was it? Perhaps it was only a small decision, perhaps only a single word, or a glance. And now Harry has his mansion and his wonderful family. While he, David, has a rented apartment, a termination notice from a mid-level job, an ex-wife who doesn't answer his letters, a string of half-hearted romances. Evidently, he made some unwitting miscalculation. And Harry has been oblivious. Intending no harm, Harry sends him the Christmas photograph each year, as happy in the photograph as if he's just discovered another tax dodge. Some Christmas, David should send Harry a photograph in return, an inscribed photograph of himself in his pajamas sitting on the shabby gray carpet in his rented apartment. At the thought, a smile crosses his face.

He does not begrudge Harry. Harry deserves what he has got. In his bumbling way, Harry was always far more ambitious than David. Let Harry keep all he has got. Let the ambitious rule the earth.

And he will not feel sorry for himself, because others are less fortunate. He has a decent apartment. He has some money in the bank. His landlady owns a diner next door, where he can get his meals without having to cook. Every week, he takes a long walk around the lake near his house, takes out books from the library.

It is just that he is searching for something, while Harry is not. Perhaps that was the unwitting miscalculation. Or maybe it was not a miscalculation. He is searching for something, although he doesn't know what it is. At moments, once every few years, he has a brief sensation of almost grasping it. A particular shape of the clouds, an unusual sound, a movement in the distance, will trigger the experience, and, for a moment, he feels something big, a flash of some totality, some grand sweeping thing like ripples moving out from a stone thrown in the lake. The whole heave and tramp of it. The sensation is not pleasant. A ringing in his ears. A weightlessness. And then, in an instant, he awakens and shudders.

Slowly, his eyes follow a crack in the ceiling. Then, in the midst of his thoughts, a voice leaks from the hallway. The director appears.

"Please," says the director, standing tentatively at the door. "I hope I didn't startle you. It's so quiet here. We like to keep it that way. You are Mr. David Kurzweil, inquiring about the . . ." The director doesn't finish his sentence, as if it would be vulgar to mention the job opening.

"Yes." He pinches his leg to rouse himself from his musings and quickly stands up from the sofa. "Yes, I am interested in the apprenticeship." He reaches out and firmly grips the director's hand.

The director is a short, overweight man with white hair and milky eyes and a kindly smile. His jacket, far too small for his lumpy body, strains at its single brass button, allowing the white shirt to billow out underneath. "You will have met Martha at the door," says the director. "The receptionist." He pauses. "Martha has a brusque manner, I'm afraid." He gives a little laugh and scratches his face with his thick fingers. "I apologize for that. But she is good at what she does, and she's been with us for fifteen years." The director waits, as if expecting a reply. "I hope she didn't put you off."

"Not at all," David says. A despicable woman.

"Good. Good. I try to talk to her about her manner, but there's only so much I can say. She's been with us for such a long time." The director leans down and straightens the bird magazine on the table. "I see from your résumé . . . Can I call you David? Please call me Martin. I see from your résumé that you've lived in the area for some time. It's a beautiful part of the country, isn't it. My wife is a birder, and you would be amazed at the species she's identified just in our little neck of the woods. She sends each sighting off to some organization and gets a certificate back. If I had a dollar for every certificate she's got . . . Do you have family here, David?"

David shakes his head no. No one except his mother, two hours away, and a sister even farther. Then he recounts a few details of his life, his father's death at a young age, his education, the places he's lived. While he is talking, his eyes are drawn to the white orchid on the coffee table. How lovely it is, sitting all by itself.

The director gently glides to the subject of David's previous employment and looks at him sympathetically as David describes the circumstances of his termination. "It was a shock," says David.

The director nods. "I took the liberty of calling them earlier today," he says. "The bank. They said you had been an exemplary employee."

"Perfect," David says bitterly. "Then why . . ." Not wanting to complain, he says nothing more.

"It must have been very upsetting," says the director. "Out of the blue, for no cause. They'll be sorry, I'm sure. Life isn't fair, certainly not on the outside. And here you are, talking to us. Their loss, our gain." The director smiles and sits down for the first time, taking the wingback chair next to the sofa. His jacket appears as if it will burst. There is something familiar about this man, David thinks to himself. What is it? The way that he smiles? The way that he sits in his chair? He can't place it. Something.

"Do you know the poetry of William Blake?" asks the director.

"I know who he is. I'm afraid I can't recall any particular poems. My mother read poems to me when I was a child, but she read only what she liked."

"Ah. You'd remember. A poet of great delicacy. Great delicacy." The director lightly closes his milky eyes and recites,

> Little Fly,
> Thy summer's play
> My thoughtless hand
> Has brush'd away.

Am not I
A fly like thee?
Or art not thou
A man like me?

"Such delicacy and simplicity, don't you think?" He pauses. "This room is where people should be soothed. People who come into this room are distraught, and they need soothing. That's why I keep the little book of Blake poems here. For people to read. It was given to me by my father, and he was given it by his father."

"Yes, it is a very soothing room." Indeed, David is beginning to feel soothed, less anxious about his unemployment, less anxious about the unsatisfactory condition of his life. He leans back and allows the sofa to envelop him, and he gazes at the white orchid.

"I'm glad you feel that," says the director. "We like to think that our funeral home is . . ." He hesitates, searching for the right word. "Comforting. We want people to be comforted here. There's so much trouble in the world these days. East versus West. Fundamentalists versus moderates." He stops and looks up, watching David's reaction. "You understand what I am referring to?" David nods, puzzled by this interesting but strange turn of the conversation. The director is an odd duck. "Savage attacks against innocent people. By both sides." Again, David can feel the director studying his face. "The outside is dangerous and uncivilized," says the director. "Uncivilized. There is much unrest, outside. That's why we feel fortunate to be here. Inside."

These last words seem like distant echoes in vast canyons, for David is struggling to combat his drowsiness. The room is far too close and warm. And it has no windows. He is beginning to sweat in his suit. He can feel the unpleasant moisture in his armpits. What was that last thing the director said? "I agree with you," says David, straining, then remembering the line of thought. "But I wouldn't necessarily say that because the world is dangerous it is uncivilized. As I remember, ancient Rome was brutal and highly civilized at the same time. It depends, I think, on what you mean by civilized."

The director smiles with satisfaction. "You're a man I can talk to." He takes a sip from a coffee cup that Martha has noiselessly delivered. "The outside can do what it wants," he says. "Let them make trouble for themselves. Here we create our own . . . world. We are all one family here, David. We create a space where grieving families can be comforted. And where we can be part of the process. It is a natural process, death. Death is a part of life. Look around you. In time, everything you see will be gone. This sofa. This building. The trees. Everything. That is the nature of things. In some way, I think we prepare ourselves for our own deaths by helping our clients. Does that make any sense to you? I hope that I'm not being too . . . morbid. Our highest priority, of course, is helping the families who are saying the final good-bye to their loved ones, sending them off. In peace. In safety." The director pauses, looking slightly embarrassed. "Sometimes I don't say things in the best way. My wife tells me that the less said about these matters the better. She has a degree in management, you know." He shifts in his chair. "If I can be straightforward with you, David . . . we usually hire people somewhat younger than you for our apprenticeships. I know that I shouldn't be saying that, but it's true." He smiles, revealing yellow teeth. "But age does bring its advantages."

"I've worked a long time," says David, "and I take my employment seriously."

"I sense that," says the director. He takes a pen from his pocket and lets out a sigh. "Some people have qualms about working in a funeral home. They have ideas about what we do—some true, some not true. It's a profession, like other professions. We are professionals here. But we are also part of the community. We personally know almost all of our clients, or their relatives. This funeral home has been in my family for four generations. I grew up in this house. The essential attitude is respect. That is what my father told me when I was learning the business. Respect. We treat the grieving families with respect. We treat the remains with respect. A human being has dignity and should be treated with dignity at every step of the way, including the last step."

"I have to admit something, Martin," David says. "I've never been in a mortuary before. I want to be honest."

"Funeral home. That's the term we prefer. Mortuary is too . . . you know." The director smiles again. "Don't worry. We recognize that our place here takes some getting used to. At first, you will be what we call a runner. You'll retrieve death certificates and burial permits for us. We're not allowed to take possession of the remains without a death certificate. Ophelia, our other runner, will show you what's involved. Later, we'll begin training you in other matters. Robert can help with that. Robert is another apprentice."

It appears that the director has just offered David the job. With a touch of concern, David wonders how many applications the director has received. Martin stands, takes out a piece of paper, and writes something down. "I have an instinct about you, David. I'd like to show you the facilities."

When he stands, David feels sluggish. The room is suffocating. He needs to go outside for fresh air, but the director is already walking ahead, leading him and talking over his shoulder. "The old part of the house," he says, running his hand along one of the walls. "There was a fire forty years ago. You can still smell a burnt odor if you put your nose close to the wall. I remember how we all had to move out and live in a hotel for three months. The food was awful, but we were afraid to complain because they gave us a good rate. There were eleven of us, counting my older brother and his family. He's gone now. After the fire, all the rooms were rearranged. Can you smell it?" David leans over and sniffs, detecting something ancient.

They go to the casket room. A dozen caskets are displayed in horizontal shelves like bunk beds in a dormitory, some as beautiful as fine pieces of furniture. Urns for cremations sit on another shelf. "Everyone has different tastes," says the director. "Some clients just want a simple pine box, and we give that to them if that's what they want. Others want a Rolls-Royce. We let the clients tell us what they want. And we sell all of our caskets only a little above our own costs. The corporate funeral homes overcharge on the caskets. They also cut corners. They use cheap, disgraceful materials for embalming. We don't work like that here. You'll see."

Next door is the slumber room, a large space with heavy draperies, a tattered carpet on the floor, two dozen chairs, a smell of perfume. On the walls are paintings of the English countryside, complete with hunting dogs and merry riders and horses leaping over fences. It is here, the director explains, that the families and friends can view the remains.

"I'm taking too much of your time," says David. In fact, he is ready for the interview to end. Although Martin is gracious, David doesn't care to see more of the mortuary today. He's perspiring and tired, and he's thinking of getting some hot tea from Marie and sitting in his reading chair with his new book.

"Oh no, no. You must come with me to the back and see our

horse-driven hearse. My great-grandfather drove Mayor Thaddeus Slatfield to his burial in that hearse."

Outside, behind the garage, surrounded by weeds, is a rusting black carriage lying on its side. Its great spoked iron wheels and harness rods stick out like the legs of a downed elephant. "It still smells of horses," says Martin. "We have photos of it in use."

David stares at the carriage and nods. "I'm really taking too much of your time," he repeats as they walk back into the building.

"Not at all," says Martin. The director looks at his watch. "Just now I need to meet a family in the arrangement room. Did I take you to the arrangement room? It's just next door, adjoining the sitting parlor. But Ophelia will show you the rest of the facility. You'll like her." The director holds out his hand. "We're a family here, David."

A few moments later, Ophelia appears, a chunky young woman with round cheeks and fire-engine-red lipstick. She wobbles a bit in her high-heeled shoes, which look like pure torture to David. He smiles at her, wondering whether she likes her job at the mortuary, whether she always wears such bright lipstick. "So, I'm to show you around," she says after the director has left. "I didn't get shown around until a week into the job. Martin thought I wasn't serious." Ophelia grins at him. "Did you notice that he always kept his left side to you? He's deaf in his right ear. Everyone knows." She takes David boldly by the arm and leads him to the hallway.

"If it would be all right with you," he says, "I'd like to go home for the day. I'm not feeling . . . I could come back tomorrow."

Ophelia makes a clownish face. "No way. Martin said to show you around, and that's what I'm going to do. Let's go downstairs. That's the interesting stuff." She looks over her shoulder. "I hope

Martin hires you," she whispers. "He usually hires stupid boys who come here just to see dead bodies. Then they leave after a few months. Rick was better, but he left to get married. Everybody gets married except me." She sighs. "But it's a good thing Rick left, because then we got Robert."

"Martin says that I am going to be a runner at first."

"Boring," says Ophelia. "You have to chase down the death certificates from this place and that. Sometimes, with the unattended deaths, you can't get the death certificate right away, and everybody freaks out. The family freaks out. The M.E. freaks out and yells at you. People are so rude. I prefer not going out if I don't have to. It's nice here. Martin takes good care of us, and he's sweet, although he doesn't pay us hardly anything. Jenny—that's Martin's wife—does the money. She handles all the business stuff. Maybe you'll get more. You're going to be an apprentice. I want to be an apprentice, but Martin won't let me."

They walk down a narrow staircase, Ophelia's heels clacking on the wood steps. The walls are plastered with photographs of birds. "You're looking worried," says Ophelia. "Don't worry. Not everyone is weird who works in a funeral home." When they have descended to the basement, they enter the holding room, a small area with two metallic racks and a drain in the floor. "This is where the remains come first," says Ophelia. A sloping concrete ramp angles upward from the floor, goes across the hall and up through a long sloping corridor to the car garage at the street level. "Sometimes they ask me to cream the face when the remains first arrive. It keeps the skin soft."

Cream the face? What a horrible expression. Suddenly, David has an image of his mother lying here on one of the metallic racks, having her face creamed. He takes a step back, steadying himself against the door frame. "Doesn't that bother you?"

"I didn't like it at first," says Ophelia. "It depends on how you think about it. Somebody's got to do it. It's only bad when the eyes are open. Usually someone closes the eyes, but they don't always close."

Leaving the holding room, they continue through the damp concrete hall in the basement. They pass a locked door with a sign: NO ONE SHALL BE ALLOWED IN THE PREPARATION ROOM WHILE A DEAD HUMAN BODY IS BEING PREPARED EXCEPT APPRENTICES, EMBALMERS, AND FUNERAL DIRECTORS.

A scent of formaldehyde. David gasps for air. He turns and looks up the sloping ramp, through the long corridor, to a door leading to the street. In the distance, he can see a small window, a sliver of sunlight.

"I hope you'll stay," says Ophelia. "We've had only stupid boys."

DAVID IS WAITING IN LINE at City Hall to get a burial permit.

The place smells of perspiration and dust. Overhead, a fan hangs from the ceiling, its blades slowly churning the thick air. The room is slow and old. The heavy front door is old. The wood desks and lighting fixtures are old. The flaking walls haven't been painted in thirty years. The salmon-colored tiles on the floor are chipped and worn along a path from the entrance to the front counter, where, year after year, people have stood waiting in line.

Already today, David has been waiting for half an hour. He has come here many times over the last month. With a sigh, he looks at his watch. It is 2:40 p.m. Behind the front counter, a half dozen clerks sit at their desks, while only a single clerk attends to the people waiting in line. David stands on his toes to see what the other clerks are doing. Most are staring at their computer screens. Two read magazines.

There are still six people in front of him. For the last ten minutes, the woman at the head of the line has been arguing with the public clerk about her property tax bill. Her house is far smaller than her neighbors' houses, she says, yet her taxes are just as high. She produces document after document of evidence, laying each out on the front counter. The clerk appears unmoved.

When David at last arrives at the head of the line, it is well past three in the afternoon. He explains that he needs a permit for the burial of a Frederick Hawkins, who died during the night, and hands the clerk the death certificate. The clerk studies the certificate and frowns. "I'm afraid that the physician has signed in the wrong box." The clerk is a thirtyish man, just beginning to bald, dressed in a rumpled white shirt and checked tie.

"What do you mean?" asks David. "His signature is on the certificate. It's right here."

"Yes," says the clerk. "But the signature is supposed to be in this box." He points to a blank space on the death certificate. "You'll have to get it signed again."

"But it's Friday," David says helplessly. "There's no way I can get the death certificate back to you before you close for the weekend."

The clerk nods. "I'm sorry," he says. "We have our rules." The clerk looks past David to the next person in line.

In his mind, David is imagining the Hawkins family at this moment, the wife and the three children, waiting to schedule the funeral. By now, the family would have been waiting for almost twelve hours. This morning, David himself received the call from the wife, sobbing into the telephone. "He was only forty-six," she kept repeating.

"The wife and three children are waiting for us to schedule the burial," says David. "There are three children."

The clerk stares at him. "All right," he says finally. "But next time make sure that the attending physician signs in the right box. It's the rule."

David watches as Martin washes and disinfects the body with germicidal soap. Both men wear face masks and blue hospital scrub suits. In the light of the fluorescent lamp, the director's forehead looks waxy and yellow. When he is finished with the washing, Martin sprays the body with a long shower hose, the water running into a flush sink near the floor. The embalming room is small and bare of ornament, except for an anatomy chart tacked to the plaster wall. On its margins are scribbled notes, people's names, telephone numbers.

Martin steps back from the operating table. He bows his head and begins muttering quietly. He is saying a prayer. Opening his eyes, he moves back to the table and begins working again. His instruments lie waiting on a silver tray: scalpels, forceps, scissors, clamps, hooks and tubes, wire, thread. First, he swabs the inside of the mouth and nose with a germicide-disinfectant solution. With a pair of forceps, he plucks all visible hair from the nostrils, nose, and ears. He then packs the nostrils with cotton soaked in disinfectant. Again using the forceps, he pulls back the eyelids and puts plastic eye caps over the eyes. An adhesive paste rubbed on the underside of the eyelids keeps them closed. More cotton is placed in the mouth, to fill out the cheeks and shape the underside of the lips. Martin is working methodically, patiently, as if he were a craftsman repairing a valuable piece of furniture.

With a staple gun, Martin drives staples into the upper and lower gums. Then, using wires attached to the staples, he pulls the mouth shut. He begins shaping the mouth with his gloved fingers, carefully working the mouth and lips against the cotton underneath. This procedure takes time. The mouth must be handled with special attention, Martin explains, because the mouth is the most expressive part of the face. The mouth determines how the relatives will view the deceased. Indeed, David is astonished at how many different expressions the face assumes as Martin slightly moves the lips this way and that—as if the deceased were passing through his lifetime stock of emotions.

When he is satisfied that the mouth has a natural shape, Martin glues the lips into position with more adhesive, then rubs them with softened wax. "Jenny was telling me about bowerbirds," he says as he makes a one-inch incision just below the neck. He peels back the skin. With a metal hook, he fishes around in the wound until he finds the jugular vein, covered in a translucent pink jellylike substance. "You see it? Under there." Careful not to rupture the vein, he lifts it up with the hook, places a metal wedge beneath the vein to prop it up, and puts thread around each end. He inserts a needle and plastic tube into the vein. Immediately, blood rushes into the tube. He is draining the blood out of the body. "I've never heard of bowerbirds. I don't know where Jenny learns all this stuff." With his metal hook, the director probes deeper into the wound, searching for one of the carotid arteries. "There it is. You see it? It's thicker and deeper down than the vein." He pulls the artery up, wedges it, puts thread around each end, and inserts another needle and tube. "The males build really fancy nests with colored grasses, ribbons, anything they can find to attract a female. Then they fly around and destroy any other nest that competes with theirs. Just like people." Pushing a plunger, he injects a mixture of formaldehyde and water into the artery. Slowly the liquid flows, two gallons' worth. From time to time, Martin leans over and massages the legs, to help circulate the fluids, he says. David doesn't want to watch, but he finds himself unable to look away. He is mesmerized. He stares at the yellow skin. He feels faint and strong at the same time. He feels alive. In the background, a ventilator hums. It breathes, like a human. Once the blood has been drained and the arterial embalming fluid injected, the director ties off the punctured vein and artery to keep them from leaking. He is moving with a kind of rhythm now. He has gone through these motions hundreds of times.

Tenderly, Martin places his gloved hand on the deceased's stomach—tenderly, as if he were touching the shoulder of a friend, or a lover. Then, just above the navel, he pushes through a long, pointed metal tube attached to a suction hose. No blood appears. One at a time, he punctures the stomach, the bladder, the large intestine, the lungs—and suctions out gases and fluids. Odors of flatulence mix with the sharp smell of formaldehyde. Some of the organs faintly pop as they are punctured. He weaves the metal tube back and forth as if he were rowing a boat. Each abdominal organ must be punctured and drained. After which a stronger solution of formaldehyde is pumped into the torso. When this process has been completed, the director deftly sews closed the incision holes. He packs the anus with cotton. He washes and dries the body again. Finally, he glues the fingers together. David stares at the fingers, long and thin, almost feminine. Later, Martin says, Robert will manicure the fingernails, comb the hair, and put cream and makeup on the face. The entire procedure has taken an hour, possibly two. There is no clock in the embalming room. A door opens. David leans against the wall, wobbly on his feet, and realizes that he has been panting the whole time.

PERMITTING HERSELF A FUGITIVE LITTLE SMILE, Martha has strung ribbons across the room so that everyone walking in must duck or be tangled in a swirl of yellow and green. For her part, Ophelia dispenses plastic cups for champagne and party hats. She wears a cone-shaped hat herself. "I'm not leaving until I'm crocked," she announces, draining and refilling her own cup every time she fills someone else's. On the round central table, usually reserved for the grieving families to ponder cost sheets and event schedules, is a coconut cake with candles, ham sandwiches, chips, sweet pickles, and some potato salad that Jenny has made. Today is Robert's birthday. By tradition, they are celebrating in the arrangement room.

Robert is tall and so thin that he looks ill, but he's as strong as a horse. He is twenty-six today. For the last two years, he's been working at the mortuary to support his night classes at the university, and he's soaked up everything that Martin has taught him, but he's made it clear that he'll be leaving at the end of this academic term to be an engineer. Robert's impending departure Martin considers a personal rejection. He can't bring himself to mention it and instead talks as if Robert will remain at the mortuary indefinitely. "In a year, Robert, you'll be better at makeup than me. We'll see." Now he puts his arm around Robert. From across the room, David looks at the two of them, Martin's hand on Robert's shoulder. Martin is relaxed with the champagne. All of the staff birthday parties are celebrated here in the funeral home, says Jenny. "Martin prefers not to go out."

Robert is talking to Jenny and David about how his parents met the first time. His father was on his way to work one morning when he saw this "fascinating" woman staring at him out the window of a bus, which had stopped briefly to discharge passengers. Seizing the moment, his father leaped onto that bus without any clue about where it was going. By chance, there was a vacant seat next to the fascinating woman. They began talking. "It's amazing how things happen," says Robert. "If my mother had been looking somewhere else for three seconds, I wouldn't be here. And now I'm going to be an engineer." Robert laughs and takes a bite of cake.

All the staff are here, people David has barely met, coming and going in the hidden rooms of the mortuary. Thayer, the sullen hearse driver, is already drunk and sits in a corner eyeing Ophelia. Just last week, Thayer was bragging to Ophelia about how he takes the hearse out on his own during his off hours, without permission, and drives at high speeds down the highway.

"This room used to be my grandfather's office," Martin says to no one in particular. "And my office now used to be my bedroom."

"We should have some music," says Jenny. "What do you think, love?"

"If it's low," says Martin. He takes a swallow of champagne.

"We always have music," says Robert. "Who's got my CDs? I brought them in, but they totally disappeared."

"Your CDs are boring," says Ophelia. "Let's play mine."

"That would be the thing," says Thayer, slurring his words. "Rouse the dead. They got a long time to be dead. Let's wake 'em up."

Even without music, Robert and Ophelia begin dancing around the room, moving slowly. Everyone watches. Ophelia is barefoot, having flung aside her high heels. Crocked as she intended to be, she droops her head against Robert and seems limp in his arms. He holds her up by her waist, struggling to wrap his arm around her thick middle.

"Ophelia is the best runner I've ever had," Martin whispers to David. "She's a little cheeky, but she's got spirit, and she cares about this place."

Martin is talking to everyone. "Robert should blow out his candles," he says, "and make a wish." Robert has already blown out the candles, says Martha. "But what about the wish?" asks Martin. He's done that as well.

"Well then, a toast to Robert," Martin says and raises his champagne glass. "Twenty-six years old. . . . When I was twenty-six, I . . ." He can't finish his sentence. Tears are in his eyes. David has an urge to put his arm around Martin as Martin did with Robert.

"What is it, love?" asks Jenny.

"I'm sorry," says Martin.

"You were thinking of when you were twenty-six."

"Yes. A long time ago."

"Let's dance," says Ophelia. She slides away from Robert, drapes herself over Martin, and pushes him into the middle of the room.

ON A SUNDAY, DAVID VISITS HIS MOTHER, taking the early bus just after dawn. For the last month, she's had trouble walking. Twice, she fell on her way to the market, causing her legs to swell and turn a dozen shades of purple. She doesn't complain, and she rarely asks him to make the two-hour trip to see her, but he knows when she wants him to visit.

When he arrives, David can see that his mother is not well. Her face is pale, despite her considerable makeup, and she barely has the energy to stand up and kiss him before returning to her chair. She's wearing her red Chinese robe.

"I don't understand why you keep it so dark in here," he says, opening the heavy curtains. She squints in the light.

"Lauren closed the curtains last week," she says, "and I haven't bothered opening them. You know Lauren does what she wants. Lauren said that people across the way can look in my window and see me in my bathrobe. Or worse." She laughs. "Phoo. Who cares about seeing an old woman naked."

He leans down and gives her a kiss. "You still look pretty good."

"I know I don't look good." She coughs and takes a sip of water, holding the glass carefully in her veined hands.

He can smell his mother's perfume, flowery and sweet, jasmine. "Did you get the fruit?" he asks.

"You shouldn't send me so many things. I can buy fruit for

myself. Lauren sends me more than you do. You know, I do go out of the house now and then."

"I send fruit to a lot of people. Okay, I'll stop sending you fruit."

At the window, David stares out at the other apartments across the way, the little path leading to the gardens, the swimming pool that his mother never uses. "You've got a beautiful view. You really should keep your curtains open."

"I already know what it looks like out there." She coughs again. "Before I forget, darling, I want you to check my last bank statement. The dumb thing isn't right. I know I should have more money than what the bank says. You're so good at figuring those things out." David nods. "Sit," she says. "Here."

He sits in the love seat next to his mother, takes off his shoes. Already, he is slipping into her world of tranquillity. He feels it and leans back into the cushions. "I passed Mr. Crawley on the stairs," he says sleepily. "I didn't know he still lived in the building. I thought he was going to move."

"Jack will never move. He only talks about moving. He must have just gotten back from mass when you saw him. He goes to mass with his daughter every week. He never used to, but he's gotten religious in his old age. That happens."

"You used to go to church."

"Phoo. I can't remember the last time I went to church." She pauses. "You should meet Jack's daughter sometime. She's a smart cookie. Unmarried too. But I won't say another word about her."

"Jack looks all right."

"Yes, he does. I don't know what he does to his hair. That's his business."

They sit for a while without talking. They could always do this together. He asks about her friends. Mary has moved away to be close to her grandchildren, his mother says. And Frances has surprised everyone by enrolling in a course in psychology at the university. Unfortunately, she has become awfully full of herself in the process and rarely speaks to her old friends anymore. David remembers Frances. She's been around since the days when his father was alive. In his mind, he pictures Frances and her husband coming to the house for drinks before going out for an evening with his parents, the women in fancy shoes and the men in jackets and ties, everyone laughing as they sipped their drinks and talked about some new comedy on television. Frances and her husband were attractive, but they paled beside David's parents. Even at that young age, David recognized envy when he saw it, and he saw it in Frances. David's mother knew that she was beautiful, but she let it all slide off her back. David's father would have been oblivious to such a thing. He seemed completely unaware of his handsome good looks, as if he'd never glanced in a mirror in his life. He was humble. People told David that his father treated the janitor in his shop the same as the owner. He managed a five-and-dime store, but that wasn't his passion. His passion was woodworking. He could make anything with his hands—a chest of drawers, a carved wooden box, a toy sailboat—and David spent hours with him in his shop in the basement, all a dim memory now. But the smell of sawdust and paint he remembers. The pieces of wood. At the pond, the toy sailboat catches the wind, its tiny sails billow. David, David, his father yells, laughing in pleasure, and David runs along the shore following the boat. How old was he then? Seven years old, eight years old, his father almost a boy himself, his sudden death only a year in the future.

David stands. For hours he sat cramped on the bus. He walks

around the living room, pausing in front of the little jade bowl that he sent his mother for one of her birthdays, and the cabinet with the photographs. There, the familiar picture of his father eons ago, so handsome and so young, much younger than David is now. A photograph of himself and Lauren. A photograph of the tiny house they lived in after his father died, with its three tiny bedrooms hardly larger than closets, its tiny kitchen and the stained linoleum floor with the peeling tiles. A photograph of his mother in her twenties, glamorous. In her younger years, she looked like Lauren Bacall, with wavy brown hair and high cheekbones and sultry eyes. Looking at the photograph, David wonders again why she never remarried. She had plenty of opportunities. Men admired her. Besides her beauty, she had a serenity. Her paramours invited her to parties on boats, candlelit dinners, dancing, and she sometimes went, but she never accepted any of their marriage proposals. It was not as though she were a heartbroken widow. In fact, she rarely mentioned David's father. It seemed to David that remarrying would have made her life so much easier—she was working such long hours at a dingy insurance company to put food on the table for her children, even though it was only macaroni and cheese out of a box, and she was always gone from the house. Marriage to any of the men would have let her spend time with David and his sister. But she preferred her independence. She wanted no attachments. It was as if the early loss of her husband had flattened the terrain of her life. Afterward, nothing bothered her. When she entered a room, people felt the air grow still. When she walked, she floated, never quite touching the ground. Both men and women were drawn to her. And when people entered her bubble, they felt that the world was a little better and calmer than it actually was. Her serenity could be maddening. Lauren hated her for it. When Lauren had her first period, she never told her mother; she told David instead. At eighteen, Lauren left home. In his childhood, David wanted to be like his mother. He would do anything to please her. She was the strength. She was the world. But she had no interest in anything. He wanted to be disturbed, while she could not be disturbed. And now, his mother was growing old, her once sensuous eyelids turned to heavy, dark bags, her cheeks sunken hollows that no makeup could disguise. For years, he was angry with her for never remarrying. And yet, he still wanted to please her. He went to law school to please her. Law is the most noble profession, she said to him one afternoon near his twenty-first birthday, the two of them sitting on a cool stone bench on his college campus. Except for medicine, she said, and you aren't cut out for medicine—you can't take the sight of blood. Sailing through the entrance examinations, he roomed with Harry. For six months he suffered through the tedious law books and lectures until he couldn't stand them any longer. Not until a year later did he tell his mother he'd dropped out.

Looking at her now as she slowly sips from her glass, he realizes that he would still do anything to please her.

"You should see your doctor," he says.

"I don't need a doctor."

"Please see your doctor."

She sighs. "Okay. If you want me to." She looks at him and smiles. "I really am doing all right. You don't need to worry about me." Her eyes move from him to the next room and linger there, as if she is expecting someone. For a few moments they sit again in silence, listening to a radio faintly playing in a neighboring apartment. It is one of the jazz singers from the 1940s, a woman. "Are you happy, darling? I can never tell."

He hesitates. "I think so."

"Good."

He waits for her to ask him something else, something more, but she merely takes another sip of water and closes her eyes.

"Darling, will you bring me my scarf?" she asks, her eyes still closed. "It's in my closet. My neck is just a little bit cold."

David goes into his mother's bedroom, opens her closet door. He finds himself embarrassed by this sudden intimacy—her dresses, her shoes, her nightgowns, her brassieres. Unintentionally, he recalls a recent meeting with a grieving family, the entire family crowded into the arrangement room, the husband, the sister, the brother, the two grown children. Lavinia always looked best in lavender, said the sister. She's got a lavender cotton dress—that's what she should wear. No, said the daughter, tears in her eyes. Not cotton. Cotton is too casual. But none of her wool suits look right, said the sister. How do you know what looks right? demanded the daughter.

Standing in the closet, David realizes that he doesn't know what clothes his mother would want to be buried in. In fact, he doesn't know whether she would prefer to be buried or cremated. He catches himself. He shouldn't be thinking such thoughts. And yet it is a practical question. Shouldn't he ask her? To avoid difficulties in the future? He stands in the closet, his eyes slowly roving over each dress and suit, imagining. He should ask her, Which dress? He finds the scarf she wants, enters the room where she sits, stares at her. "Here, Mother," he says. "Here's your scarf."

A PRISM OF LIGHT JUTS THROUGH THE WINDOW, folds over the open casket, and bends up the opposite wall. In the air, a scent of flowers. It is late afternoon. In a couple of hours, family and friends will gather in the slumber room to view the deceased, but now, at this moment, David sits here alone. He is tired but not overly tired. Some days, he likes to come here before the visitors arrive. His duties are finished until the night viewing, and he could go home and take a shower, but he would rather be here in this quiet, alone with his thoughts. To his surprise, he has begun to appreciate the life of the mortuary. He is beginning to grasp the many different responsibilities, the possibilities, the capacities of human feelings. The presence of death seems to bring about some clarifications, as well as some mysteries. Here, he is always a student.

It is so quiet now that David can hear the clock ticking in Martin's office. Somewhere, fainter sounds—a flute, wind chimes. Unconsciously, he matches his breathing to the ticking of the clock, a rising and falling, a rising and falling. In a way, it is the quiet rhythm of the mortuary itself, a rising and falling, the unhurried breathing of the mortuary. He leans back in his chair and lets his muscles go slack. He floats on an ocean of liquid lapping, the waves coasting in and the waves coasting out, the slow curl of the waves, rising and falling, rising and falling. Thoughts sprinkle the wave crests like foam, thoughts bubble up in the air and dissolve.

The flowers are star-gazer lilies. He chose them himself. Get something pale, the husband said, without further instructions. Not too many, he added. Ophelia usually buys the flowers, but today she has been occupied with other activities. Just since this morning, some of the flowers have opened, like fragile mouths. He always gets some that are still closed. Bethany used to bring lilies home with her and put them in a vase on the dining table. When she was a little girl, she said, she fantasized that she lived in a jungle of flowers, and she wanted to preserve that memory, the one pleasant memory of her childhood. Bethany's star-gazer lilies on the dining room table. He stares absently at the casket and wonders whether Bethany still puts lilies on her dining room table, wherever she is. In his next letter to her, he'll ask about the lilies. He tries different addresses, a stationery shop where she used to work, her father's company, her old school, her mother, her brother, neither of whom speak to him. Perhaps she receives some of his letters. His letters form a small history of his life. As he looks across the room, he can see the face of the deceased, a faint rosy color even in this half-light. Bethany also liked pale, as he remembers. She avoided bright things. They found an abandoned railroad car, miraculously sitting in an open meadow as if it had been dropped down from outer space, sacks of white flour inside, and she took off her clothes and rubbed her body with the flour until she was completely white. Don't ever leave me, she said, holding him against her white skin. He never left her, but she left him.

It was a late afternoon, like this one, when with a clatter of chairs he sat down at the end of the table, wedged between people he didn't know, and first met her, introduced by Harry. All friends of Harry. Not one of them past the age of twenty-two. And himself, in his infinite possibilities. Twenty-two! How delicious! With life stretching out to the galaxies, the tinkle of beer glasses on the table, slices of pizza and sandwiches, telephone numbers passed around on folded slips of paper. She was a bird, a sparrow, light in the air, fascinating and beautiful when she perched near his chair for a few moments. She thought him handsome and brilliant and sad, she said later. After the others had left, they stood together on the sidewalk, not quite touching, and felt that something momentous had happened. When he told her his father was gone, tears came to her eyes.

Already, the angles have changed. The prism of sunlight has broadened and slipped over the casket, sweeping across the folded hands. David can see the hands, right over left. To him, the hands are even more expressive than the mouth. He has suggested to Martin that they consult the family on how to position the hands, but Martin says that there are certain decisions the family shouldn't make, decisions they don't want to make. Clothes, the family can choose, but not how to fold the hands. Martin ponders these things. He lives with Jenny in the back of the mortuary and rarely leaves the premises. According to Jenny, Martin has an inexplicable fear of people and places he doesn't know. When Jenny is away on one of her birding excursions, Martin sends Robert or Ophelia to do his shopping and collect his medicines. For the outside funeral services, he appoints Jenny as his representative. Martin and Jenny have no children. From time to time, David has visited Martin's apartment in the back, suprisingly ramshackled and cluttered for someone as meticulous as Martin. The tables are covered with stamps from all over the world, Martin's hobby. Through his stamps, he travels the planet. He can tell you when a particular stamp was issued, the language and currency of the country, the type of government. Some of the stamps are quite rare, and he carefully lifts them with his forceps. The stamps are beautiful and delicate, like the poetry of William Blake. Raising them to the light, Martin holds forth on countries and governments and his political philosophy. He announces that he is an antinationalist, that much of the world's problems have been caused by geographical boundaries between countries. He favors not only disarming the world but also eliminating national boundaries. Cultures should mingle, he says. People should mingle. After his lectures, he carefully puts away the stamps in semitransparent cellophane wrappers, dimming their colors. The stamps leave sticky patches on the tables where the glue has come off.

The waves coast in and the waves coast out. David has taken off his shoes. He breathes in and breathes out, matching his breath to the tick of the clock. At this moment, he is possibly alone in the building. Martin and Jenny would be resting in their rooms. When the family and friends arrive, they will stay half an hour. A few people will linger longer, after the casket is closed. Coffee and doughnuts are served in the next room. Sometimes the visitors talk about small things the deceased did, or particular words spoken. Particular days. How does one measure a life? Is it the few moments in which decisive events happpen, or is it the slow drip of years? What will be remembered about himself, he wonders, and who will remember it? She was completely white, except for the pink of her mouth and the two pink tips of her nipples, and she held him against her white body. She was a goddess. Even then, years before they parted, she felt that he didn't desire her enough. We are living like an old married couple, she said. I don't want to be old. I want passion. I want you to crush me. You're the only woman in my life, he answered. That's not what I mean, she said. She was born into money, and David always felt that her parents looked down on him. When he had dinner at their home, they served him premium wines and then smiled at him as if he could not possibly appreciate what he had drunk. In return, he brought them cheap wines, which they never opened. After dinner, he would go on about the vintages and bouquets of his cheap unopened wines. David is training to work in a bank, Bethany said to her parents. Why? Bethany's mother asked. Her father kept pushing him to take a position in his insurance company, but David would rather be destitute than trapped under Frank's thumb. Frank pushed and pushed, with that condescending smile, and David pushed back. During the entire decade of their marriage, Frank sent a large check to his daughter each month, larger than David's salary, as if to say that David was financially inconsequential. Whenever Frank called their house, he immediately asked to speak to Bethany. Why don't you say something to him? David asked Bethany—he treats me like garbage. I can't, said Bethany. He's my father. He's an asshole, said David. Please don't talk about my father like that, she answered.

He hated it that she said they were living like an old married couple. He should have been more unpredictable. But he is not now what he was. If she were here at this moment, he would crush her, he would envelop her. She might be remarried. She might have children. He would envelop her.

He tries to remember what she took when she left that last time. By then, she was so bored that nothing seemed to matter. She had worked at one job after another—a bookstore, a lawyer's office, a hospital, a stationery shop—each as far from her father as she could get. He should have been more unpredictable; he was like one of her boring jobs. He never knew what she wanted. What did she take that last day? You keep the house, she said, and the furniture. I don't want it, he said—you paid for it. I'm leaving, she said. I don't need any of that stuff. Within a month, he sold the house and the furniture and sent the money to her parents. What did she take? She took her clothes. She took her omelet pan. She took a photograph of them soon after they had first met, standing on a wooden dock out on the lake. I'll keep this, she said. I want to remember the way that you looked at me that day. Please, he said, I'll do whatever you want. You were so sweet, she said, looking at the photograph. You're still sweet. I still love you. Then why are you leaving? he asked. I'll keep this photograph, she said, and she placed it inside a book with her clothes. She also took one of his sweaters. When they went walking on cool days, she often wore one of his sweaters. Leaves fell into her hair, and she would put them one by one into her pocket. She was perfection, everything. She held his hand, said hello to people they passed on the street. You are becoming very dignified, like your mother, she said to him, stabbing a knife into him. Didn't she know? He should have made love to her in the railroad car, when her body was white with the flour. That was the moment.

Leaves fell into her hair. Leaves fall on the grounds of the mortuary and are gathered up in white bedsheets. Martin himself burns the leaves in the back, next to the overturned carriage with the weeds growing up all around it. A small pleasure, he says. On some Mondays, slow days, David helps Martin burn the leaves, the smoke turning and shifting about their heads with the wind. Martin reminisces about his childhood growing up in the funeral home, his grandmother's insistence on warm milk every night before bed, soured with a few drops of lemon juice, his father's picture of Thomas Edison tacked to his office door, the goat that they kept on a ten-foot chain in the backyard and who periodically slipped off its chain and came wandering into the building. On one occasion, the goat accidentally ate a freshly inked burial certificate, delaying the burial of an elderly gentleman whose body then sat in the basement for three days. The disappointment and loneliness because Martin's friends, and later his would-be paramours, were frightened to come to his house—the Double-Deckered Spook House, they called it. Often, he played alone in his room. At times he was angry at his father for bringing him into the world in a funeral home, but it was hardly his father's fault, because he had been brought into the world in a funeral home by his father, and back to the great-grandfather who had started it, unwittingly, wanting only to make a living. All in all, it's been an interesting life, says Martin with a sigh. I wouldn't want it any different. This is a personal business, he says. This business is a matter of listening. The grieving families will tell you what they need. The Italians are emotional, the Germans are stoic. Some people want to joke with you. Others want no joking at all. So. Are you attached? Attached? A woman. You know. I was just wondering if you had a . . . girlfriend. Yes, David says. Ellen. She works at the library. I hope you don't mind my poking into your business, says Martin, laughing, his shirttails hopelessly loose from his pants and flapping about his waist. I know that people have lives outside, and I was just wondering, hoping that you had someone. You should bring your Ellen here. I'd like to meet her. Next weekend, we'll have you and Ellen to dinner. Jenny will cook her grilled trout. Looking away, David feels oddly conscious that he may have revealed something of himself that he shouldn't have. He wants to confide in Martin. There's a dearness and comfort in Martin's attention. Is this what it feels like, he thinks, to talk truly with Martin? But . . . He glances at Martin, as he happily gathers the leaves and takes a contented breath of the leaf smoke, and wonders if Martin simply acts interested in everyone. He wants to trust Martin, and he pictures the four of them, Ellen and himself and Martin and Jenny, at Martin's table . . . Leaves. The smell of lilies hovers in the air.

There is a dampness too, a blend of lily and fresh rain. The odor of rain that evening he went to the concert with Ellen. Rain on her face, on her bare arms. Even with her hair matted against her forehead, she was beautiful. Somehow, the wetness only emphasized her fragility. It's fun to get dressed up, she said, turning all the way around to look at the other concertgoers. Umbrellas clattered to the floor. Above them, in the gold balconies, people streamed into their chairs like a flock of birds swooping into a tree. She leaned up, a full head shorter than he, and kissed him. I adore Schubert, she said. Especially his lieder. What a good idea you had for tonight. It was your idea, said David. She laughed. I was afraid you might take me to that Wagner concert. What's wrong with Wagner? he asked. Oh, I like Wagner too, she said, but his music is pretentious. Look, she said, nodding toward a couple taking their seats in the next row. She must be twenty years younger than he, don't you think? And that dress she's got on. She's falling out on top. She might be his daughter, he said. Not a chance, Ellen said. Look at the way he's touching her. At intermission, Ellen wouldn't get out of her seat. Can we just sit for a while, she said, with her head on his shoulder. I feel like I'm soaring. I feel like he sees into my heart. He must have been in love when he wrote those pieces. He was in love with poetry, said David. It was a great time for German poetry. That wouldn't be enough, she said. There had to have been a woman. Schubert would have been in love with you, he said, and he buried his face in her hair and breathed in the sweet damp.

The light has dimmed further. He should turn on another of the lamps. In this light, the English hunting paintings on the wall have faded into mist. The body is just a shadowy shape in the casket. He stares at the casket and listens to the ticking of the clock, the rising and falling, like the slow breathing of his mother as she sits in her chair. Her legs have improved since the fall but will never be right, says the doctor. Age. Lauren says that it's time their mother moved into a "facility," but they both know that she will never do such a thing. She will always live by herself, live alone in her majesty and calm even as she dwindles away. With her legs as they are, she is using a cane. The last time he visited, she met him at the door, then walked across the wood floor to her chair, the strange sound of the cane tapping on the floor like a third person in the room. From a cabinet she took out some of his old school papers and gave them to him, adding that she was doing the same with Lauren—as if that justified everything. Making room, she said. A friend had sent her books from abroad, she explained, not that she was a reader, and she needed more space. Although hurt, he could hardly object. The school papers were faded and smudged, with a reedy dryness about them, yet they still contained something of those many nights he stayed up too excited to sleep, his mind blooming with what he was reading and thinking—English literature, Latin, chemistry, the history of China—while the small light of his lamp stretched across the dark sleeping hallway to the closed doors of his mother's and sister's rooms. What would he now do with the papers? I am fine, his mother said, smiling and trying on a new hat. To demonstrate her mobility, she commenced to walk from room to room, followed by the tap of her cane. He remembers her when she was a beauty. He remembers her on the arm of his father, the smell of the gel in his father's hair. The day that he managed to balance himself on a two-wheeler for the first time and ride unsteadily across the front yard, the elation of his triumph after so many defeats, clouds singing in the sky, his blood ringing in his ears, his father cheering him on and waiting for him at the bottom of the hill. Then, in his father's arms. I did it straighter than he did, said Lauren, pouting. You rode like a prince, his father said to him.

He looks around the slumber room, listening to the tapping and the ticking of the clock. The chairs have been arranged, two dozen empty chairs in a semicircle about the open casket. The casket is the dot at the center of the circle. The casket is the pivot. Robert has done his grooming well. The hair is neat but not too neat. One of the thick velvet draperies is not fully closed, and David can see a street lamp, a glow in the dusk. Beyond, a dark row of trees gathering the night. The dusk seems to pour into the room. He stares at the casket and listens to the ticking of the clock. In the dim dusk light, the air is thick and soft, as at the bottom of a deep pool. A semicircular pool, with the casket at the center, the pivot. He breathes in and breathes out, following the waves. The white waves and the white of her body. That was the moment. The smoke drifts and curls in the wind. Ellen. He thinks he might be falling in love with her, falling through space like the leaves. But slowly. He leans back in his chair. The other chairs in a half-circle, carefully arranged like everything in this place, the chairs in a round cut in two, the casket the dot at the center. His eyes rest on the pivot, he breathes out, he breathes in. The silence.

"MRS. ABERNATHY HAS BEEN SITTING by herself all day, just staring at the wall." What can be done for her? David has offered her tea and sandwiches, but she only waves him away. While the hours pass, the rest of the family waits in the sitting parlor, goes out to do errands, has lunch, comes back, goes out again. The funeral service isn't until four-thirty, and Mrs. Abernathy has been sitting in the arrangement room since nine o'clock this morning. She refuses to view the body.

In the sitting parlor, the family camps out with doughnuts and soft drinks. Michael, son of the deceased, has been weeping and arguing with his wife. Every ten minutes, he excuses himself to go to the bathroom and comes back with a wet handkerchief pressed against his swollen eyes. "I can't believe Dad is gone," he mumbles.

David talks quietly with one of the nephews, Bartley Ryan, a school acquaintance whom he hasn't seen for years. In his younger days, Bartley was quite an athlete, and he had the girls swooning over him. He was one of those guys David envied from a distance, not a man he could be friends with, like Harry—he didn't have Harry's modesty and sincerity. Talking to him now, David is not unhappy to see that Bartley has lost nearly all of his hair and gained a great deal of weight. Life gets so insanely busy, says Bartley. These days he never spends time with his old friends, never does anything he really wants to do. He asks about Bethany. No, he hadn't heard that David split up with her eight years ago. Sorry for that. He was close to his uncle, Bartley says. They used to go fishing together. "Hardly ever caught anything." But that didn't stop Uncle Richard. He was the most patient man, says Bartley. Uncle Richard would prop up his fishing pole underneath a cross strut of the boat, lie down, and tell jokes. He always laughed at his own jokes. His aunt is taking it really hard, Bartley says. They should do something for her. She's been in that room for hours and hasn't eaten anything all day. Bartley reaches for a Kleenex on the table, unabashed about the tears in his eyes. How astonishing, David thinks. Bartley was a star football player who would never do anything he considered the slightest bit feminine, and here he is with tears in his eyes. It is the men who are crying today.

An army lieutenant has just arrived with his bugle. He stands in the reception area as if he has a steel rod down his back.

"Would you like some tea?" asks Jenny, unnerved by the lieutenant.

"No thank you, ma'am," says the lieutenant. He walks into the sitting parlor, his medals swaying, seems uncomfortable with the family gathered there, and says that he'll wait outside. "I didn't know the major but . . ."

But Mrs. Abernathy, the major's wife, is still sitting by herself. What can be done for her? Martin goes to the arrangement room, looks in, and comes back. "Everyone grieves in their own way," he whispers to David in the hallway. "Sit with them, David. I've got to make a call about the service."

In the sitting parlor, Michael is shouting again at his wife, Sarah. "I didn't get to say good-bye," he says. "You should have told me he was going so fast."

"You keep saying that," says Sarah. "But I didn't know. Nobody knew." She puts her arm around her husband, trying to comfort him, but he pushes her away.

"Don't coddle me," shouts Michael.

Sarah, who has not shed a tear before now, appears stung by her husband's rebuke and reaches for a Kleenex on the table. The other family members wince or look away in embarrassment or sit silently with their own sadness. But Michael and Sarah don't seem to be finished with each other. David senses that something worse is in progress. He has seen this before—family members covering their grief with anger, acting crazy. He hurries into Martin's office. "We've got a bad situation with Michael." Martin hangs up the telephone and shakes his head.

In the hallway, Martin greets some of the family members who have just arrived, calling them by first names. Martin's manner has temporarily silenced Michael's ranting. But a nervousness holds in the air. The sons and daughters, brothers and sisters and cousins, put down their coffee cups and lean forward in their seats to see what will happen.

"Michael isn't himself," says Sarah. "He didn't mean to start shouting."

"Don't tell me what I meant to do," says Michael. "I said that I didn't get to say good-bye to my father."

"I understand how you feel," says Martin. "We want to say good-bye to the people we love."

"That's right," says Michael.

Martin sits down in an empty chair next to Michael. "The important thing is that your father understood that you loved him," he says gently. "Every day, year in and year out. Think of all the happy moments you spent with him." Martin pauses and looks at Michael. "That is what life is. Life is a collection of moments strung through the years. No one can take those moments away from you,

Michael." Michael nods, softening. "Your father had those same moments. They belong to you and him. Remember those moments. They can never be taken from you."

Michael's anger is beginning to ease. He will continue to grieve, but his anger is slipping away. For a few minutes, no one speaks. Then Michael gets up and goes to the bathroom to wash his face.

Now Martin is talking to Sarah about her children. David listens to him in amazement. With a few words, Martin has soothed the family. He is a magician. How does he do it? David wonders. Already, he knows that he will never be an embalmer—he doesn't have the stomach for it. But this other skill he can strive for.

Robert comes into the sitting parlor with a folded flag, looking for the lieutenant. Where's the lieutenant? He's outside, says David. The lieutenant's stiffness has not helped the general mood.

"I never thought I'd want to go to a military funeral," says Sarah. "I hate all that stuff. But now it seems right."

"We have a lot of military funerals these days," says Martin. "The veterans from World War Two."

"Dad had no pride about being a soldier," says Michael, back from the washroom. "It was Mom who wanted the military funeral. Is she going to sit in that room all night? It's nearly time to go."

"Give her another few minutes," says Martin.

Outside, the cars are waiting in a line with their engines rumbling, like a jointed animal snoring in its sleep. "Wake up," David shouts at Thayer the hearse driver, who is nodding off in the backseat. Supervising Thayer is the job he likes least. It is dirty work that Martin would rather not do himself.

Thayer snorts awake, looks at his watch. "What are you doing?" says David.

"I was just getting a few extra winks," says Thayer. "Don't talk so loudly. You're hurting my eardrums." Thayer gives David an ugly look. "Hold your water. Nobody's walked out yet."

"Come on, Thayer. You're supposed to be ready. Drink some coffee."

"I'm not drinking that black piss you got in there."

"Well, wake yourself up and get ready to drive."

"I wouldn't mind driving if they had a real car. This piece of junk is older than I am." With a surly expression, Thayer picks up his hat and gloves and moves to the front seat of the hearse. "Hurry up and wait," he mutters.

It is four o'clock. Outside, the light is already beginning to fade. As David and Bartley put on their coats in the coat room, just the two of them, Bartley says, "So, you and Bethany hit the skids eight years ago. You know, I was surprised that you married Bethany in the first place. She always seemed so sour to me. I hope you don't mind me saying that." David stops and stares at him. "All that money," Bartley continues, "and she never seemed satisfied with anything." Sour? thinks David. Bethany was never sour a second of her life! Suddenly David wants to smash Bartley in the face—he can feel the blood surging—but he merely turns away and leaves the room. Bartley must be extremely distraught, he thinks, because he's talking nonsense. David remembers something that Martin said: At the mortuary they come into people's lives at the worst possible moment.

Finally, they must rouse Mrs. Abernathy from her private lamentations. David and Martin stand in the doorway of the arrangement room. David is worn out from the scene with Michael, his encounter with Thayer, the meanspirited lies of Bartley. And the day is far from over. Softly, Martin speaks to the drawn form of the woman sitting in the arrangement room. "Louise."

She moves slightly in her chair and sighs. "I know, Martin." After a few moments, she stands, surprisingly erect for a woman in her late seventies. Her face is worn, but she has no tears in her eyes. "I met him when he was only a boy," she says.

The plaque beside the great arched door of the church reads: WE ARE THE BODY OF CHRIST, EMPOWERED BY THE HOLY SPIRIT, LIVING IN FAITHFUL COVENANT WITH GOD AND ONE ANOTHER.

In a rare outing, Martin has consented to accompany Louise Abernathy and her family to the funeral service. They mount the stone steps two by two, Louise and Michael first, then Martin and Jenny, David and Robert, followed by the rest of the family and friends. "Hello, Martin." "Good to see you out." "Martin!" Martin doesn't stop to talk and keeps his gaze straight ahead, frozen, while Jenny whispers to him as they walk, her arm around him.

Organ music vibrates in the air, jagged, and David looks up at the sky to see clouds in collision, and he thinks of his church wedding with Bethany, billows of silk, women with bare arms. How happy he was at that moment.

Once inside, dozens of people swarm toward Louise, trying to offer their sympathies. Everyone is talking at once.

Suddenly Martin and Jenny are engulfed by the crowd. They are surrounded. A frantic look clutches Martin's face, as if he were drowning, and he grips Jenny's arm.

From across the room, David can see Martin's panic. Martin

begins to flail, he staggers, he shakes free of Jenny then grabs her again. "Here," David calls out. "Our seats are over here."

Martin looks up and spots David and pushes his way through the crowd, keeping his eyes fastened on David. Now his face is flushed red. Finally, he gets to his pew and sinks down on the red cushion, breathing heavily. Jenny puts her arm around him again. Martin is gasping for breath. He leans against Jenny, his eyes closed, and he swoons in his seat.

Even though David has heard about Martin's fear of being in public, he always found it difficult to believe. Now he is stunned. Something hidden in Martin, beneath the calm and control, has erupted. Just minutes ago, Martin was himself. Now he seems small and afraid, like a child. David wants to say something to reassure him, but he doesn't know what to say, and he feels shaken and disoriented himself by Martin's behavior. Anxiously, he turns around in his seat to see who has noticed, who is watching. It is almost painful to listen to Martin's breathing. But Jenny just holds him and whispers into his ear.

Finally, Martin's gasping subsides. With Jenny on one side of him and David on the other, he moves to an upright position and seems to feel safe. He opens his eyes. Now his breathing is almost normal; he takes long breaths and lets them out slowly. He looks up and begins to survey the space. The altar. The flowers. The side windows with their semicircular slatted tops, like Oriental fans. He cranes his neck up and stares at the chandeliers high overhead. Then he looks across the aisle at Louise Abernathy and smiles at her. She smiles back. Yes, he is here, despite everything. This is why he is here.

At the altar stands the pastor in his robes. He is illuminated by a patch of colored light, streaming sideways from the stained-glass window on the opposite wall. To David, it seems that the pastor must be aware of the effect, for he moves this way and that to stay in the light.

People have settled into their seats. "We will start with 'Faith Is the Victory,' " says the pastor. A rustling, as the hymn books are opened.

Faith is the victory!
Faith is the victory!
O glorious victory,
That overcomes the world.

The voices are accompanied by the organ, whose magnificent brass pipes adorn the front wall of the church. David hasn't been in a church for many years. Once, he recalls, his mother told him that she didn't need "a hundred other people moaning" around her to feel close to God.

WHEN DAVID FIRST TELLS ELLEN about what he saw at the mortuary, they are having dinner in the little Indian restaurant. Or perhaps it is later, in her apartment beside the lake.

"Your hands," she says. "You're shaking. I didn't see you shaking before. Poor thing." She takes his hands and holds them in her hands. Besides his mother, Ellen is the only person who physically touches him. Already, she seems to know everything about him, although they met only a few months ago, at the library, where she works acquisitioning and deaquisitioning books. Did he act strangely in the restaurant? he asks. Don't worry, she says. He was fine.

"I don't know what to do," David says.

"Why do you need to do anything?" She kisses his hands, then resumes brushing her hair at her mirror. Standing behind her, watching her in the flickering candlelight, he remembers that Bethany also sat brushing her hair, although Bethany was not as conscious of her appearance. Undeniably, Ellen is a beautiful woman, small but perfectly proportioned, fragile and fair-skinned, with dark hair falling halfway to her waist, dark and almond-shaped eyes that make her look almost Asian. She must be in her mid-thirties. He once asked her her age, but she wouldn't tell him. Ellen makes him young again. Not the immaturity of a schoolboy, but the raw energy of youth, the daring, the adventure of doing things one shouldn't, like walking up creaking staircases in the middle of the night to share a bed. Ellen tells him that he is handsome, that his slight paunch is sexy. She has a sweetness and a generosity. She takes him dancing—he, who hardly danced when he was a teenager, who never danced even when he and Harry went to parties—and she wears for the occasion a silver sequined blouse and a tuxedo jacket with tails. She takes him to concerts. One day, they rode the bus together with no particular destination, just going wherever the bus went, happily eating sandwiches and reading to each other from *Gulliver's Travels*, pretending that each place they stopped was a new country. She may be beginning to love him. He needs her, especially now. Is he losing his mind? He's afraid to tell her that he may be losing his mind. The thing that he saw a few days ago, he wants it to go away. It burns in his brain. What should he do? In the flickering light, objects jump on the walls, her silhouette at the mirror, the little bottles of perfume on her vanity, the books on her bedside table. He doesn't know what is real anymore. Taking the brush from her, he strokes her hair.

"Do you believe me?" he asks.

She leans back until her head rests against his chest. "I believe you. If you believe yourself." She looks at him in the mirror, then gently takes the brush back and continues stroking her dark hair. "Like this."

He paces the room. He sits down on the bed. He gets up and paces again. The light is jumping.

"I hate to see you like this," she says. "What can I do to help? Tell me."

"I'm not sure," he says. "Maybe I imagined it." He paces. "But I saw it." A wave of nausea sweeps up from his stomach. He sees it again. "Do you believe me?"

"If you think you saw something, then I believe you. But you said yourself that you aren't sure."

"How can you be sure of anything?" he fires back. "You see things with your eyes, and you know you saw something. That's what I know. I saw something with my eyes. What's being sure? What does that mean?" Why does she keep coming back to that, he wonders, the being sure? She doesn't really believe him. He can't blame her, for something crazy like this. He can't blame her. Is he losing his mind? She's beginning to love him, he feels it—a small plant that must be nourished. But now she'll think that he's nuts. He shouldn't have told her. He doesn't know what he's doing now, what he's saying. Everything is upside down. He kisses the back of her neck. That is real. He wishes he could stay forever in this room with her. "You don't believe me, do you?" he whispers. "Just say it."

"I do believe you."

Still, she sits at her mirror in the jumping light, brushing her hair. It occurs to him that she hasn't made direct eye contact with him. Why didn't he notice before? She can say whatever she wants while she's not looking directly at him, looking at him only in the mirror. She is using her mirror as a sly misdirection.

"Please don't say that you believe me when you don't." There, he's said it. People should be honest with each other. Suddenly, he regrets every dishonest thing he's ever said and done, with Harry, with his mother, with Bethany, with Ellen. His sweet Ellen is not being honest with him. How does a person truly know the mind of another person? he wonders.

Finally, she stands up, a full head shorter than he. Turning, she embraces him. "I don't want you to be upset," she says softly. "I want to help. Maybe you'll see it again, whatever it was. If it's real, you might see it again."

"But what if I don't see it again," he says, keeping his arms around her, holding her.

"Then you should write it down. Write down what you saw."

"That's not proof."

She nods her head, as if agreeing with him. But . . . he doesn't know what she thinks. Despite his strong feelings for her, he realizes that he doesn't really know her. Does she believe him, or is she just trying to take care of him, as she did when he was ill with the flu and she came to his apartment and sat with him through the night? During that night, in his fever, he was beginning to give himself to her, even though he knew she was flirtatious, even though he knew she was the kind of woman who enjoyed the constant attention of men. She's confessed that she's had a half dozen relationships. "None of them keepers," she says. There is so much about her. The way that she touches him. Like him, she is a reader. They talk about books, something he never did with Bethany, and she tells him that he is the first man who hasn't been threatened by her intelligence.

I should tell somebody, he says. You've told me, she says. But shouldn't I tell somebody else? Maybe somebody else has seen something like this. What am I saying? It's all impossible. I saw something impossible.

On the wall, the bedposts are leaping.

"David. Be careful who you talk to about this. Some people won't understand."

"We shouldn't discuss this anymore tonight." He is exhausted and floundering, and he needs to mull over the confusions and fear by himself. Something has opened that should have remained closed.

She begins to unfasten her earrings, the small gold seashells that he gave her, and he helps her, placing them in the turquoise enamel box on her table. His hands are still shaking. Her friend Claire's boy will be visiting for a few days, she says. He'll be sleeping on the sofa in her living room, so they'll have to be discreet. It is just that Ralph and Claire are having "married troubles," and they thought it would be good if Sam got out of the house for a few days. Maybe David shouldn't stay over for the next few nights, she says, not that she doesn't want him to.

"Do you mind?" she asks.

"Of course I don't mind. It's your friend and your house." She is too generous, he thinks.

"I was surprised that you ate lentils at the restaurant tonight," she says, rubbing lotion on her bare shoulders. "I thought you didn't like lentils."

"I like lentils."

"You do? You didn't eat lentils when I cooked them here a few weeks ago."

"Really?" He tries to remember the night and summons up a vague image of cookbooks on the kitchen counter, the immaculate table with each plate and fork perfectly set. She had on some Buddhist meditation music that he liked.

"Don't you remember? The Indian dinner. There was a lentil-and-potato dish. And chickpeas and onions."

"Yes. I don't know why I didn't eat your lentils. I like all of your cooking. You know that."

"I put love into my cooking. I don't cook for everyone, you know." She laughs and musses his hair. Now she is kissing him, undressing him, touching him. He closes his eyes and lets himself fall.

Cliffs hang over him on both sides, glittering with strange things in packages, in boxes, in plastic cellophane wrap. Colored wire and glass, metal brackets, machines of various kinds, lightbulbs and plugs, scissors, thermometers, envelopes, clothespins, marbles. His father's store. His father's gentle voice, like a hand on his shoulder. He wanders down the aisles, touching the treasures, lost and found at the same time. He sleeps in the warmth.

A few days later, Martin asks to see him in his office—a difficult morning when two families have initiated new cases and Thayer has just quit. David waits in the hallway outside Martin's door, above which is a seventy-five-year-old sign in flaking gold paint spelling FINAL PEACE.

Martin stands up from his computer screen. "Is anything the matter?" he asks. "You haven't been yourself in the last few days. You seem . . . nervous."

So it is obvious, as David thought. Of course it's obvious. He's been nauseated, exhausted, having trouble remembering routine tasks. He could say that he's been worried about his mother, or that he and Ellen are having problems, but he lacks the energy to prevaricate. With a sigh, he sits down in the Windsor chair next to Martin's desk, on his good left side, and tries to tell him what he saw in the slumber room. However, just as when he talked to Ellen, he finds it difficult to put the thing into words. While the image still vibrates and burns in his mind, he cannot easily describe it. Somehow, he felt the thing as much as he saw it.

Martin listens, saying nothing. After David is finished, Martin still says nothing, but he has taken up his glass paperweight and is turning it over and over in his stubby fingers. He seems to be staring at the bookcase on the other side of the room. "What do you want me to do?" he finally remarks. He is concerned, he must admit.

David is the best employee he's had for years—even better than Robert, but that's confidential—he's been teaching David everything he knows, like his father did for him. . . . It's not just David's growing importance in the funeral home, he wants to make clear, it's not just a business matter. This is an extended family. He has a great deal of affection for David, he wants him to be happy and safe here, and any problem of David's is his problem as well. They'll put their heads together on this.

But despite his caring words, Martin seems shaken, as if he's been betrayed. He rises and lumbers around his desk, then across the room. "Why don't you take a few days off," he says. "Give yourself a little holiday."

"I wouldn't do that," says David.

Martin nods, a worried expression on his face. He smooths back his white hair. "I'm not doubting that you think you saw something." He hesitates. "Funeral homes have their own . . . ambience, an unusual ambience. Let's face it. We live here with the recently deceased. For most people, that takes some getting used to. That takes a mental adjustment. And you were probably tired. You have to consider that, don't you think? It was the end of the day, and you were tired. I've imagined things when I'm tired. Sometimes I see double when I'm tired. I see two doorknobs when there's only one. That kind of thing. Don't you think . . . something like that could have happened?"

"It's possible."

"Good." Martin returns to his desk and sits down. He seems partly satisfied, partly relieved, but he is gazing at David with his milky eyes as if he's not completely sure that David is with him. And David can see that Martin doesn't believe him. From now on, Martin will never fully trust him. All of this is conveyed without words, in a subtle shift of the face. "I want to make another suggestion," says Martin. "You know, David, you have a great range of abilities."

"Thank you."

"I mean that. Jenny tells me that your new accounting system is brilliant. And you're wonderful with the families."

Martin picks up his glass paperweight again. "I want to make another suggestion, just a suggestion. I'm wondering if it might be a good idea for you to see someone." Someone? A doctor, a therapist or a psychiatrist, Martin explains. "To help with the stress you're going through now. Some help of that kind would be worthwhile in any case," says Martin, "whether you actually saw something or only imagined that you saw something."

"Martin, Martin." A knock on the door. Jenny enters, holding a suit of clothes wrapped in plastic. "Hello, love. The cleaners said that they did as much as could be done with the spot, so here it is, ready for tomorrow. I took a peek, and they did a pretty good job. You'd have to be really close to see anything. That's one advantage of always wearing black." She gives a little laugh. "David, I didn't see you. Sorry." She glances back at her husband and can see that he is disturbed, not by her intrusion but by something else. With her good nose for problems, Jenny stands for a moment and then sits down in the second Windsor chair. "Thayer has quit—I know that." She waits, understanding that the issue is not Thayer.

"David saw something in the slumber room a few days ago," Martin says. "Something . . . not normal." And he repeats everything David told him in a flat, level voice, careful to use the same words David used, as vague as they were.

"That's amazing," says Jenny. She turns to David. "You saw something?"

"Yes."

Jenny has an expression of excited shock.

"David has been quite upset the last few days, understandably," says Martin. His voice is anxious, not a voice David hears often. "I think he should take a little time off. I also suggested that he might see someone, a doctor. He could see that fellow your sister went to last spring."

"You mean Dr. Gupty?"

"Yes, that's his name. I couldn't remember it."

"Dr. Gupty is a shrink," says Jenny.

"Yes." Martin pauses. "I thought a psychiatrist could give us some help. Whether David actually saw something or—"

"Why should David go to a shrink?"

"Well, I just thought—"

"That's insulting, Martin." She turns to David. "Forgive us, David, for talking like this in front of you. It's just a friendly little squabble between two old married people." She turns back to her husband. "David has had an extraordinary experience. He doesn't need to see a shrink. It sounds like you don't believe him."

"Come on, Jenny, that's not the point."

"Of course that's the point. You either believe him or you don't."

"I'm trying to help him," says Martin.

"No, you're not. You just don't believe him. You don't believe in anything that's not right in front of your face."

"That's not fair, Jenny. That's not fair. David told me himself that he's not completely sure. Didn't you say that, David?"

The conversation has made David even more uncomfortable than he was before. He's lost part of Martin's trust, and now he's wedged himself between Martin and Jenny, something he never wanted to do—he's been on such good terms with both of them, he's eaten dinner with them. Now everything is in doubt, just when he was starting to settle into his life here. But how could he expect anything to stay the same after what's happened? The world has been cut in half. This is just the beginning. A ticking. For the first time, he hears the clock. He looks up at the clock on the wall, the enameled face in its wood and brass case, the ticks moving outward like circles in a pond.

"David? Didn't you say that you're not sure of what you saw in the slumber room?" It is Martin's voice.

"How can you be sure of anything?" says David. "I guess it's possible that I imagined it. Yes, that's possible. But I don't think I imagined it." He cannot look Martin in the eye.

"I believe you," says Jenny. She turns to her husband. "There are too many stories of this kind for it all to be made up."

"How can you believe what David says when you weren't there?" says Martin, waving his arm in frustration.

"Why do you believe things that I tell you?" says Jenny.

"That's different," says Martin. "If you told me you saw a ghost, I wouldn't believe you."

"Really."

Martin doesn't answer.

For a moment, Jenny stares at her husband. "Okay," she says. "Let's agree to disagree. But David is not going to a shrink. If he wants to take a few days off, he should. But he doesn't need to see a shrink."

Somehow, word has traveled around the apartment building. From behind the counter of the diner, Marie gives David a sheepish look as she puts toast and fried eggs on the platters. So it was her.

"Be a good guy," says Henry, a huge red-faced man who has lived on the second floor across from David for longer than anyone can remember. "Tell us firsthand what you saw. Tell us straight."

Marie scowls at Henry and slaps a pot of coffee down on his table. "Don't hassle him," she says.

"I'm not hassling," says Henry. "You're one to talk."

"Yeah," says Raymond, who is still wearing his pajamas under his raincoat. Raymond usually doesn't get dressed until midafternoon, when he saunters into the lobby and watches movies on the video player. "David has his own pair of lips. He can talk if he wants to. Tell us, David. We want to hear it from you. What did you see?"

"I'd rather not talk about it," says David.

"Come on," says Henry. "Tell us."

"Leave him alone," says George, who is sitting at David's table. George slices a knife through his eggs, letting the yolk ooze and run, takes a bite, and frowns. He looks over at Marie and winks at her. "If David doesn't feel like talking about it, then he doesn't have to talk about it." He puts his arm around David.

"I heard that you saw some goddamn ghost," says Freddie. He starts laughing. "Hoo, boy."

"So what if he did," says George.

"Don't tell me you believe in ghosts," says Freddie.

"I don't have to talk to you about what I believe and what I don't believe," says George. "I'll tell you one thing. I don't believe in stupid people who think they know what's what about everything. David says he saw something. Let's leave it at that."

"How do you know David saw something?" says Henry. "Let David speak for himself." Some of the other men nod in agreement—by this time, about a dozen have walked over from the apartment building and are sitting and eating at the Formica tables or standing around David, friendly, trying not to crowd him. A CD machine in the kitchen is playing Wagner, the usual morning fare, and Gunther, the German cook, who has apparently been listening to everything despite the music, comes out of the kitchen to hear what David has to say.

"I don't want to talk about it," says David. "Please. Aren't there things you don't want to talk about? It's like that."

"But you told Marie," says Henry.

"He told me in confidence," says Marie, standing next to Gunther.

"Look, we're all in confidence here," says Henry. "Anything said here in this diner right now is in confidence. We're friends talking to friends. All I'm asking is for you to tell us what you saw, David. You told Marie. Tell us."

"It's not easy to describe," says David.

"Show some regard," someone says. "David doesn't want to talk about it."

"Okay," says Henry. "You don't want to talk about it. Okay. I'd just like to know whether I have to worry about a ghost floating into my room tonight. If it does, I'm calling you."

Freddie howls with laughter. Some of the others are laughing as well.

"This is great stuff," says Alfred, the retired dentist, from his table across the room.

"Maybe somebody would like to mind-meld with me," says someone else. "I'm feeling paranormal." There is more laughter.

"You guys are bigots," says George.

"Yeah. A lot of people have seen spirits," somebody says.

Freddie whistles and flaps his arms while weaving in and out between the tables. "I'm not too happy about living with some loonies who believe in ghosts," he says. "That's all I've got to say." He looks around the diner. "Who in this room believes in ghosts? Raise your hands."

"Don't, Freddie," says Marie. "You're making fun."

"No. This is serious," says Freddie. "Everyone who believes in ghosts, raise your hand."

Marie raises her hand. Gunther raises his hand. After a few moments, about half the men raise their hands. And half don't. Everybody is eyeing one another.

"Well, I'll be a goddamn fish," says Freddie. "I'm living with a bunch of loonies."

A call comes in from a reporter at the newspaper. A reporter! David is summoned to the telephone by Martha the receptionist, who remains standing within earshot. The reporter wants to ask just a few questions about what David saw on the evening of April 23. April 23? What's this about? Who's talked to her? Out of respect for confidentiality, the reporter says, she can't discuss sources. Is David familiar with the newspaper? Of course David is familiar with the paper. They keep a copy in the sitting parlor. "Excellent," says the reporter. When might David be available? She could drop by any-time in the next few days. No hurry. She's especially interested in seeing the dream room. She corrects herself. It's the slumber room. It's called the slumber room, isn't it? She wants to visit the slumber room. Would that be possible? No, thank you, David says. No, thank you? The reporter doesn't understand. David hangs up. You've made your own bed, says Martha.

Later that day, while David is planning the arrangements for a service, Martin comes to see him. "I just got a call from someone at the newspaper," Martin says. "She says she spoke to you."

"I didn't tell her anything," says David.

Martin gives David a long, searching look. "I appreciate that, David. But somebody talked to her." With a glance into the hallway to see who is listening, Martin begins pacing the sitting room, circling the table with the white orchid and the William Blake. "This is bad, very bad. . . . She wants to come here, into our funeral home, our place. She's intent on coming." Martin is pausing between sentences, thinking through what should be done. Evidently, he was having his late-morning tea when the reporter called, and he seems unaware that he's still holding his teacup. "Why would a reporter want to come here—with all that's going on in the world?" He shakes his head and sighs. "I just can't believe it. I'm afraid that we're going to have to notify the staff. I hate to do that, to get people upset, but . . . the reporter might try to talk to some of the staff. Who knows what these people will do." Martin's neck is flushed red against his white hair. Strategies, reactions to crises, financial decisions, are not Martin's forte. He much prefers to manage quietly, to attend to the embalming procedures, to soothe the grieving families through their distress. "Here, hold this," he says, handing David the teacup, still oblivious that it is a teacup. Jenny has been called, he says. By telephone, Jenny has advised that they be polite to the reporter. They should not deny whatever "information" the reporter has, but they should not confirm any information either. Ideally, they shouldn't say anything at all. Jenny has been out at the dressmaker's, getting a dress for her grandniece's graduation, and will be returning as quickly as possible. Martin gingerly explains that although he and Jenny have some disagreements about the nature of David's "experience," they completely concur that no one should talk to the reporter. Martin takes pains to emphasize this unanimity, as he always does when invoking the authority of his wife—after all, she has a university degree in management and he would be foolish not to heed her advice. "I appreciate your cooperation, David. That woman gets in here, publishes a story, no matter what, and it's going to be very bad for us. I don't know what she's going to do." Martin glances into the hallway again, an unhappy expression on his face. Then he returns to his office and closes the door.

HAS DAVID BEEN GIVEN INSTRUCTIONS? He isn't sure. Is it he who is supposed to notify the staff? There is an unfamiliar vibration in the air, a faint hum, a sense of invasion. The tranquillity has been disturbed. As David meets with a grieving family in the casket room, he finds himself brooding about the reporter. Who is she? Who talked to her? What did they tell her? It must have been some-one at the apartments—who else could it have been? Or possibly one of the staff at the mortuary. Although they haven't mentioned anything, Ophelia and Robert have been looking at him strangely these last few days. Not to mention the despicable Martha. And even Andrew, the new driver, has given him funny glances. Without wanting to, he recalls a scene from grade school long ago, when he was punished for talking in quiet study hall and sent to the princi-pal's office. There, he sat by himself while his classmates gawked at him through the glass window. He was already considered different, the boy whose father had died, the boy with the glamorous mother who had boyfriends. In the principal's office, people stared at him, and that smell—a chalky, mildewy odor.

Only Marie and Jenny are in sympathy with him. And Marie doesn't quite count, since she believes that she has received signals from her dead mother. And now, this reporter, who probably wants only a sensational story to entertain her readers, who could never put the thing into proper perspective. But what would that be? There is no proper perspective. What did he see, what did he see? He wishes he had never seen anything. If something impossible happens for only five seconds, why can't it just be snipped out like film, with the frames on both sides spliced together as if it never existed? Couldn't he just tell everyone that he made a mistake? What exactly happened in the slumber room on April 23—odd that he has never thought of the date until now, when the reporter mentioned it. Somehow, a date attached makes it more monumental and definite, like the date Japan attacked Pearl Harbor. He wishes that he hadn't told anyone. Maybe, in time, he would have come to understand that he didn't see anything at all. But . . . he did see something, something impossible. A few seconds of something impossible. And, he now realizes, he is frightened. What he saw frightens him. Someone is talking, Mr. Brockman or Brockford, the brother of the deceased. His voice sounds like a dog barking in the distance, yippety-yip, with a note of sadness at the end of each bark. The voice resonates with the pervasive vibration in the air, the new tilt of the building. The brother is saying that the family wants something "simple but regal." His sister was an unpretentious woman, he says, but she achieved important things in her life. Has David read her obituary in today's paper? She was on the Board of Selectmen. What? Obituary? No. Wasn't the funeral home involved with the obituary? David should read it, Mr. Brockman or Brockford says. His sister was a significant person. But down-to-earth at the same time, says another family member. She died in her sleep, the way we all want to go. Something simple but regal. Evidently, none of the caskets in stock will do. David takes out a catalog. What did he see that late afternoon? April 23. At dusk on April 23. Five seconds. He closes his eyes and he sees it again. Is he losing his grip?

When he walks out of the casket room, he finds Martin waiting for him in the hallway. "Have you received any more telephone calls since this morning?" whispers Martin.

"No," David whispers back. Inadvertently, he has placed himself on Martin's right side, his deaf side, and he must repeat himself on the good side before Martin hears him. After which Martin hurries back to his office and closes his door. It occurs to David that he's never seen Martin hurrying before.

At least Jenny is back. Jenny is the calm center. She smiles at David when she passes him in the hall, smiles and shrugs her shoulders as if she doesn't understand what all the fuss is about. Jenny will take care of things with the reporter.

There's a funeral this afternoon for the Kane family. The pallbearers and traffic assistants, hired on a half-day basis, stand about in the hallway in their black coats and gray gloves. Even they seem nervous, keyed up, sensing the unusual oscillation in the air. The front door opens and closes, opens and closes. Bouquets of flowers arrive, and the men hold the flowers in their gray gloves.

In the arrangement room, David finds Ophelia and Robert. For the first time, he can see that there is something between them. Youth, of course, but more. "Tell us the truth," says Robert. "What did you see?" David hesitates. Does he have to struggle through another unsatisfactory explanation, another attempt to describe what can't be described? "I'm sorry," says Robert, seeing David's discomfort. "You don't have to go over it again. But you do think that you saw something strange?" David nods. "See," Robert says to Ophelia.

"See what?" says Ophelia, beaming with pleasure. "I'm the one who told you, remember. Something's finally happening at this place. Isabelle Poole said it to me this morning. Something's finally happening at the funeral home. And she didn't even know that we might be in the papers." In the papers? Well, Ophelia blurts in excitement, Martin has told them not to speak to any reporters. But he wouldn't be saying that out of thin air, now would he. Reporters! It has to be about what David saw—nothing else interesting has ever gone on. Something's finally happening, says Ophelia, just when it was becoming impossibly dull. She was going to leave early today after the funeral—she's been getting a touch of flu—but she thinks she'll stay around and see what's "on the agenda." Indeed, Ophelia's face does appear a bit flushed. The soft red of her cheeks and the bright red of her lips contrast strongly with the blue-green of her eyelids and the habitual dark mascara. Strands of her straw-colored hair, held up in a bun, slip down into her face.

"Lower your voice," says Robert. In the hallway, the men are drinking coffee in paper cups and laughing.

"Don't you want to be in the newspaper?" says Ophelia. "If you tell me you don't, I won't believe you. Everybody wants to be in the papers. Mostly, it's just a bunch of rude celebrities who're in the newspaper. Why shouldn't it be us? Actually, it should be David. David, you're the one the reporter wants to talk to. You're the one who saw the ghost." She pouts. "I've been here a lot longer than you have, and I haven't seen any ghosts."

"Ophelia." Robert leans over and gives Ophelia a quick kiss on the cheek.

"Yes, I know. I'll shut up. At least something interesting is going on. The last interesting thing that happened to me was the yellow hat I got on sale after Christmas. But I haven't had any place to wear it."

"What do you think it was?" Robert says to David. "What you saw?"

"I don't know," says David. Although Robert seems friendly, David can feel an edge of skepticism in his voice.

"I heard you saw a ghost," says Ophelia.

"I never said it was a ghost," says David.

"But it was a ghost, wasn't it," says Ophelia.

"I don't know what it was," says David.

"Sometimes light can have weird effects," says Robert. "It was late afternoon, wasn't it. The sunlight in late afternoon can be weird. You can see things that aren't there." He takes a forbidden cigarette out of his pocket, fingers it, and begins talking about mirages in the desert, the "refraction of light," and how people can see entire cities teetering over the hot sand when there's nothing at all.

"Don't try to talk him out of it," says Ophelia. She turns to David. "Robert is going to graduate at the top of his class at college. He'd never tell you that himself. He's a genius, like you. And after that, I'll bet he gets married. But not to me. I'll never get married. I'm twenty-four, and nobody's even asked me."

"Kenny asked you," says Robert, grinning.

"Oh, Kenny was just a stupid boy."

"Well, I think it was some kind of weird light effect," says Robert. Ophelia frowns at him. "Listen," says Robert. "We work backward from what we know. Right? I'm betting a zillion to one that there aren't any ghosts and there's never been any ghosts. That's where we start. So if you saw something like a ghost, either it was some weird light effect, or you imagined it. It's got to be one of those two things. No offense, David. That's my opinion."

Martha comes to the door and says that it's the reporter again on the telephone. This time she wants to speak to Ophelia. The reporter is going down the staff directory, says Martha. She says there're no train wrecks today and she's got nothing else to do. She wants to speak to Ophelia. She wants to speak to me! says Ophelia. She hesitates. Tell her that I'm not here. You should tell her yourself, says Martha. I'm not the errand girl. Please, Martha, says Ophelia. I'm not allowed to talk to her. I don't get paid enough for this, Martha mutters under her breath.

Looking out the window at Andrew as he backs the hearse into the driveway, David realizes that he dreads going to his apartment building tonight. It's been a horrible day, and the men will jab and jeer at him as they have for the last week. He should go to Ellen's. But her friend's son will be there on the couch. What should he do? In the driveway, the hearse kicks up bits of gravel, which pelt the window like hard rain.

FOR HOURS, A BLUE MIST HAS FLOATED over the lake, like gauze caught between the glass of the sky and the glass of the water. Every few moments, the mist slightly parts and David can see the faint outlines of things on the opposite shore, the roofs of houses, trees, automobiles.

Ellen, sitting next to him, reads from her novel. At each chapter, she pauses and eats a few grapes left from their lunch. This place is as precious to her as to him. In the midst of all the confusions and dislocations, they have stolen this afternoon for themselves. The low-lying branch of a gum tree hangs just over their heads, giving them a feeling of being hidden, a secrecy. The afternoon is cool, with the absence of sun, and she pulls her sweater more tightly about her and moves closer to him. He reads as well, books that he's signed out from the library. He is surrounded by books, happy with books even when he's disturbed.

"Linda is pregnant," she says, looking up from her novel.

"Your sister Linda?"

"Yes. Three months. Mother and Dad are ridiculously happy. This will be their first grandchild."

He nods. But he is only half listening and stares out at the mist. He studies how things shimmer and fade, then slowly come into existence again. What happened that late afternoon? Was it a trick of the light, as Robert said? Or was it something else?

Someone is grilling nearby, and the smoky smell of roasting

meat moves through the air. The smoke sails out over the lake and mingles with the mist, which grows thicker and thicker until nothing can be seen. The lone canoe on the water, together with its canoeist, vanishes.

"Linda is five years younger then me," says Ellen with a sigh, "and she's already having a baby."

"I'd like to meet her sometime."

"You will." She looks at him reading. "You think you're going to figure it out with books? Maybe you will. I've never figured anything out from a book."

He reads from Lavoisier's *Elements of Chemistry,* a crumbling nineteenth-century edition that sends up a puff of red dust when it's opened: *We may lay it down as an incontestible axiom that, in all the operations of art and nature, nothing is created; an equal quantity of matter exists both before and after the experiment.* What could be clearer? Nothing appears out of thin air.

And from *Leviathan* by Thomas Hobbes: *The world . . . is corporeal, that is to say, body; and hath the dimensions of magnitude, namely, length, breadth, and depth . . . every part of the universe is body, and that which is not body is no part of the universe.* Body and matter, that is all that there is.

But in apparent contradiction, the words of Charles Darwin in *The Descent of Man: A belief in all-pervading spiritual agencies seems to be universal, and apparently follows from a considerable advance in man's reason . . .* What spiritual agencies?

He closes his books. Looking out, he watches two green-headed mallards glide out of the mist and touch on the lake in a wraith sweep of dream wings.

———

An article appears in the newspaper. MORTUARY WORKER CLAIMS TO SEE GHOST. Marie is quoted, speaking guardedly about her conversation with David—his privacy must be protected, she says—but elaborating on her own experiences with the spirit world. "Ignore it at your peril." Several men at the apartment building are also quoted, describing in much more detail what Marie told them about what David told her. Ophelia is quoted at length. Described as "a pretty and engaging young woman," Ophelia, in fact, appears to be the principal source, and she goes on for two columns about the ghost that David saw, how it rose out of the body of the deceased and floated about the room for nearly half an hour while whispering the names of various spirits in the "other world." According to Ophelia, the ghost was a shimmering, cloudlike thing that slowly changed colors from blue to pale yellow. Finally, it sailed out the window.

Inside the mortuary, the newspaper article explodes like a bomb. Martin begins shouting, something no one has ever heard before. "How could you!" he shouts at Ophelia, behind his closed office door, but everyone can hear.

"She followed me on my way home," wails Ophelia.

"Even so. Why did you tell her . . . that preposterous story? How did you come up with all that malarkey?"

"I don't know," cries Ophelia. "It just came out."

"I should fire you," says Martin. "Not once in a hundred-odd years . . . And now . . . Our name . . . used like that . . ."

Ophelia comes flying out of the office in tears.

And the telephone is constantly ringing, for Ophelia and for David, but mostly for David—people he's never heard of, strangers wanting to speak to him, wanting just fifteen minutes of his time.

When Martha stops picking up the phone, people leave long messages on the answering machine describing their personal experiences with the netherworld. A man says that his dead wife comes back each night at bedtime to check on her family. She walks the upstairs hall, opening and closing doors. A woman claims that she once walked through a solid door. Some of the callers invite David to séances. At the front entrance, people leave cards and notes and a picture of the Church of the Holy Sepulchre in Jerusalem.

David's initial anger at Marie and Ophelia has partly been replaced by embarrassment and shame. Martin is walking from room to room in a daze, mumbling that he has disgraced his father and his father's father, while Jenny follows one step behind and tries to comfort him. "Nobody really believes what they read in the papers, love."

Robert, Ophelia, Martha, Lloyd, Andrew, are all attempting to maintain business as usual. David can't look any of them in the eye. He is the fool who caused it all. He should quit his job at once and leave the premises. But there is a man with a camera outside, apparently trying to take pictures of people coming and going.

Trying to hide, in his embarrassment, David goes downstairs and looks for a room where he might remain unnoticed until nightfall. As always, he is perplexed by all of the passageways and doors. It seems that every week he discovers a new room in the mortuary; the place is an endless warren of rooms, some of them hidden and accessible only by interior doors, some without windows, some the former bedrooms or sitting rooms of past generations of the family. He decides to cloister himself in one of the downstairs washrooms, which he can almost imagine as the principal's office—the toilet seat is the bench, faces jeer through the four walls.

It is cool and silent in the washroom, and he has just taken off his tie when Martha knocks on the door. The evil woman has found him. But even Martha seems subdued and shaken, almost docile. "Mr. Kurzweil, I'm sorry to disturb you." The Holland family, scheduled for an appointment with Martin, has asked to meet with David instead. It is not that Martin is indisposed, Martha explains; it is just that the family would prefer to meet with him. I can't see anyone, he groans through the closed door. They say they'll wait to meet you at your convenience, says Martha. They have some "special requests."

It is almost midnight when David arrives at Ellen's house, taking his shoes off as he tiptoes around the dark shape of Sam sleeping on the couch. A tiny light in the kitchen faintly illuminates the path through the living room to Ellen's bedroom. For a few moments, he pauses by the window and looks out at the lake. At this hour, it appears as a shapeless black desert, with lights flickering like campfires on the opposite shore.

"Do you think Sam saw you?" whispers Ellen.

"No, I was very quiet. I had to be with you tonight."

"Do you want to take a shower?" Ellen has been in bed and is wearing her nightgown. He can't answer any questions now, please; he can't think. In the darkness, he feels for the drawer where she keeps his pajamas. When it comes to organization, Ellen is a perfectionist. She has a certain drawer for scissors and tape, another for paper and pens, a certain box for batteries and candles. Her own clothes she keeps neatly folded in drawers. He puts on his pajama top and leaves off the bottoms. Her breath. She envelops him. She is his flower, and she has not chastised him once about the article, even though she must be as embarrassed as he is—her colleagues at the library surely have discussed it, and he can't imagine what they've said, the whisperings and ridicule she must have endured today as she sat at her desk. But not a single disapproving remark from her. "I'm so sorry" is all she says, and she kisses him at the base of his neck.

With the fragrance of her all over him, they lie side by side in her bed. They lie listening to each other breathe. Slowly, David begins to recover his mind. For a few minutes today while he sat in the basement washroom, he had the fleeting sensation that whatever happened on April 23 was *it*, or close to *it*. Has he been offered a glimpse of the meaning that always eluded him? The thing that he saw, whatever it was, surely meant something. It has frightened him, but it meant something. Why him? Perhaps because he has been searching for something in a way that other people have not. He was prepared. He was a cocked spring. Not that he ever considered himself special. But he has made certain decisions in his life. People are the sum of their decisions, aren't they? Harry has gone one way, and he has gone another. Bethany has gone one way, and he another. At times, he has felt the world opening up around him, shifting, cracks forming in the wall of experience, and he has been poised to see through those cracks. The supernatural he cannot accept. But he does believe that there is something unseen behind common experience, some *totality*, which can be glimpsed only between the cracks. He has read that people near death understand something. What is it they understand? Do they understand the flash of their lives against the totality, against the infinity of time before and after their single chirp of life? Do they feel a connection? Sometimes he strains to remember fragments, sounds, anything from before he was born—an absurd idea, of course, but isn't it equally absurd to think that the world existed before him, that there was a time when he didn't exist, when he had no thoughts, when the impulses and bursts in his brain, whatever constitutes thought and consciousness, did not exist, when the billions of tiny cells of his brain and his body were just random atoms scattered in the soil and the air? How do those bits of unfeeling inanimate matter congregate to make something living and thinking? What meaning is in it? Surely there must be a meaning for something so elaborate and complex. Could it all be an accident? Perhaps a fissure in the wall appeared in front of him that late afternoon in the slumber room. He saw it. What did it mean? He saw something, he almost understood something. The grand sweep and the totality emerged for a moment from the haze, and he brushed up against it.

In the lobby, Raymond is playing computer games in his pajamas. Overhead, the floorboards creak as the tenants move around in their rooms, getting dressed and ready to go to the diner for breakfast and then out to their jobs—the sudden whoosh of a toilet being flushed. Too tired to mount the stairs to his rooms, David walks next door to the diner. Gunther is already at work in the kitchen, and his music escapes through the swinging door along with the smell of bacon, eggs, pancakes, coffee. But the diner is empty. It is only 6:30 a.m., and the tenants of the apartment building—the diner's only customers—don't start coming over until 7:00. Marie walks from one table to the next, humming a song, wiping the red Formica tops and filling the paper-napkin dispensers. In the slanting light of the morning, her hair shines and glows. He stands at the door and she sees him. By now, after the night with Ellen, his anger has completely dissolved. Marie meant no harm. She looks at him with her usual cheerfulness, but also with an uncertainty, a tentativeness. "The guys have been asking about you," she says. She turns to the kitchen door. "David is back."

Gunther comes out of the kitchen, a big smile on his face. He walks over and shakes David's hand, the first time he's ever done so, his hand oily with butter. "I'm making blueberry pancakes this morning. In your honor. You take whatever table you want."

"Isn't it early?" says David.

"No problem," says Gunther. "You hungry?" David nods. "Well, you take a seat anywhere you want, and I'll bring out the pancakes." A Christmas ornament permanently hangs from the kitchen door, and it swings back and forth as the door opens and closes.

David sits down and Marie sits next to him. You've seen the paper? asks Marie. Yes. "I'm not the one who called that reporter lady," says Marie. "I wanted to tell you straight off. I'm sorry. I know you told me those things in confidence." Her upper lip is quivering, as if she's about to cry.

"Marie, don't worry about it." He places his hand over her hand. Marie's lip is still quivering.

Gunther brings out the pancakes. He puts a plate in front of David and a plate in front of Marie, the fancy plates he reserves for birthdays.

Marie is beginning to regain her composure. "But you did do people a service," she says. "People should know. People have no idea." Marie pours syrup on her pancakes, just a little, she says, because she's watching her weight. Her husband, Sterl, would like to meet him, she says, if he wouldn't mind coming to their house. Perhaps she could make dinner for him some Sunday at her house. It would mean the world to her. Sterl has never given much credence to her "experiences," she says, but it's different with David, an educated man, and Sterl would like to talk to him. Please, would he come? David feels himself being drawn into a swamp, but he can't say no to Marie. She has been so kind to him, and she has so little of a life outside the diner and apartments. Just now, she tells him, her son is in jail for writing bad checks, and she has no idea how she will get him out. She doesn't even know if she wants to get him out. Yes, he'll come, David says. Any Sunday.

A few of the men begin wandering in. "Blueberry pancakes in David's honor," Gunther yells out from the kitchen. Marie brings out the pancakes, and the men begin eating.

"Why can't we have blueberry pancakes more often," complains Henry. "I've asked for blueberry pancakes a million times."

"Pancakes ain't got no protein," says Winston, eating his pancakes.

"You one of those health freaks?" says Raymond. "Or you just watching your figure?"

"Winston is watching his figure," says George.

"Good article in the paper," someone says.

"That's 'cause your name was in it. I talked to that gal too, and she didn't put my name in it."

" 'Cause you're a jackass."

"Good article."

"Yeah. I sent a copy to my girlfriend."

"Like shit you have a girlfriend."

"We got a bunch of celebrities," Henry says, and grins at David. "Hiding-out celebrities. Somebody ought to get us a book deal."

"You have any more pancakes back there, Gunther?"

Upstairs in the apartment building, David finds several notes under his door. "I take my hat off to you. You've got steel balls," one note says. Another note: "I'm not changing my mind about ghosts, but we're all friends here in this rat's nest." An envelope contains forty dollars, a payback of the money David lent Raymond two years ago. Raymond isn't taking any chances.

In the shower, the embarrassment returns, and the confusion. His life has been flung out of control. How thin the surface between sanity and insanity, he thinks. How quickly the membrane can break. From one instant to the next, a person can fall through the ice. He feels like he has walked into a novel by Kafka.

With a clenching in his stomach, he wonders who has read the newspaper article. Perhaps even his mother has read it—and if she hasn't read it herself, she has friends who will happily recite it to her, the same friends who were always jealous of her beauty. They would be polite, of course, but they would be vengeful and pleased. "Poor Madeleine," he can hear them say to one another, the pit of snakes. "Madeleine's son, David, an intelligent boy when he was younger, divorced for some time, no children, thank God—we don't see him very much these days—he must be in his forties now. For years he worked in a bank but now, apparently, he works in a *mortuary*. Yes, that's right, a mortuary. Madeleine's son is an assistant in a mortuary. And evidently he's seen a ghost! Ha, ha. It's all in the papers. Madeleine must be absolutely red with embarrassment. We should give her a call."

It was at his uncle's house, the summer after he graduated college, and his mother and her friends were gathered there, laughing and talking and drinking Bloody Marys around the outdoor table, and the air sagged with that sleepy haze of summer, that heavy blue light. They were talking about somebody's daughter, from a family of means. The girl had gotten secretly engaged to a cocaine addict and brought him home one day, a terrible idea. The young man was all dressed up in a suit and tie, but his eyes were dilated and he chattered nonstop "like a monkey." Then one of the women with her Bloody Mary said that parents never know what is going to happen to their children, regardless of the example they set at home. And another woman looked directly at Madeleine, with David sitting there, and said not to worry. "David is a straight arrow."

They will relish his downfall.

What will his mother think? She will handle her friends; she is much too self-assured and serene to let her malicious friends get under her skin. But what will she think of him? Certainly she'll guess that he's lied to her all of these years about his exalted position at the bank. He must speak to her. What will he say? He doesn't know, but he must speak to her. He dreads the encounter.

But his mother will have to wait. Today he must assist with another funeral. Julia McConoghy has died at age forty of breast cancer. With the rain coming down in buckets, everyone enters the front door of the mortuary with mud on his or her shoes. First, an hour early, is the grieving family—Patrick McConoghy, Julia's husband, and their two daughters—then three women friends with their hats and coats and umbrellas sloshing about, a florist delivering flowers from an uncle who is too frail to attend, Andrew with water pouring from his cap and cursing the foul weather, two pallbearers. As soon as Martha has cleaned up the carpet from one person, another walks in the door. To make matters worse, they are short on staff, for three of the pallbearers have abruptly canceled for the day, and the McConoghys have no family to do the job.

David has been in and out of the garage helping Andrew clean the hearse, then searching for umbrellas. "Did you count them?" he asks Jenny. "I found only twenty-three." The umbrellas were all supposed to be in the garage shed, but David has been discovering them scattered about in coat closets, in the basement, in the trunk of the hearse.

"We might have enough," says Jenny. "Only a few people have called in."

Martin has just come in from the rain after checking on the cars. He's taken off his boots and is walking around in his wet socks. For the last hour, he's been making phone calls, going through the list of temporary help to hire a couple more pallbearers for the day. Martin seems to be ignoring the embarrassment of the last few days, covering his humiliation because he is a professional and because he will not fail the grieving families. The rhythm of the funeral home, carrying on its dignified business, is what he knows. And his spirits have been boosted by an angry letter from Bertram Bigelow, director of one of the rival funeral homes, who complained that the ghost article was just a "sneaky ploy" by Martin to increase business. Years ago, Mr. Bigelow visited Martin's funeral home on the pretense of some kind of merchandise partnership and took the opportunity to have a good look around, tramping from room to room and viewing the decaying shabbiness with satisfaction.

Jenny gives Martin a kiss in the hallway. "Take off those wet socks, or you'll catch a cold."

Ophelia, weepy for the last three days, is dispatched to buy more umbrellas. Of course we're not going to fire you, Jenny whispers to her in the coat room. "Martin was just emotional. He'll get over it."

IN THE BASEMENT, DAVID HAS FOUND three more umbrellas, one of them broken and of little use. "I'm on my way up," he calls to Jenny, and begins mounting the stairs. "You've got the last ones," she shouts down. "I don't know what happens to our umbrellas." While he climbs the stone steps, David can hear Andrew in the garage, the engine of the hearse coughing, stopping, then coughing again. Evidently, something is wrong with the car. Something is always wrong with the car. But to everyone's relief, Andrew can repair automobiles as well as drive them. A smell of gasoline drifts through the air. The staircase is narrow and winding, barely wide enough for a person. And now the broken umbrella won't close. As David continues to climb up the stairs, he fiddles with the latch, trying to fix it. The umbrella, half open, drags against the opposite stone walls. "The carburetor is shot," Andrew shouts up. "Tell Jenny I'm going out to buy a new carburetor." "All right," says David. "Will we be able to drive today?" "Yep," says Andrew. "I'll be back before we have to leave." David continues up the spiraling staircase. Its stone walls are deeply indented with branching grooves, like the channels of ancient dry rivers. Its spiraling stone steps are also notched and grooved, uneven. Around and around he goes. His shoes tap on the stone steps like the tapping of his mother's cane. Every few moments, he looks back at the steps behind and below, which vanish after six or eight feet because of the tight twist of the staircase. Today, he thinks, the soil at the grave site will be mud.

There will be mud getting into the cars, mud getting out, mud on the path down to the grave. Doubtless, some people will slip and get mud all over their suits. Even with the umbrellas, everyone will get muddy and wet. He fiddles again with the bad umbrella. Unable to fix the latch, he forces it shut. With a crack, the supporting struts snap. At least the thing stops scraping the walls. The gasoline smell stings. He pinches his nose, but the sharp odor remains. Upstairs, a man's voice can be heard talking to Martin in the reception area, apparently one of the new pallbearers. Then Martin's voice as he dictates instructions. "Ophelia is back with the umbrellas," Jenny calls down to David. "Two more will be enough." "That's all I've got," David shouts back. For some reason, he remembers a day he and Lauren were taking their mother to lunch in the rain, just after Lauren's divorce. They had two umbrellas between them. His mother kept shuffling back and forth, squeezing first under David's umbrella, then Lauren's, never able to remain dry. While they walked, Lauren enumerated all of the shortcomings of her former husband, as if to convince herself that the divorce was justified. Their mother listened without comment. Then Lauren began wondering how her children would adjust. In an unusual settlement, the court had decided that one child should live with Steve and one with her. Steve hardly cared. In fact, he was already dating another woman, who had her own children. Lauren began weeping, and their mother tried to comfort her, but she hurried ahead to the restaurant. Ten years ago, maybe twelve. Only shortly before, it seems to him now, Lauren's second marriage, and the outdoor reception with the tinkling of bells and a train passing by in the distance with its windows glinting in the sun and the guests barefoot in the grass. David listens to his shoes tap on the steps as he climbs. His shoulder brushes against a protruding ledge in the wall. He steps away, then continues up. It will be a mud-filled day. And at the end of the day, he and Andrew will have to clean the cars. Then, for him, a long night with the preplanned funerals and the obit files. He hears Andrew again in the garage, tools clanking. "I'm back," shouts Andrew. "I'll let you know in a minute." The engine of the car comes alive and throbs happily. "That was the problem," says Andrew. "Glad to hear it," David shouts back. Another pungent whiff of the gasoline. He holds his nose as he climbs. Everyone will get wet and complain, but he actually enjoys rainy days. In the rain, flowers and grass appear their most exquisite, as if they breathed water instead of air, more alive in the wet and the mist, with the rain softening the edges of light, coating the leaves with silky soft gloves. He touches the grooved wall with its ancient riverbeds, lets his fingers trail the stone crevices as he follows the spiraling steps. Tap, tap, his shoes tap on the stone steps. Twisting in their tight turns, the steps vanish ahead and behind.

In the hallway, David goes directly to the sitting parlor, where he's been visiting with Patrick McConoghy and his family. As the mortuary always does for poor families, it has taken this case pro bono. Pathetically, Patrick keeps repeating his gratitude to David and the rest of the staff. "You are good people." Patrick is a large man with red hair and freckles, bushy red eyebrows, a gap between his two front teeth. Both daughters have red hair as well. Sitting on the sofa together, the three of them look like a garden of red plants.

Over the years, David has often been a customer at Patrick's shoe shop but has never engaged in more than two minutes of conversation with the man. In person, Patrick speaks in a quiet, halting voice, but once David heard him and his wife shouting at each other in the back of the shop. Patrick has a famous ability to match faces with shoes. Out of a hundred pairs of refurbished shoes on his rack, he can retrieve the right shoes for each customer without glancing at the tag. Patrick himself wears the shoes his customers have discarded. For today, he's borrowed shiny black patent-leather shoes, and his curly red hair is neatly trimmed and combed. But his eyes are swollen, and he keeps jabbing at them with the knuckles of his left hand. "Shop's been closed the last six weeks," he says to David. "Nothing to be done for it. I had to take care of my Julia." His breath smells of alcohol.

Two of the women friends talk quietly to the children, paging through a picture book, while the third sits in the wingback and knits. "There's no sense in this," the knitting woman says to David. Mille Halliburton is her name, and she's knitting a sweater for one of the red-headed girls. A strand of saffron-colored thread wanders lazily from her lap to a ball of yarn in her purse. "A woman with two young children, taken away at forty years old," says Mille. "Can you tell me what meaning there is in that? I don't understand it. It makes me angry."

"God knows the meaning of it," says one of the other women.

"Well, I wish God would tell me," says Mille. "Because it sure doesn't make any sense to me. Sometimes I wonder if there even is—"

"Don't dare say it," breaks in the other woman. "It's not for us to figure these things out."

The younger of the two daughters—she must not be older than four—looks up from her book and tells David that her mother is up in the clouds and that she can see them but they can't see her. "Can you talk to my wife?" Patrick abruptly asks David. The three women friends exchange glances. Then, one by one, they step out into the hallway, as if they shouldn't witness this moment of privacy, or perhaps they don't want to hear whatever lie David is about to tell.

Patrick and his two daughters are staring at David. Suddenly the world turns totally silent. Voices stop midsentence. The footsteps in the hallway come to a halt. Even the clock in Martin's office seems to freeze. In the terrible silence, in the purity, David looks helplessly at Patrick, remembering the sight of Julia McConoghy stretched out on the embalming table. No, he mumbles, he doesn't think he can. Patrick continues to stare at him, not accepting David's answer. The two daughters stare at him. He's fallen through the ice.

"What's going to happen to those girls?" Martin whispers in the hallway. "Mr. McConoghy can't possibly take care of those girls."

"You don't know that," says Jenny. "Have you talked to the friends?"

"They live quite a distance, they told me. And they don't think the girls should be moved. You remember that family two years ago, the three children?"

"We're doing what we can," says Jenny, fussing with one of the flower arrangements. "You can't carry the world on your shoulders, love."

"I know that Mr. McConoghy can't take care of those girls," Martin says, shaking his head. "It breaks my heart to look at those girls. And there's no family, other than an old uncle."

David, still shaken from Patrick's question, stands in the hallway and remembers the face of Julia McConoghy. She was pretty. Once he asked Martin what thoughts went through his head as he "prepared the remains." Martin replied that he thought only of making the deceased look as good as possible for the grieving family, giving the deceased a natural and peaceful expression that would comfort the family. But what about the face? asked David. The face. There's a person lying there. What do you think about when you look at the face? Martin shrugged his shoulders. I don't think about the deceased, he said. I just think about the grieving family and doing my job. David was not satisfied. He wasn't getting the answers he wanted. You don't think at all about the person lying there? No. No? You don't? David became almost angry with Martin. If you're only thinking about the family, why do you say a prayer at the beginning? My father always said a prayer, replied Martin, and his father always said a prayer. Martin paused for a moment. "I guess I say a prayer because it feels right. The body is a sacred possession the family has entrusted to me."

Patrick McConoghy, his two daughters, and their three friends are gathering their coats. It's time to get into the cars and to leave for the cemetery. No, they'll go in their own car, thank you. David looks out the window. It is so dark in the rain that he can barely see the cars waiting on the street. He glances at the handwritten poem Patrick has asked him to read at the grave site. *In dreaming, we journey to distant blue shores.* He recites the line softly and hears his mother's voice instead. His mother read poems to him before bed, after reading a story to Lauren. Why she read stories to Lauren and poems to him he never knew, another of his mother's mysteries. He in his bed and she in the corner chair with the single lamp glowing above her head like a halo. Wordsworth. Dickinson. Coleridge. More than once she read to him *The Rime of the Ancient Mariner*. It was one of her favorites, and he would occasionally come upon her in the little hallway between the bedrooms, when she thought she was alone, and find her reciting the lines to herself. She said that you could tell a poet's style from one line, and style was everything. Neither of his parents was cultured, but his mother liked poetry. To mark the poems she wanted to read, she used little scraps of paper torn from old phone books. The sounds of the words calmed him, but their meanings stirred him and made him want to leave their small house and go to far places. It was a strange sensation that he can still remember, the being calmed and stirred at the same time in different parts of his body. When his mother turned out the light, he would still be stirred and awake, imagining, and he would listen to her footsteps going down the hallway. Even her footsteps weren't like the footsteps of other people. She seemed to glide when she walked. It was part of her grace. She was never completely attached to anything. She rarely kissed him good night. He can see her as clearly as if she were sitting five feet from him now—his young, glamorous mother with the halo of light above her head, her hair its rich brown natural color, on her left hand the wedding ring that she stopped wearing the week after his father died, the jade necklace around her neck. Until this moment, he had completely forgotten that jade necklace. She hasn't worn it for thirty years, and yet he sees it now around her neck as she sits in the corner chair and reads to him, her voice calming and stirring.

SOME OF THE FILES, FROM THE MORE illustrious families, bulge with newspaper clippings—business promotions, garden parties, honors and awards, photos, children's achievements in athletic competitions, wedding announcements. Others contain only the single page of notes from the initial interview. "Father and two children together in one plot/mother with her own family." The skinny folders sometimes get lost. Folders get lodged within other folders, folders get misfiled, folders slip down to the bottom of the drawer. Lives are shuffled like playing cards. At Jenny's request, David has been going through the preplanned funeral files, weeding out the extraneous material. "Martin clips everything," she said this morning in that mildly disapproving tone she uses when referring to Martin's excesses. It should all be scanned and digitized anyway. David sits at Martin's desk, in Martin's chair, late in the evening, a pile of folders nearby. He glances sleepily at the glass paperweight that belonged to Martin's father, the photograph of Martin and his father and grandfather at some country inn, a well-used book titled *Stamps of the World*. Breathing deeply to stay awake, he reads the first paragraph of each clipping to see if it should stay in the folder or be tossed. But how to know? Sometimes families ask for the most random thing to be included in the obituary, a vague memory of some event or accomplishment, and it can be found or not found only in the folder. In one photograph, a boy, now in his fifties, grins at the camera during a high school football game.

The boy reminds David of Bartley Ryan, who was always handsome and blond until he lost his hair—David is still astonished by how much Bartley has changed, seeing him just a month or two ago, weeping without embarrassment and making his ugly comments about Bethany. And Bartley has just called about the newspaper article that appeared last week, the second one, this time containing a twisted statement from David. The reporter, the same who had done the first story, apparently energized by the public enthusiasm for the topic, followed him one evening to Ellen's apartment. Do you deny that you saw a ghost? she asked. I never said it was a ghost, David blurted in frustration. "It?" That was all he needed to say. "It" was certainly something. "It" was not nothing. "It" was a subject that commanded a verb. Whereupon the newspaper considered the sighting "confirmed by the original source." "Mr. David Kurzweil, a respected former bank employee with advanced education, did not deny that he witnessed a supernatural event on April 23. Whether ghost, spiritual messenger, or energy aura, this newspaper will not speculate." As further support for the veracity of the sighting, the newspaper went on to describe the venerable history of the mortuary itself. A day later, a remarkable image appeared in the paper. Somehow, a photographer had gotten into the slumber room and taken a picture. Martin and Jenny had been turning down all requests for photographs, but an outsider could have posed as a grieving family member and hidden a small camera. The published photo showed a faint haze hovering in midair.

The business of the mortuary, which for three quarters of a century was a meandering stream, has turned into a small flood. Families who have buried their loved ones with other funeral homes for generations are now calling Martin's establishment for appointments. People want to sit for an hour in the slumber room, to meet

David and plead with him. They want him to talk to their dead relatives. They want him to describe the nature of the other side. I can't help you, David says over and over. I wish I could help you. The grieving families don't accept his denials. "We just want to know if Mother is okay," a man implored David yesterday in the arrangement room. "Don't, Paul," said the wife. "You're embarrassing me. Your mother is dead."

Martin has grudgingly lifted his moratorium. Anybody can talk to whomever. Including Ophelia. Go ahead, blab away. Just don't tell me about it, he says. I don't understand the world anymore. "Well, you should understand one thing," says Jenny. "We're doing a firesale business." If this continues, she adds, we'll finally be able to refurbish the furniture. We can buy a new hearse. We can put new tiles in the bathroom. But I don't want new tiles in the bathroom, Martin says. They are tiles my mother got for us and I love those tiles. They're ugly, says Jenny. Your mother had horrible taste. Admit it. And what a lovely article in the paper about the funeral home. Very respectful. "People had no idea it had been in one family for four generations," says Jenny. "What do you think, love? Don't say you aren't pleased." Martin won't comment, but he's not discouraging the increase in business.

On her signature cream-colored stationery, David's mother has written a cryptic response to his request to talk to her. "I'm not in a good state of mind for you to visit at the moment."

Gallison, Gallois, Garrity, Girabaldi, Grady. David trudges on, barely through the G's, with a hundred or more folders to go and so many new people calling up for appointments and it now being nearly midnight. His hands are smudged from the newspaper print. Martin's desk. He once sat at the desk of his father. It had a big ledger book, where the accounts were kept, and he imagined how nice it would be to write all of those numbers in their neat boxes. The telephone rings. A silence at the other end. "Shaw Funeral Home," David says. He can hear someone breathing. "Yes, what is it?" He waits for a few moments, then hangs up.

He is lost in the M's the next day, somewhere near *Montegut*, when Ellen calls.

"Guess where I am," she says.

"I can't guess. Aren't you on your lunch break?"

"Yes, I am. And I'm sitting on the bed in room three-seventeen of the hotel on the east side of town. I've rented it for the day. And . . . let me see what else. I'm not wearing any clothes. I thought you might like to come over."

He pauses, trying to imagine her there. He knows the hotel. "I'll have to tell Martin something to get away."

"Tell him anything. Just come. Room three-seventeen."

"I got that."

He hurries down the street. He can hardly wait to see the maroon awning of the hotel, the large terra-cotta pots on the curb. In the lobby, people lounge about, waiting for lunch. There, past the front desk, he spots the staircase, and, without looking at anyone, bounds up the carpeted stairs.

He knocks.

"Is it you?"

"Yes."

Invisibly, the door opens. Ellen appears from behind the door, naked, and rubs her body against him. She watches as he undresses. "Mr. Kurzweil, you shouldn't meet strange women in their hotel rooms in the middle of the day."

"Only this once," he says, grinning.

"We don't have much time." She pushes him to the floor, on his back, and straddles him. "Isn't this better than whatever you were doing in the mortuary?"

"Much better," he says. He can't remember what he was doing, what he was worrying about. Her silky dark hair sweeps across his chest, her nipples. The world has shrunk to this room, this small area of rug on the floor. As she begins to sway back and forth, a patch of light comes through the shutters and falls across her shoulders.

He sees blood and sits up. "You're having your period."

"I am. But it's a light day. Is it a problem?"

"We've never made love when you were having your period."

"But I want to. I want to now."

"I didn't know."

"Does my blood bother you?"

"I just wasn't expecting it."

"I want you to know everything about my body." She goes to the bathroom and gets a towel and puts it beneath them, and she is delicate even doing this common thing, she is a sculpture of ivory, touched with the dark triangle of her pubic hair. When she sits astride him again, she massages his penis, splotchy with her blood, and puts him inside of her.

"Oh," she moans. "That's what I wanted, Mr. Kurzweil."

"Happy to oblige, Ms. Merriwether."

"Doesn't it feel good to you?" she gasps. "Like this? With my blood?"

"Yes, it does."

"Say it again."

"Yes, it does. Yes." She is right. He wants this, he wants all of her.

A SCREECH OF TIRES. Martin, who ventured out this morning to be fitted for a much-needed new suit, comes bolting through the front door and throws his coat to the floor, dashes into the first room he sees, which happens to be the visitors' washroom, and locks the door behind him.

"We'd better send for Jenny," says Ophelia.

"It's me," Jenny says softly through the locked washroom door. There's no answer. "Martin, are you in there?" She knocks on the door and waits. "Just say something if you're in there."

"Yes," comes Martin's voice.

"It's okay," says Jenny. "You're back now. You're safe."

Martin says nothing.

"You stay in there as long as you want," says Jenny.

Alarmed, David stands in the hallway with Robert and Ophelia. "Is there anything we can do to help?" he whispers. Jenny shakes her head no.

"Call a doctor," Martin says. "I'm having a heart attack."

"You're not having a heart attack, love," Jenny says to the door. She brings a chair into the hallway and sits down next to the washroom. "He just needs some time by himself," she whispers.

"Are you still out there?" comes Martin's voice.

"Yes, I'm right here," says Jenny.

"Poor Martin," whispers Opheila. "Something wicked must have happened to him when he was little."

"Nothing that he's told me," whispers Jenny. "I know that he had some problems with his older brother years ago. But I don't think that's it. He just doesn't like new people or places."

"It's really weird," says Ophelia. "He never gets like this with the grieving families. There's tons of new people."

They see the light go out under the door.

"Are you still there?" he calls out.

"Yes, I'm here," says Jenny. "I'm not going anywhere. I'm just sitting outside the door."

"Please don't leave."

"I'm not leaving," Jenny says to the door. "Do you want anything?" Martin doesn't answer. She begins whispering things to him through the door.

An hour later, Martin says that he would like a ham sandwich. When Jenny brings the sandwich, Martin opens the door a crack, a hand comes out of the darkness and takes the sandwich, the door closes again and locks. Jenny remains by the door, whispering to him in a steady stream.

In another hour, Martin comes out of the washroom. Without saying a word to the staff in the hallway, he goes to his office and closes the door.

ONE MORNING, DAVID IS CALLED to the reception area. Some people are waiting for you in the sitting parlor, says Martha. I don't know who they are. I don't know anything about it. Then why did you let them in? says David, annoyed. Martha shrugs her shoulders. They look like, you know, lawyers.

Theresa Gaignard and Lester Mewhinney. Both of the visitors appear to be in their mid-forties. Ms. Gaignard is wearing a smart, tapered jacket over a white blouse, stockings and black leather shoes, peach-colored lipstick, not a hair out of place, while Mr. Mewhinney has on a gray silk suit and silk tie, with a small gold pin in his lapel. When Mr. Mewhinney opens his mouth, David can see gold fillings in his teeth. Ms. Gaignard and Mr. Mewhinney are refined-looking and relaxed, much more relaxed than any lawyer David has met. They apologize for not calling in advance to make an appointment—they didn't, in fact, expect to be able to speak to him on their first visit.

"Can we sit down?" says Ms. Gaignard, gesturing to the sofa. She glances at the coffee table and smiles. "I see that you appreciate William Blake. Something that we have in common. I like his drawings as much as his poems." She turns to her colleague. "Do you know Blake, Lester?" Mr. Mewhinney shakes his head no, with a trace of irritation, as if he resents the suggestion that he might be less cultivated than his colleague.

Ms. Gaignard hands David one of her cards, which has an

embossed logo of two overlapping circles. Ms. Gaignard and Mr. Mewhinney explain that they represent a nonprofit organization called the Society for the Second World. "It's an international society," Ms. Gaignard says, "a philosophical and scientific society devoted to a comprehensive view of existence."

"What does that mean?" asks David. They certainly have the mumbo jumbo of lawyers as he remembers it from his one semester in law school.

"Bear with us, Mr. Kurzweil." The society includes philosophers, doctors, lawyers, scientists, theologians, artists, and "more Ph.D.'s than a small university." Ms. Gaignard does most of the talking. Her voice is pleasant and earnest at the same time, similar to the voice of one of the executives at the bank where David used to work. She has placed her small, elegant briefcase on the coffee table next to the volume of William Blake.

"We've read the recent articles about you," says Ms. Gaignard. "I wouldn't imagine that you were too happy with them." She pauses and smiles. "I wouldn't be. My word, everything was such a mishmash of secondhand information."

"Newspapers have become irresponsible these days," says Mr. Mewhinney. He leans forward on the sofa, placing his well-manicured hands on his knees. "Journalists have no interest in the truth anymore. They're only interested in sensationalism and popular culture, movie stars and all that. I used to be in publishing, and I've watched it happen. It's a disappointing decline."

David nods. Mr. Mewhinney and Ms. Gaignard, whatever their business, are clearly not here to arrange a funeral. They shouldn't have come during regular hours, but he'll be polite and spend another few minutes with them. And he does like Ms. Gaignard. He decides that she is more attractive than Sally Jacoby, his colleague at the bank. In an indirect manner, she is flattering him, making him feel important, but he has his guard up. So many people have come to talk to him in the last month.

"Still," says Ms. Gaignard. The word hangs in the air. "We take the subject seriously."

"What subject is that?" David asks.

"The subject of the articles." With a graceful sweep of her hand, she smooths her pleated skirt. "We respect you, Mr. Kurzweil. We've looked you up a bit—nothing confidential or invasive—and we know enough about you to have a high regard for you. That's why we wanted to come talk to you."

But David does feel invaded. They've looked him up. There's no privacy anymore, he thinks to himself. Every letter a person has written, every word spoken is recorded somewhere. Everything is public. He's hardly a prominent figure, and yet he's been "looked up."

"We want to earn your trust," says Mr. Mewhinney. At that, he opens the briefcase and takes out some pages, the résumés of some of their members. There are names David has never heard of, but with impressive credentials. He will keep his guard up.

"We'd like to ask you something," says Ms. Gaignard. "Actually, we've come quite a long distance to talk to you." She pauses. "Did you see something unusual here?"

"Yes." David is surprised at himself. How baffling it is that a person can utter a word before any conscious decision has been made to speak. Evidently, the brain and the mouth are not connected. His intention was to say nothing to these people, but he finds himself mesmerized by the sound of Ms. Gaignard's voice.

"You saw something . . . with no rational explanation, here in this mortuary?"

"Yes." Who are these people?

"That's what we wanted to know, Mr. Kurzweil." Ms. Gaignard and Mr. Mewhinney exchange glances, and Mr. Mewhinney takes out a small notebook from his breast pocket. "We weren't sure from the newspaper accounts," says Ms. Gaignard, "so we wanted to ask you in person. We look into these reports when we think there's reason to look into them, when the people involved are thoughtful people, such as yourself. As you can imagine, there are a lot of kooks out there. But we were especially impressed by your . . . seriousness."

"We'd like you to assist us," says Mr. Mewhinney. "And maybe we can be of some service to you." Mr. Mewhinney places the résumés back into the briefcase. "Let me say that you're in good company, Mr. Kurzweil. We've all experienced events that, one way or another, don't have . . . any rational explanation. And why should we expect everything to have a rational explanation? The world is complex. More than we can imagine. There are things beyond our human comprehension. We're ants, Mr. Kurzweil. Does an ant understand what has happened when, one day, a man puts his boot down on the anthill? Think about that."

The image of the ant and the anthill is so compelling that, for a few moments, David pictures himself as an ant, scrambling over the mound of an anthill. Suddenly, a giant boot descends from the sky . . .

Ms. Gaignard explains that they would like to help David cope with what she calls his "second-world experience." Such experiences, she says, can be disorienting, similar to a person's first flight in an airplane. Isn't it strange, she says, how huge buildings can dwindle to toys in a dollhouse, how a hodgepodge of highways and fields can take on an orderly pattern. Clouds, once impossibly high, lie far below in a white fluffy carpet. Do you remember? she asks, smiling—not a condescending or fabricated smile, but a genuine smile. At an altitude, says Ms. Gaignard, you see things that you didn't see before, things that were there all along but not visible on the ground. What we call the "second world" is like that, she says. The Society believes—in fact the Society *knows* from its own research and observations—that there exists a second world, parallel to the first world. Parallel but very different in nature. The second world is not a physical world, she says. It has its own laws. The second world may or may not be the work of a deity. We keep an open mind, says Ms. Gaignard. We've found that certain people, and sometimes certain special locations, have access to the second world. Of course, those people usually can't immediately comprehend that experience. We want to help in that comprehension. We want to facilitate those communications and contacts. We want to learn. From time to time, we get brief glimpses of the second world, but we want to know so much more. "Tell us," she says, "have you been disoriented since your experience?"

David stands up from his chair. He finds himself greatly disturbed. *From time to time, we get brief glimpses . . .* Hasn't he had the identical thoughts? In his mind, against his will, he sees it again, the terrible seconds burning in his mind. Do Mr. Mewhinney and Ms. Gaignard know what he saw? He's afraid to describe it, yet he wants to tell them. Now they are staring at him as if they can gaze into his mind, staring and smiling as they recline so easily on the sofa. Why do they sit so easily? He looks away, into the hall. He feels nauseated all over again. For the last month, he's been spending afternoons in the slumber room, twisting the draperies this way and that in an attempt to create one of Robert's "weird light effects," but he hasn't succeeded. It was not a special effect of the light. No lighting produced what he saw. Could he have imagined it? The thought constantly thrashes about in his mind. He must have imagined it. There is only one world. The world of tables and chairs, the earth spinning hard on its axis, blood throbbing in veins. And when the heart stops the animal dies. Many times now, he's seen death on the embalming table, final death. Cells without oxygen cease their convulsions. Tissues dry up and rot. Atoms scatter. Cause and effect. The Pythagorean theorem. And yet . . . Ms. Gaignard and Mr. Mewhinney are persuasive. She strikes him as genuine. Mr. Mewhinney he doesn't much care for—he's a little too smooth and he seems to be on somebody's payroll. But she is genuine and attractive, and he wants to believe her. She has a family, she tells him, a husband, a daughter, a son. She eats dinner with her family when she's not traveling, she says, at six o'clock every night. She cooks and her husband does the cleaning. She has advanced degrees. He wants to believe her. Other people have reported experiences like his, she says. Could they all be imagined? What are the probabilities? Yes, that's it. He should think of it all in terms of the probabilities. Solid material. "Are you all right, Mr. Kurzweil?" Is he losing his mind? What is the probability that he imagined that thing on April 23? What is the probability for ten people at ten different mortuaries? Somewhere a telephone rings. Martha's voice. He should take the vacation that Martin has offered—not to be treated, but to rest. He would like a rest; that's what he needs, a rest to settle his mind. What are the probabilities? "Mr. Kurzweil?" And after his rest, he'll visit his mother. She's aging rapidly these days, she's a diminishing stump of a candle, and he shouldn't stay away any longer. He can picture her holding her glass of water in her veined hands. "We hope we didn't upset you, Mr. Kurzweil." What? What did they say? What are the probabilities? It must be a question of the probabilities. Now they're standing, Ms. Gaignard and Mr. Mewhinney. Can they see into his mind? "We'll be in touch. With your permission, we'd like to conduct some experiments." What?

Ophelia cannot contain herself. For the last hour, she's been pleading with Dr. Tettlebeim to let her watch the experiments in the slumber room. "I'll sit in the back and won't say a word," she whimpers. "Or I can help."

Dr. Tettlebeim, a small, gentle man dressed in a suit and bow tie, waves Ophelia away with apologies and repeats that the Society prefers not to have spectators. "Interferes with the intentionality," he says. His pimpled assistant nods in agreement and continues his work positioning the mirrors and candles. The sound-absorbing panels Dr. Tettlebeim installs himself. "Mr. Kurzweil, are you prepared?"

As he's been instructed, David practices closing first one eye and then the other in front of the mirror. He's also been told to wear loose clothing, to take off his wristwatch, and to think only quiet thoughts. A light meal of fruit and vegetables beforehand was highly advised. With reluctance, David has agreed to participate in the investigations, after Ms. Gaignard talked to him in the lobby of his apartment building for over an hour. After which Jenny argued with Martin for two days to allow "those people" into their funeral home.

Ophelia knocks again. "Dr. Tettlebeim, I have some tea for you." She comes into the slumber room, her eyes growing big as she regards the mirrors and candles and acoustic panels. "All my life, I've wanted to see something like this," she says.

"All right," says Dr. Tettlebeim with a sigh. "All right. How can I say no to such a determined young lady. But please, dear, sit in the back and try not to make any sound." Ophelia is ecstatic. She winks at David and crosses her fingers in a good-luck sign.

From a CD player, Beethoven's "Moonlight Sonata" quietly begins ebbing and flowing through the room. "I hope that you like Beethoven," Dr. Tettlebeim says softly. "I find that the first two movements are excellent for promoting a restful atmosphere."

As the opening adagio moves through his body, David tries to think calm thoughts. The steady bass triplets sound to him like an old man with a cane walking down a long road to unfasten a gate. The old man is so enduring and steadfast. As he walks in triple beats—left foot, right foot, cane/left foot, right foot, cane—the gate continues to retreat in the distance. But the old man will not give up. On and on he walks toward the gate—left foot, right foot, cane/left foot, right foot, cane. Why does he want to unfasten the gate? David wonders. What's on the other side? But he will not give up. In steady and patient triplets, he keeps walking. And then the melody to accompany the bass triplets, so sad, a lamentation. The melody knows why the old man wants to unfasten the gate, knows what is on the other side, and the knowing is sad.

"Lights," whispers Dr. Tettlebeim. His assistant walks around the cavernous room, turning off each porcelain lamp one by one. Then the heavy velvet drapes. It is dusk, the optimum time according to the doctor, and the room is illuminated only by a single candle behind David.

David leans back in the chair, listening to the old man walk down the road, and stares into the mirror. He sees the candle flickering, he sees the dim moon of Ophelia's face in the back of the room, he sees Dr. Tettlebeim sitting quietly in a chair. In this light, the doctor's hair is silver, the wrinkles in his face silver shadows, his blue eyes shining dark dots. This will take some time, Dr. Tettlebeim says softly. These are sensitive matters. We are told, he whispers, that Nostradamus used a mirror and candle to gaze into the future. Our Society cannot accept such unverified reports, but they are suggestive. What is the future, Mr. Kurzweil? The second world does not obey the same laws for time as the first. The separation between past and future, in fact the very concepts of past and future, may simply be a human construction, a figment of how our limited brains grasp the world. But I am intruding on your experience.

Dr. Tettlebeim's ideas do not seem so unreasonable to David. He has often wondered about the split between future and past. Why, in a sliver of a second, does something that was once in the future become something now in the past? And why does it not also go in the opposite direction? What causes that razor-sharp line between future and past? It seems to David that nothing in nature is so sharp. If he looked at that line with a high-powered microscope, he imagines, he might well find that it is not really so sharp. It might have fuzzy filaments, crooks, and valleys that allow events to slip across in either direction, or perhaps to get snagged in the boundary, neither future nor past. And if there isn't a sharp boundary between future and past, then maybe what we think of as the future is already determined. If so, then the act of making a decision to do one thing or another is only an illusion. Perhaps our decisions are already made. In which case our lives are like railroad tracks already laid. Was it like that when Ellen called from the hotel? Did he have to say yes? But he wanted to say yes. Why did he want to say yes? Was he simply following the track? And if there isn't a sharp boundary between future and past, then maybe what we think of as the past never actually happened, or maybe it hasn't yet happened. In which case, he never went to room 317 with Ellen. But he feels. He feels the chair against his bottom. He feels his shoes against his toes. Are his feelings future or past? What is a feeling? Does it take place in his brain? Is a feeling a feeling before it is consciously recognized as a feeling? His head aches. . . .

The second movement, the allegretto.

You needn't strain, Mr. Kurzweil. If there are spirits in tangential contact with our sphere, they will make themselves optically known in due course. And please, do not be alarmed by anything you see. Are you beginning to relax? Yes, says David. He must stop thinking of future and past, of decisions and feelings. The music streams through his body. Dr. Tettlebeim's voice itself has become part of the music, steady and smooth and touched with a sadness. Does Dr. Tettlebeim know why the old man wants to unfasten the gate? As you relax, says the doctor, your arms will begin to feel heavy. Just let your arms lie at your side. Let your arms be heavy if they want to be heavy. Describe to me what you see in the mirror. It looks like a deep lake, David says. Good. The mirror may turn cloudy. That is what some people report just before contact. Or the mirror may darken. If you see an image of something or someone, just let the image trickle by you like water. Don't try to control the images. You may see someone you know, someone who has departed this physical world, a deceased father, a deceased mother, a grandparent, or possibly a stranger. You may see only a peculiar sign, or a pattern of some kind. These too can have great significance. Is the mirror clouding or becoming darker? David stares at the mirror. It does seem slightly darker to him. Yes. But no new images have appeared. Behind him, the doctor is whispering something to his assistant. David continues to gaze into the mirror. For a long time, he gazes into the mirror. What would he wish to see? he wonders. Certainly not the thing that he saw on April 23. He might like to see his father. And if his father appeared to him now, what would he look like? How old would he be? Would he be the age that he was when he died, in his late thirties, or the age he would be now, seventy or so? Is it his father who walks down the long road to unfasten the gate?

In his mind, he sees a vivid picture of his father. He sees his father on a night long ago. Well past midnight, he woke up to go to the toilet and heard a faint sound from the basement. Opening the door, he saw a dim light below, smelled wood oil and sawdust. When he tiptoed down the stairs, he discovered his father in his basement shop, working his lathe. The lathe made no noise as it spun, his father also moved without sound, it was all like a silent film, and his father's face glowed in the light. Then he looked up and saw David, gave him a strange smile, almost embarrassed, as if now they shared some secret between them. He motioned for David to join him, but David, feeing a discomfort he didn't understand, returned to his bedroom. That glowing face of his father David would like to see now. But when he looks at the mirror, he sees only the flickering candle, the dim chairs behind him, the small face of Ophelia. He wants to see his father. He would like to say many things to his father. Do you see anything? whispers Dr. Tettlebeim. No. David continues to gaze into the mirror. He feels as if he is floating, has lost all sense of his body. He floats with the music, the melody over and over, and the melody is like Ellen's voice when she sings in the kitchen. Sometimes I wonder if your job is challenging enough for you, she said to him last night. You have such a good mind. I learn a lot at the mortuary, he answered. Tell me about it. You see people in extreme conditions, he said. You learn what people can withstand. And there are other things. The place makes me think about life and death, the line between. That sounds so morbid, David. I can't believe the things you think about. But it's beautiful, he said. What? Beautiful. Like the *Rubaiyat of Omar Khayyám*. God, David, the *Rubaiyat* is so dismal. Everything is passing away. Yes, but it's beautiful too. A flower is all the more beautiful because it lives only a season, don't you think? Are you ever going to get married again? she asked suddenly. What made you think of that? I don't know if I'll get married again. I might. Just checking, she said. Something moves in the mirror. It is the moon of Ophelia in the back. He continues to stare. But he sees nothing unusual. Dr. Tettlebeim whispers again to his assistant. You can get up now, says the doctor. It's been an hour. An hour? David is surprised. We're finished for today, says the doctor. Thank you for your participation.

In the back of the room, Ophelia sighs with disappointment. "But he saw a ghost before," she says. "In this room."

"We don't want to leap to any conclusions," says Dr. Tettlebeim as he begins putting away his equipment. "We will do different tests."

The next experiment is also performed in the slumber room, a location that may possibly be a gateway, according to Dr. Tettlebeim. "We will wait and we will see."

The black box, Dr. Tettlebeim explains, contains something called a random number generator. "We at the Society call it the R box," says Dr. Tettlebeim. "A company makes them for us." One hundred times a second, a small computer within the R box randomly generates one of two numbers—either a zero or a one—like an electronic coin flipper. The results are recorded and graphed. After a few minutes, the machine has created thousands of numbers. According to the laws of chance, the little black box should spit out an equal number of zeroes and ones, randomly spaced, with no discernible pattern. However, says the doctor, certain people have the ability to alter the outcome of the box merely by the influence of their mind—by their concentrated "intentionality." Such people can change the string of numbers from random noise to a pattern, or produce a preponderance of zeroes or ones. "Intentionality is a powerful force," the doctor says. "We in the first world get only inklings. It is possible that some intentionality created the universe."

Dr. Tettlebeim places the black box on a table in front of David, not too close and not too far away. It is the size of a small book. Wires trail off to another computer and a printer, operated by the doctor's silent assistant.

"I don't get this," objects David. "What does this box have to do with what I saw before?"

"Everything is connected to everything else," says Dr. Tettlebeim. He takes off his glasses. "Have patience, Mr. Kurzweil. We are proceeding."

"This stuff is silly. Silly. I didn't agree to do this."

"Mr. Kurzweil. Please. We are exploring your powers. When you step into the second world, everything is connected—it is all part of the invisible world, the nonmaterial world. The R box, you see, is an excellent gateway between the two worlds because it is permeated with reason. It is subject to logical analysis. And when that analysis shows an anomaly, it shines out like a floodlight in the dark. A lovely paradox, don't you think? Please, have patience."

First they must calibrate. At the doctor's instruction, the R box is turned on. It makes a faint humming sound. Across the room, lights blink on the computer, and the printer whines. After five minutes, the printer has produced a graph. Dr. Tettlebeim puts his glasses back on and carefully examines the graph. Totally random, he says. "We are calibrated."

There's a knock at the door. It's Martin. He stands in the doorway, consternation on his face. "I thought we were finished with all this," he says.

"We have finished the first round of tests," Dr. Tettlebeim says in a soft voice. "We are conducting a second round now."

"This is a funeral home," says Martin. "This is not a hotel where conference rooms can be rented out for this and that."

Dr. Tettlebeim's assistant walks to the back of the room, as far from Martin as possible, and sits on the floor.

"We realize that we are interfering with your establishment," says Dr. Tettlebeim, "and would not be doing so without a good reason." He pauses. "I believe Ms. Gaignard has spoken to you about our work."

"She certainly has," says Martin. "And I can tell you that I'm not happy about it. I'm not happy about any of this." He waves his arms at the equipment, frowning when he sees the black box, a strange and possibly dangerous object smuggled into his funeral home. Then he turns to David, as if asking his opinion.

David shrugs. "I guess I'll go ahead and finish the thing up," he says.

"Two more hours," says Martin. "That's it. Two more hours. I think I'm being generous."

"Thank you," says Dr. Tettlebeim.

Martin leaves, closing the door behind him. Dr. Tettlebeim puts his hand to his forehead. "Unfortunate," he says softly. "Let's take a moment to collect ourselves." He walks over to David. "These things happen. People don't understand. Can you concentrate?"

"I think so."

"Then we will continue."

Dr. Tettlebeim turns on his CD player—this time it is a nervous little fugue from Bach's "Well Tempered Clavier," far less soothing than the Beethoven but, according to the doctor, more conducive to the projection of patterns. Bach was a maker of patterns, says the doctor.

Now please concentrate, Mr. Kurzweil.

But how should he concentrate? What should he think about? Think about the box, says the doctor. The R box. David stares at the R box. It is simply a little black box. How does a person think about a little black box? It looks like a book. He stares at the black box, and he thinks about the William Blake book and the poem that Martin once recited to him. Something about squashing a fly, a little fly on the little black box. He must concentrate. Dr. Tettlebeim is so gentle and kind. He must concentrate. Are we running? Dr. Tettlebeim whispers to his assistant. Concentrate on the box. Faintly, it hums.

At the end of ten minutes, Dr. Tettlebeim switches off the box and walks to the printer. He studies the graph. Then he beckons to his assistant. For a few moments, they confer. "Yes," says Dr. Tettlebeim, smiling. "Mr. Kurzweil, you have influenced the box. There are far too many zeroes compared to ones. Several standard deviations too many. Congratulations. You have swamped the probabilities of chance with your mind."

"This proves everything," says Ophelia. "Isabelle Poole told me she would pay you one hundred and fifty dollars to concentrate on her boyfriend and make him introduce her to his parents, which by the way he's never done in nine months. And she said I should get your autograph because you're going to be hyper-famous."

Distressed, elated, and suspicious, David calls Ronald Mickleweed, the smartest person he knows and a former classmate in school. Ronald was born with an untreatable form of lazy eye, but he read faster with his one good eye than anyone else with two. Furthermore, he didn't need full binocular vision to think brilliant thoughts. Since a young age, he quietly suffered the inevitable ostracism and cruel jokes that went along with his disfigurement. His sense of humor saved him. Excelling at school and then in college, Ronald went on to advanced studies—science turned out to be his greatest strength among many—and he was now a distinguished professor in the department of chemistry at the university.

Yes, yes, of course, he's been reading about David's "exploits" at the mortuary, Ronald says on the telephone in a good-natured manner. The newspaper people have certainly blown it way out of proportion, but they're having fun. I've hallucinated myself after too much grog to drink, Ronald says, laughing.

I'd rather not talk about that, says David. But there is another matter, and he explains the experiment with the R box, the ones and the zeroes. What does Ronald think? One experiment doesn't prove anything, says Ronald. Those people get excited over one atypical result, but they never mention the hundreds of typical results before and after. I'd be impressed if they repeated the experiment five times and got several standard deviations away from the norm every time. But it won't happen. It won't happen? asks David. No, says Ronald, because it's a random number generator. But Dr. Tettelbeim says that some people can alter the results with their minds. Come on, David. You don't believe that, do you? No, says David. Actually, I'm not sure. That's why I called you. Could there be some kind of mental force, or something like that? It's a random number generator, David. It produces numbers in random sequence. At times it will produce more zeroes than ones. At other times it will produce more ones than zeroes. It all averages out. In the long run, it produces an equal number of zeroes and ones. It's exactly like flipping a coin. On rare occasions, you'll get a long run of heads. And vice versa. It all averages out. But, asks David, doesn't it seem a little surprising that a rare occasion should happen just when I'm sitting in front of the box? But, David. Listen. *Somebody* is going to be near the black box every time a rare event occurs. Rare events do happen once in a while, you know, and somebody is going to be near the box. This time that somebody happened to be you. Do you understand what I'm saying? I can tell from the sound of your voice that you're upset about this. I can sympathize with that. Maybe I'm not explaining it well enough. I'm trying to understand, says David. I want to understand. We agree that a rare event happened. Yes, says Ronald, from what you've told me. Yes. A rare event happened. Why are you so sure that it didn't have anything to do with me? asks David. If you're asking me if I think that you can affect a little box or anything else outside of your body with your mind, with mental telepathy or whatever, absolutely not. We have a good understanding of the forces of nature, and that isn't one of them. But you weren't there, says David. How can you be sure? Dr. Tettlebeim was there, and he told me that I was influencing the box. It's a bunch of baloney, David. They're using you. Who are these people? They call themselves the Society for the Second World, says David. You've gotten mixed up with some nuts, says Ronald.

BUT SOMETHING DID HAPPEN with the R box. David feels it. After all of his misgivings, he did finally concentrate on the box. Something passed from him to the box like an electrical current leaping through space. He felt it, and no one can tell him he didn't. The experience was so extremely intense—with the jittery throbbing of the Bach fugue and Dr. Tettlebeim staring at him through his spectacles and the black box there on the table—he felt that he had a power. And then the announcement by the doctor that he had indeed "swamped the probabilities" with his mind. Isn't that possible? A force unknown to science? Isn't that possible? If he has the power to control a small box, what else can he control? But . . . now he's thinking nonsense. He is a mortal man, flesh and blood, nothing more. *There is nothing more.* There are atoms and molecules and the known forces of nature, as Professor Mickleweed says. He is deluding himself. Yet . . . that feeling will not go away. Surely there must be some things unknown, some things as yet uncomprehended.

When the letter from Ms. Gaignard arrives, asking him to attend a conference of the Society, he hesitates only a moment. It is a two-hour bus ride, barely longer than the trip to his mother's. He can leave on Friday afternoon and be back on Sunday in time to have dinner with Ellen at their favorite Indian restaurant.

———

On the bus trip to the conference, David is scarcely bothered by the unpleasant diesel fumes, the uncomfortable seats with the torn vinyl coverings, the rolling glass bottles on the floor. Instead, he is setting off on an adventure, and he has something to learn. Certainly, Ms. Gaignard and Mr. Mewhinney will be there, as well as some of the accomplished members and scholars of the Society whose résumés he has read. Absently gazing out of the window at the dingy gray towns streaming by, he wonders whether any of the gathered experts will be able to explain his "brief glimpses."

"Mr. Kurzweil." It is Ms. Gaignard, dressed beautifully as usual and carrying a handsome umbrella, although no rain is predicted. "I wasn't sure that you'd come," she says, and gives a little laugh. "I admire your courage." She touches him on the shoulder as if he were an old friend. "This is a challenging group we have here, fascinating but challenging. Now you'll see us in our full glory. We have so much to share with you, Mr. Kurzweil. May I call you David? Everyone is thrilled by your experiments with Sam Tettlebeim." David nods, remembering how Ms. Gaignard always manages to flatter him without being superficial. "Sam is actually here, to present the results. I hope you won't mind."

"I didn't know . . ."

"You shouldn't worry," says Ms. Gaignard, seeing his concern. "Sam is very professional."

"I won't have to say anything, will I?"

"That's completely up to you."

Does he sound like a whining schoolboy who's afraid to get up in front of the class? What does Ms. Gaignard think of him? Is he simply Exhibit A? He looks into her face and can see only confidence and sincerity. She has an intelligent face. And she takes care of herself. The inevitable age lines have been artfully covered by makeup, while her hair has been left to turn silver naturally. To David, Theresa Gaignard is a woman in control of her life, and at peace with it. Never, he thinks as he watches her gently twirl her umbrella, has he been at peace.

"We want you to be comfortable, David," she says. "It must be difficult for you being here by yourself. I really don't like traveling alone." She pauses. "My husband never comes to the Society's events. Not that he doesn't support me one hundred percent. It is just . . . you know. I wish he would come, but he won't." She hesitates, as if she were about to say more, but then excuses herself to greet another arrival.

In the hallway, David sees Dr. Tettlebeim. The doctor smiles and nods, but only in a formal way, as if he were a psychiatrist acknowledging the acquaintance of a patient outside the office. Wearing his customary tan suit and bow tie, Dr. Tettlebeim paces back and forth down the corridor with his hands in his pockets, mumbling. Apparently, he is practicing for his presentation. Yet when each attendee passes, he stops and smiles and says a few friendly words.

Before the opening session, the guests gather in the ballroom for cocktails, complemented by grilled mushrooms and tiny salmon cakes—all served on elegant pewter plates. Soft, atonal music wafts over the speaker system. The music drifts without recognizable melodies but establishes repeating patterns of its own, like a water-fall. At the front of the ballroom, flowers adorn the podium. There must be two hundred people, clustering in threes and fours, many obviously having known one another already, drinking and eating, laughing or talking thoughtfully. People range in age from their twenties to their seventies. Some wear suits and dresses, others jeans and flip-flops. The gathering is a bazaar. It is a cross between an outdoor school picnic and a symphony audience at intermission. But David senses something serious here as well. There is an expectant buzz in the air. One man, apparently an academic of some kind, holds forth to a group of admirers circled about him, pausing every once in a while to gaze off into the distance. People seem spellbound by whatever he is saying. Two young women stroll past David drinking wine, deep in conversation. In the corner, a man in a pinstriped suit leans against the wall tapestry and ponders a manuscript.

David sees no one he recognizes. He tries to listen in on conversations, but he feels awkward and misplaced. Where are Ms. Gaignard and Dr. Tettlebeim? Within a few moments, however, he finds himself in conversation with a sympathetic Asian man named Jason Chee and his wife, Ling. "My third conference," says Mr. Chee, dabbing at the wine he's just spilled on his navy-blue blazer. "It is a stimulating occasion. I look forward to it every year." David says that this is his first. "Oh, you'll find these people delightful," says Mr. Chee.

"I don't find them as delightful as you do," says Mrs. Chee.

Mr. Chee is a stout, shortish man. The pink color of his fat cheeks rises up to his forehead, where it scatters in red splotches and contrasts with his glossy black hair. His eyes gaze out eagerly behind the polished lenses of his glasses. Mrs. Chee also wears glasses. Hers are decorated with a flower design on the rims. She is taller than her husband, and sinewy, with brown weathered skin. Holding a straw to her lips, she sips a soda.

"How did you get interested in the Society?" David inquires.

"Oh, that is a story," says Mr. Chee. "If you really want to know." It involves his mother. Ever since childhood, he says, his mother was enthralled with butterflies. She painted butterflies on paper and canvas for years, she collected butterflies, she knew every species and color. Butterflies were her passion. She was also a seamstress, and she once made a dress for a queen, but he won't go into all of that.

"Madame Chee was highly artistic," says Mrs. Chee. "Unfortunately, her talents were not passed down."

"Our daughters, Wan and Yen, did inherit their grandmother's beauty," says Mr. Chee. "Beauty is artistry enough."

"Just what a man would say," says Mrs. Chee. "A woman needs more than beauty."

Mr. Chee looks at his wife, perplexed, and continues with the story. A week after his mother died, he says, he was walking through a field and suddenly had an overpowering sensation that she was near. A moment later, a Monarch butterfly alighted on his shoulder and remained there for ten minutes, its wings gently rising and falling like the beating of a heart. Finally, the butterfly flew away. "What do you make of that, Mr. Kurzweil? I think it was my mother, that's what I think."

"It's a lovely story," says David.

"Maybe it is a lovely story," says Mr. Chee. "But there are many lovely stories. I believe it was my mother. I keep thinking about that day. I'd like to know if it was her."

"It was her," says Mrs. Chee.

"That's the thing of it," says a woman nearby who has been listening. "Even though we're in the first world, things in the second world can communicate with us. And vice versa." Her name is Maggie Hoppsfield, and she's wearing black leggings and a black sweater with a diamond pin on her shoulder. Her boyfriend comes with her to "these things," she says, but he just goes straight to the bar and gets smashed.

"What did it feel like when the butterfly was sitting on your shoulder?" asks David.

"It felt like my mother's hand touching me," says Mr. Chee. "It was strange, like my blood was rising up in me. I felt a peace come over me. I had been suffering so much since my mother died. We were very close. I hadn't been eating much, and I was weak. Every night, I was dreaming about her. I think that my consciousness was higher than usual. Then I was walking through this field, just wandering around to get some exercise, and I had this weird feeling, like when you know somebody is standing behind you. I felt my mother there. When the butterfly landed on me, it was the touch of my mother. The butterfly came from nowhere, and I felt that my mother had come back to me from wherever she had been. A warmth came over me, as if the sun were shining right on me. I had walked into the light. I was given a good-luck chance, Mr. Kurzweil, a chance to be with my mother again. I thought of all the things that I wanted to say to her but never had. I knew that she wouldn't stay long. It was just a good-luck chance to spend a few moments with her. She touched me like she did when I was a child, that feeling of someone older and wiser who loves you very much. Just imagine the warm sun shining on your body. There was a certainty to it. I had no doubt at the time. Now I'm not sure." He shrugs his shoulders.

"It was her," says Mrs. Chee.

Listening to Mr. Chee describe the tender relationship with his mother, David cannot help thinking about his own mother, dreading again her reaction to recent events, to the terrible articles in the newspapers. What did she mean when she wrote that she was "not in a good state of mind" for him to visit? Is she so horrified and embarrassed that she cannot bear to see him?

The session is about to begin. A tall middle-aged man goes to the microphone, introduces himself as the president of the Society, and welcomes everyone. People take their seats. The president waves quickly to a few friends who have just arrived. He has an affable, confident manner, an SSW pin on his lapel. "We are all truth seekers," he says. There is a modest round of applause. "The Society for the Second World seeks a comprehensive view of existence." Exactly the same words that Ms. Gaignard used, as David remembers. "I'd like to welcome members of our sister societies," says the president. "We have representatives here from the Paranormal Society, Mind over Matter, Spirits and Auras, Origins, Advocates of Modern-Day Miracles (AMDM), and the Sixth Dimension." The president grins. "At SSW, we have a big tent."

The first speaker is a philosopher. "How do we know what we know?" he begins, without waiting for an introduction. Even though we live in the first world, he says, we should be able to prove the existence of the second world, just as Descartes proved the existence of God. Descartes began with the one thing he was certain of: that he was a thinking being. What we are certain of, says the philosopher, are two things: first, that we are thinking beings, and second, that we have intense feelings and sensations of a reality beyond our understanding—an acausal and immaterial world lying side by side with a causal and material one. A world that does not necessarily obey traditional logic. In other words, the second world. Suppose we accept only our own thoughts, which we know exist because how could we be thinking at this moment if it were otherwise? We can conceive of a four-dimensional world even though we cannot visualize it. We can conceive of invisible forces even though we do not see them. Indeed the physicists have proved the existence of such forces. We can conceive of a soul. We can conceive of a world in which solid matter passes through solid matter. In these mental constructions, there is no distinction between causal and acausal worlds, material and nonmaterial. There are no hard and fast boundaries. These are equal mental conceptions taking place in the only realm that we know to be true, our own thoughts.

The philosopher looks up from his notes and takes a sip of water. Evidently, he is just getting his engines warmed up, but someone seems to be signaling that his time has expired. Already? A look of dismay crosses his face. Reluctantly, he sits down, a victim of the relentless march of time in the first world.

David frowns, trying to unravel the philosopher's argument. It is compelling. But there seems to be some missing logical step, which he can't put his finger on. Then again, the philosopher was talking about the nonlogical world. Perhaps one shouldn't require logic when thinking about illogical and acausal concepts. But how can convincing ideas be presented in an illogical framework? David is puzzled. Others in the audience are not so concerned. The philosopher's remarks, even if interrupted, have struck a chord, and there is an appreciative applause.

"Did you understand that?" David whispers to Mr. Chee, who is sitting next to him.

"Hocus-pocus to me," Mr. Chee whispers back. "It seems to me that what he's really talking about is the imagination. Don't you think? The imagination is connected to the metaphysical, and the metaphysical is connected to the second world. That would be my argument. My imagination is like one of my children. I'd never give up my imagination."

"Hold on there," whispers David. "Aren't we talking about what's real and what's not real? There's a difference between what we can imagine and what's real."

"What do you mean by 'real'?" says Mr. Chee.

"Will you guys be quiet," a man says in an annoyed voice.

"It seems to me," whispers Mr. Chee, "that there's just got to be a lot more out there than what we can understand. Our brains are so limited. I know mine is."

"And it gets more limited every year," says Mrs. Chee. She swivels her lanky neck to see if she's disturbing the man behind them. "Here's what I have to say," she whispers to David. "There has to be another world because there has to be something after we die. Death can't be the end. All of this beautiful life. To have it end would be such a waste. And so sad. There's got to be something else. That's what I think."

But Mrs. Chee has evidently spoken too loudly. The irritated man behind them stands up and rattles his chair. Scowling, he pushes his way to the end of the row and moves four rows away to reseat himself.

Strange images are appearing and dissolving on the stage. With a PowerPoint presentation, a physicist is explaining something he calls the "many worlds" interpretation of quantum mechanics, which is apparently supported by some leading lights in the field. Unlike the stereotype, the physicist looks like a prosperous banker, with a crisp white shirt and gold cuff links. As he explains in his prefatory remarks, for the last ten years he has worked "independently, without formal institutional affiliation, because the universities and government laboratories are not nearly as open to new ideas as one would like." At each moment of time, the physicist says, an infinity of universes exist parallel to one another. These parallel universes branch off from one another with each conscious measurement, no matter how small. A glance will do. The second world, in fact, may be only one of an infinity of parallel worlds.

The audience is totally silent, trying to absorb these ideas.

The physicist moves briskly to gravitation and cosmology. He explains that some scientists currently believe that everything we experience in our physical world is simply a lower-dimensional space trapped within a larger space of six dimensions or more, as if we were all water bugs skating on the surface of a lake, spending our entire lives on that ruthlessly flat surface while oblivious to the third dimension. "There's a lot of extra space out there," says the physicist, with a smile on his lips. "It gives one room for thought."

"Yes!" shouts a woman in front of David.

"The soul, the spirit, the sacred, all reside in the immaterial world," says a theologian who has taken the stage, "whether we are talking Christianity, Judaism, Islam, Buddhism, or Hinduism. Surely, these intangible phenomena don't exist in the corporeal world of earth and flesh." For that matter, continues the theologian, what about the abstract but beautiful Platonic concepts such as love, goodness, truth, beauty? These too have an existence on some other, nonearthly plane. And history, unfortunately, has shown that human beings could not have originated these concepts. Where did they come from? From God, says the theologian, the prime being of the immaterial world. "In many ways, the immaterial world has more substance than the material."

"What did you think of that?" whispers Mr. Chee.

"It's hard to believe that the immaterial world, or whatever you call it, came along just to take care of goodness and love," says David. "As far as God is concerned, I've always been an agnostic." David hesitates, not wanting to offend Mr. and Mrs. Chee. "It seems to me equally impossible to know for sure that God exists or that God doesn't exist."

"I agree," says Mr. Chee. "I don't think we can ever know any of that with certainty, as you say. And exactly for that reason, Mrs. Chee and I are not buying into the first world one hundred percent. That's why we're here. To us, there are just too many uncertainties. And strange connections between people and things. When you go outside at night, why do the stars appear beautiful instead of frightening? Why do people feel connected to one another over long distances? Why did I feel that my mother landed on my shoulder? There are too many connections like that. I don't think they can all be accidents, do you?"

David sighs. "I don't know. How do you tell when something is accidental or not?" Mr. Chee takes off his polished glasses and shakes his head in frustration, unable to answer David's questions. David stares at the red blotches on Mr. Chee's forehead, and the shapes move and shift on the screen. The investigators are projecting their images. These men and women, many with good credentials, have gone to sites where unusual or unexplained phenomena have occurred. There, they have measured and documented with infrared thermometers, cameras, gauss meters, and other scientific instruments. Some of their photographs show faint, gauzy images of humanlike forms beside normal, solid images. Others have wisps and cloudlike shapes floating in the middle of rooms, or shining filaments winding through space against familiar landscapes like mountains and trees. The strange shapes appear and dissolve. An audio device plays "electronic voice phenomena" that have been recorded at some of the sites, none with any visible sources. Strange sounds fill the auditorium, more disturbing and evocative than the visual images. Invisible doors open and close. A person whispers, repeating a nonsensical phrase over and over: "Kinley spakle leedlemake, kinley spakle leedlemake, kinley spakle leedlemake." A child cries for her mother, the voice hollow and echoing as if coming from a deep well. There is a silence, then the child cries again, this time more softly but more desperately. The cry hovers in the room, penetrates the bodies of the men and women gathered there. Who is it? Another recording produces strange hums and whines that David has never heard before. Afterward, he's left with an unsettled feeling in his stomach. The president is talking. He says that the following testimonials have not been confirmed independently by the Society, but there has been a screening process and, of course, all of these people are members. A Mr. Francis Robb, who speaks so loudly and boldly that he has no need of the microphone, says that when he plays card games, especially with people he doesn't know, he sometimes hears a voice telling him what particular cards the other players hold. This mysterious voice, which is always a woman's voice with a slight stutter, has been amazingly accurate. He wants to know if others in the Society have ever had a similar experience.

"I could use that voice with my poker game," whispers Mrs. Chee.

"She's a good bluffer," Mr. Chee whispers to David.

Mrs. Chee smiles proudly. "That's because I don't take off my glasses," she whispers. "I don't let anybody see my eyes. It's in the eyes you can tell if somebody is bluffing or not."

"Shoosh." A woman on the stage is describing her discovery that the formation of ice crystals responds to words. In her investigations, she says, she writes a word on an index card and attaches it to a container of water. Next, she freezes the container. Then she examines it with a magnifying glass to see the shapes of the ice crystals formed. The words "love" and "harmony" cause beautiful patterns with rounded edges, while "fear" and "hate" cause chaotic and ugly shapes. She shows a few slides, which bring forth an approving murmur in the audience.

"What do you make of that?" whispers Mr. Chee.

"I don't believe it," says David. "It's ice. It's not alive. It's inanimate matter."

"Maybe there's some kind of vibration from the words," says Mr. Chee.

"Vibrations?" whispers David. "But the words are in English. The vibrations wouldn't know any language."

"That's a good point. Maybe the vibrations come from her mind and not from the words on the index cards."

"I don't believe it either," says Mrs. Chee. "But I'm going to try it when I get home. We'll see."

A Dorothy Ann Farrar, who describes herself as an amateur biologist "but not all that amateur," tells the audience that one day she was looking through a microscope at a living bacterial colony when she was astonished to see a word spelled out by the microscopic cellular organelles. The letters of the word were a little misshapen, and they jiggled as the microorganisms throbbed and pulsed, but there was no mistaking it. The word was HELP. All capital letters. Unfortunately, she didn't get a photograph at the time. For years, she's been haunted by the experience. "I believe there is an entire microscopic civilization," she says. "And they are intelligent, possibly more intelligent than us. But they need our help. What should we do?" Someone in the audience suggests that she report her findings to a government agency. Or maybe the Society should launch its own investigation.

David feels a tap on his shoulder. He turns around and is surprised to see Theresa Gaignard, who has apparently been sitting behind him for hours. "I hope you're feeling more at home with your experiences," whispers Ms. Gaignard. "You see, the Society can provide a context. I've been watching you, and it seems as if you've been enjoying yourself. Not that you have to believe all of this." She smiles. "It's like getting reports from the first trips of Columbus, or Magellan. Some of it is true, some of it is exaggerated, some probably downright false." David nods, thinking that most of what he's heard may fall in the last category. "Sam's up next," she says.

Before David can prepare himself, Dr. Tettlebeim moves toward the stage. Unlike some of the previous presenters, he doesn't clamber up like an excited teenager but climbs the steps slowly and with dignity. Evidently, Dr. Tettlebeim is one of the more distinguished investigators and is held in high regard. Speaking softly into the microphone, he announces that he has some "interesting" new results to report. He explains the R box, at which point some of the audience nod their heads knowingly. Then, putting on his spectacles, he gives a brief introduction of David. "Mr. Kurzweil, will you please rise." David stands uncomfortably. People are waiting to see the results. Then Dr. Tettlebeim projects on the screen the cumulative graph of the ones and the zeroes, comparing David's results against those expected by random chance. The column of David's zeroes rises gigantically above the other columns, like a skyscraper in a small town. "Ladies and gentlemen," says Dr. Tettlebeim quietly, "here is stark evidence of the force of the mind." The crowd breaks out in applause.

"That was something," says Mr. Chee, applauding with the others. "You should have told us."

"What do you think it means?" asks David.

"It could mean that you are connected," says Mr. Chee. "You are in touch. Who knows? You should be careful."

The session has ended. "Congratulations," says Ms. Gaignard, standing. Immediately, a dozen people come up to David wanting to speak to him, leaving their cards and addresses. People who an hour ago regarded him with a friendly disinterest are now fascinated by him. "I can tell that you aren't used to this attention," says Ms. Gaignard afterward. "I'm sorry."

"There's nothing to be sorry about, Theresa," says David. "But . . . I was hoping to have things explained a little."

"You were hoping for a logical analysis?" asks Ms. Gaignard. But you should have more respect for your experience than that, she says. Everybody wants to learn the purpose of existence. Everybody wants to know why there's something rather than nothing. Everybody wants to know why we're here. They won't find answers in logic or science or anything in the first world. We're at the frontiers. You're at the frontiers. You've got a foot in the second world.

David looks for Mr. Chee, but he's slipped out with his wife, leaving only a scribbled "Thank you" on his chair. David wants to talk to him further, for it seems that they have a similar skepticism combined with a powerful and unexplainable experience. In fact, David is ready to talk about April 23. But he won't have the opportunity. He hurries into the lobby looking for Mr. Chee. There is something wrong about this Society, David thinks, even with their caveats and disclaimers. Is it that they are too persuaded by their photographs and testimonials? Shouldn't they be more cautious? He believes that something has happened to him, but he doesn't know what it is, and he wants to explore it slowly and gingerly, like an ambiguous but riveting smile in the distance. What is it? He has glimpsed something, but what is it? Surely something more profound than the wispy photographs, or the coaching voice heard by the man playing poker, or the ice crystals that respond to words. Jason Chee seems to understand. But the Society is too certain. Ronald Mickleweed is also too certain. David feels caught in between, like a pedestrian stranded between two streams of traffic rushing at great speed in opposite directions.

On the bus back, his books. From *An Enquiry Concerning Human Understanding* by David Hume:

> It is universally allowed by modern enquirers, that all the sensible qualities of objects, such as hard, soft, hot, cold, white, black, etc. are merely secondary, and exist not in the objects themselves, but are perceptions of the mind. . . . If this be allowed, with regard to secondary qualities, it must also follow, with regard to the supposed primary qualities of extension and solidity.

Is everything in the mind? Is there no external reality?

Footsteps somewhere above. The smell of formaldehyde and gasoline. David sits in one of the hidden rooms downstairs; he can't even remember exactly when and where he wandered in—at times the rooms seem like a nest of secret underground tunnels, and he drifts from tunnel to tunnel without ever stepping into a hallway, without ever seeing a window. Faces of the deceased flicker through his mind. Again he wonders, as he listens to the tiny movements and the breathing of the rooms, why Martin never thinks of the person. A woman with an oval face. A man with thin arms. Yesterday a boy with blond hair. In one moment, a person is living, a life, a voice, a way of talking and acting, a holder of memories. In the next, there is only a motionless body, a thing, solid matter. How does it happen so suddenly? The movement from living to not living. A world, and then nothing. How does it happen? Where is the line and the break, the moment of crossing? A world, and then nothing. The thousands of memories suddenly gone, certain words of parents, the nervous piano recitals, the rows of shoes in a closet, the little Japanese bridge, the first lovemaking, the sight of a bird, a favorite song, the way that the fog looked on that day in that place, the sound of the ocean at that moment—all of it gone in an instant, gone not just for now but always. The generations of parents and great-grandparents and cousins and uncles stretching back through time, gone in an instant. Could it be possible? A life, and then nothing? Do the bits of dead matter know anything? Who allows this to happen? A life, and then nothing. It is like time. At one moment, something waits in the future, unknowable. The next moment, it is past. How does it happen, the sharpness, the worlds in destruction?

In late morning, while David is gulping a roast-beef sandwich in the arrangement room, Ellen calls. She sounds distressed. Did you see the newspaper today? she asks. No. Well, there's a long article about the Society for the Second World and your experiments with that box. And there's a picture of you. David's heart begins pounding. He feels betrayed. Why didn't they tell him? Perhaps they tried. Several unanswered calls have come in from Dr. Tettlebeim and Ms. Gaignard in the last week, buried among the calls from people wanting his service for various things. What does it say? David shouts into the telephone. Am I quoted? This is all such a nightmare. No, they don't quote you, says Ellen. But there's a mention of the "ghost incident" on April 23. And there's a graph of the zeroes and ones. Dr. Tettlebeim, who is quoted extensively, points out that a number of significant world events happened within a few days of your "extraordinary" session with the random number generator. A religious riot at a temple in southern India. A surge in the Japanese stock market. A tornado in the Midwest. "We must treat such correlations with some caution," says Dr. Tettlebeim. "If true, the intentionality force is enormous. But we haven't yet learned how to harness this force."

What's this all about? asks Ellen. This is ridiculous. And they're making you look like a fool. I hate that. Yes, it is ridiculous, says David. They're exploiting you, David. You need to do something.

Strangers begin appearing on the sidewalk outside the mortuary, in ones and twos, at odd times of the day. When David approaches the building one morning, a woman standing there calls out to him. Are you David Kurzweil? she asks with an odd look in her eyes. Without answering, David hurries past. Inside, he looks at her quickly through a window and finds her staring back at him.

Martin is shocked. What can we do? he says. He directs all the draperies and curtains to be drawn. Now no natural light enters the mortuary. He calls the police. Nothing to be done, say the police. It's only a few gawkers. But they are disturbing my establishment, says Martin. They're on public land, say the police, and they're not damaging anything. They have their rights. But if there's any violence, if they set foot on your property, call us.

One of the "gawkers" manages to get into the building. After a few such unpleasant incidents, Martin reluctantly institutes a screening process before letting anyone in the door. He says that he can't think and he can't work with the gawkers outside. Business is better than it's ever been before, Jenny reminds him. This is not how I want to conduct business, says Martin. It's just temporary, says Jenny. You'll see.

DAVID DECIDES THAT HE CAN NO LONGER delay speaking to his mother. "I realize that you might not be in the best state of mind, but . . ." Come, then, she says.

At the door, she greets him with more vitality and health than on his last visit—she is almost aggressively alive, dressed in a suit and scarf as if she were about to go out to lunch with a friend, thumping furiously about on her cane.

"The place doesn't smell right," she says. "I'm sorry about that." Gloria, the woman who cleans on Wednesdays, had to come yesterday because of an illness in the family, she explains. The odor of furniture polish and detergent wafts through the apartment, mingling with the jasmine of his mother's perfume. "Gloria is a luxury I don't need. But if you and Lauren want to spend your money that way, it's your business."

"Mother! Do you think you can get down on your hands and knees and clean this place yourself?"

"I'm not being appreciative, am I. I do appreciate it."

He looks around the apartment and sees the piled boxes of books sent from his mother's friend, books that she'll never read.

Where should he begin?

"You look good, Mother."

"I feel good. I've been taking vitamins. I don't know whether they're really doing anything, but I feel better. I've been going out. I went out with Frances yesterday."

"I thought Frances wasn't speaking to you anymore."

"It seems that she's started talking to her old friends again." His mother laughs. "She started back about an hour after she flunked out of her course at the university. She needs us again."

"So how is Frances?"

"Fine. She's getting old, like the rest of us. She doesn't get on with one of her children, and she's trying to figure out how to keep him out of her will. I told her: You have to treat your children equally, no matter what." She glances toward the kitchen. "I've got some lemonade in the fridge."

"I'll get it."

"No, I'll get it, darling. You've been on a bus for two hours."

His mother goes to the kitchen, comes back with a glass of lemonade. But suddenly she seems tired. She sits down, pats her hair into place, and places her cane across her lap. David still hasn't gotten used to seeing his mother with a cane. It seems impossible. Lightly closing her eyes, she seems completely content, as if she could sit in her chair for hours doing nothing at all. And once, she worked all day at the insurance company, shopped, made dinner for Lauren and him—and then went dancing on weekends.

After a few moments, she says, "I've seen the articles in the papers. In fact, I've got extra copies if you want any." She smiles, her eyes still closed. "I imagine that's what you came to talk about."

He feels as if he's dived into a cold lake, knowing beforehand it would be cold.

"I feel terrible that I didn't talk to you until now," he says. "Some things I should have talked to you about a long time ago. My job."

"Don't worry about that."

His mother is so composed, sitting in her chair with her eyes closed. He cannot bear to puncture her. How does she do it?

Why has he come here to disturb her? Everything he says is a knife. Say it. Say it. "Mother. I was never the manager of the bank. I wish I had been. I was just an assistant. And then they fired me. About six months ago, I started working at the mortuary." Like a knife.

She nods, her eyes still closed. "You were trying to make me happy." She pauses. "But you needn't have."

"Mother." Tears come to his eyes. He puts his hands over his face. He hasn't cried in front of her since he was a child, since his father died. In his mind, he sees his father again, the toy sailboat, his father howling with pleasure as the little sails catch the wind. There on the bookshelf, the photograph of his father. She must have loved him, like he did. She must have grieved for him. It is just that he never saw her grieving. And then all of the men afterward, in and out of the house. They never got close to her. How he wanted to make her happy. Didn't she want him to make her happy?

Now she's opened her eyes. She is looking at him with sympathy, even with tenderness, but also with a terrible distance, as if he were a visitor in her house. It is her serenity, untouched.

"I'm so embarrassed," he says.

"I'm sorry, darling. I can see how you would be embarrassed. But you didn't do anything wrong."

"People made me look like a fool."

"Well . . ." She looks toward the window and sighs. "You shouldn't let yourself care what other people think." She closes her eyes again.

"What did your friends say?" he asks, almost whispering.

"Oh, you know. They have their opinions. They try to cause trouble sometimes. One thing I've learned is that you don't have to spend time with people you don't enjoy. Life is too short." Her cane falls to the floor, and she leaves it. "Lauren has been wanting to talk to you. She knows all about it. She wanted to visit today when she heard you were coming, to be here so that she could talk to you in person. But then something came up."

"She should have come."

"Lauren does what she wants."

David's head is throbbing. He feels totally emptied, a dead battery. He can barely speak. But he isn't finished.

"What do *you* think about the newspaper articles, Mother?"

"What about the newspaper articles?"

"About what I saw in the mortuary."

"I don't know. If you saw something, you saw something."

On the bus home, David tries to sleep. His headache is now a constant pressure, just strong enough to keep him from dozing. Someone is playing bad music, a baby is crying. So, it's done. His mother has heard everything now. It could have been worse, he tells himself. But the pressure in his skull will not subside. All of those years he thought that he was making her happy and proud, and it didn't matter. Something is moving in him, a sorrow for her that he's never felt before. It is a sorrow that pushes him down and stings in his body. Nothing seems to have meaning for her. Maybe she doesn't want any meaning. She can sit in her chair until she dies. Or she can go to lunch with a friend. It is all the same. The minutes and hours and days and years are all the same. Isn't that how she survived those interminable hours at the insurance company? What was it like with his father? he wonders. Behind their closed bedroom door? Was she empty then too? And how did his father live with that emptiness?

Late that evening, in the small living room of his apartment, he stares at the painting on the wall. Where he got the painting he cannot remember. It is a night scene. A piece of countryside in the night. In the background, the dark outlines of trees huddle together, holding the night mist within their branches, deep and mysterious and beckoning. In the foreground, a snow-covered field, a solitary bush. A moon overhead casts shadows, blue against the silver-gray snow. For miles and miles there is nothing, it seems, except the snow-covered field and the trees and the night, and a great silence sweeps over the scene. But far in the distance, a tiny light glows. Someone lives there, a house, a dining table with food, beds to sleep in. Perhaps a person sitting by the window of that house looks out on the night fields just as David does now. Perhaps that person also sees a tiny light in the distance, David's house, a man in the window.

David dreams that his mother is getting married again. At last, she is remarrying. Lauren and he sit in the chapel as she walks down the aisle. She walks alone, a whiteness trailing behind her. Her husband-to-be stands at the front of the chapel, waiting. Who is he? Which one of her many suitors? Harry and Ellen and other friends lie on cushions on the floor, as in a Roman banquet, drinking wine. Lauren is weeping. And then the bride's veil is lifted. For a moment, it is the face of his mother. Is she happy? He tries to see her face. But the face suddenly turns into Bethany's face. Bethany, in white.

When he goes downstairs in the morning, he finds Saturday's mail in his mail slot. He flips through the letters, distracted by the buzzes and beeps of Raymond playing computer games in the lobby. Come look at this, shouts Raymond. Just a minute, says David. The friggin' mail can wait, says Raymond. I've just conquered an entire planetary system. Raymond stands up in his pajamas and grandly stretches out his arms. Bow down to me, he says. Just a minute, says David. A letter without a return address. He opens it. It is from Bethany. She wants to visit him. A telephone number.

SHE LOOKS OLDER, OF COURSE. She has some gray streaks— he's grateful that she hasn't dyed her hair. The flesh slightly sags under her chin. She wears a blouse with a scoop neck, and the delicate cleft between the tops of her breasts, once smooth as silk, is beginning to crease. But she is still light in the air. For years he has imagined this moment, imagined crushing her in an embrace, but now he only hugs her quickly. His body is shaking.

Neutral territory. They sit in a café. It will be quiet here; it is midmorning, and only a few people occupy the other tables, speaking in hushed tones. She puts a pair of reading glasses on the white tablecloth. So she wears glasses now.

"I didn't expect to hear from you again," he says. "Do you want to order anything? I can get the waiter."

"No, I'm not hungry."

What is on her mind? he wonders. Who is she? He hasn't spoken to her for eight years. Continents lie between them.

"Did you get any of my letters?" he asks. "I wrote you a lot of letters."

"I got some," she says. "I didn't want to stir things up. I'd really rather not talk about the letters if you don't mind."

"All right. I don't know what to say." He pauses, shaking. "Are you married?"

"I am. I remarried five years ago. To a physician. His name is Charles."

David feels something break inside of him. "Is he passionate?"

"That's a very personal question."

"I know it is." He is staring at her. Despite the years, she's still beautiful. Images of their life together flicker through his mind. The turning on of lights at dusk in the Spanish town where they took their honeymoon. The dusty mirrors in the hallway of their first apartment. Twelve years they were together. He is waiting for an answer to his question.

"No. He isn't. Can we not talk about that?" She looks away, across the street, and he can see that her profile has changed. Her face is longer. "I think I'd like some coffee now," she says. David motions to a waiter and orders coffee. "So you're not at the bank anymore."

"No," says David.

"A funeral home now, isn't it." She pauses. "That's unexpected, to say the least."

"Why did you want to visit me, Bethany?" It's the first time he has spoken her name since seeing her again, and he feels the name working through his body like liquor.

"I've been reading about you."

"That's why you wanted to see me? So it has nothing to do with me, actually."

"It does have to do with you," she says.

The coffee arrives. He watches as she puts two cubes of sugar and cream in her coffee, stirs the coffee. For some reason, he thinks of the lilies, how she placed lilies on their dining table. She liked pale lilies, and he notices now that her face is pale, beautiful but pale. Her lips glisten with just the slightest pale lipstick, her cheeks are pale.

"I read the articles," she says, "and I knew that you were probably embarrassed as hell about all of it. I know how you are. I tried to imagine how it happened. I guess something must have happened to begin with." She looks up at him, and he nods. "So, I was thinking, something really strange happened to you, and you could have kept your mouth shut about it, or you could have convinced yourself that nothing happened, or you could have jumped off a cliff. But you didn't. I was impressed."

"And that's why you wanted to see me again?"

"Yes."

"Well, that's something. That's the first good thing that's come out of it. I hope it's a good thing."

"Maybe," she says. "I just wanted to see you after I read the articles." She picks up her spoon and then puts it back down on the table. "Are you married?"

"No. I never got married again."

She nods and smiles faintly. Both of them are afraid to ask more questions.

"I think I'll stay around for a few days," she says.

Patrick McConoghy has left a message asking if David would please come see him, handwritten on an old shoe-repair invoice and left at the reception. It has been two months since Julia died.

Because the weather is fine, David decides to walk to Patrick's shop, leaving from the rear exit of the mortuary. He's told Martin that he'll be away for a while, and he badly needs some time out in the air to mull over the extraordinary meeting with Bethany, Bethany married to someone she doesn't love, and there, just moments ago, sitting across from him at the table. Against the vision of Bethany, his mother's words *you needn't have* still play over and over in a disturbing counterpoint. He vibrates with new possibilities and thoughts. But there is something else. What is it? What is this sensation? Is it the power he felt before? A child runs by on the sidewalk with chocolate on her mouth. Yes, he notices. At this moment, he feels as if he observes everything, as if his mind were a razor. He has the sensation that he can dissect a thousand sounds and images at once, slice each of those thousand into yet another thousand. He feels that he is connected to everything around him and, at the same time, separate, with a mind of his own, different from every other mind. Why does he have such intense feelings? Where do they come from? Perhaps this is part of the totality, the simultaneous merging and separateness. He is connected, as Mr. Chee said, and he is separate at the same time. Is this what it feels like to be alive? Do other people feel this way? So much has happened since he saw what he saw that dim afternoon. Everything new began at that moment. Could it be that his father's early death, the tedious assignments in school, the drunken parties with Harry, his marriage to Bethany, his job at the bank and then the undeserved dismissal—could it be that all of it led to that moment in the mortuary? Could the world be created again after such moments? What does the Pythagorean theorem say about that? What does Professor Mickleweed say? The child with the chocolate on her mouth skips by. Now everything is new. The world teems and gyrates. Sounds, smells, tactile sensations, scream at him on the high wire. A bicyclist rides by carrying a block of ice, a long stream of water trailing behind. A seedling hung from its wispy parachute drifts by in the air. As he walks along the sidewalk to Patrick McConoghy's shop, David's legs float as if suspended by strings, the barkings of dogs down a side street crash like explosions, the white onions and yellow squash in front of a market flutter like colored shells tossed up on a beach, a child runs by with chocolate smeared on her mouth—oh yes, he remembers that—the hum of a sewing machine at a tailor's shop, shards of broken pots on the floor of a pottery shop while an old woman sweeps them up with a broom back and forth and the smell of wet clay in the shop expands in his lungs and he feels that he could inflate like a balloon and become lighter than air and be carried up over the houses and shops, so high that everything appears like a toy, as Ms. Gaignard described. What are the limits of this power?

With the colors still shouting, he finds himself at Patrick's shoe shop. The bell rings. He waits in front of the rough wooden counter carved with the initials of all the assistants who have labored there. T.S. S.N. L.B. Isn't it odd, he thinks, that a life can be reduced to two letters. But, of course, it cannot. Two planets perhaps. A life is more than a planet. He has glimpsed . . . Harry never wondered about anything. That was always the difference between Harry and him. On the wall, spools of leather twine. Rough, smooth, mottled. In the back room, the harsh steady sound of a hammer splits through the odors of leather and shoe polish. Dozens of shoes occupy the racks, shoes that Patrick can match to a face. A customer arrives, the bell sings at the top of the door, an assistant fetches the shoes, and the customer leaves, the bell jangles again. See how precisely he observes each detail. Past and future, future and past. Taped to the side of an ancient cash register are pictures of a bloodied Jesus and the Virgin Mary.

Jesus and Mary. Could it be that simple? Should he become a believer, after all? He is anxious about this visit with Patrick. Why did Patrick invite him to his shop? Most likely, he wants him to communicate with Julia. But he cannot. He couldn't communicate with her at the funeral, and he can't now, whatever this feeling of power. What does he know of the dead? He knows the prayer Martin says at the beginning of each embalming procedure. He knows the facial expressions of the dead as Martin moves their lips this way and that. He knows the stillness.

Then Patrick comes from the back room. He wears an apron stained with shoe polish, and his hair is a wild mass of red curls. "Please," he says softly, and he motions for David to follow him. Back through the workroom they go, under a low beam and up a staircase to Patrick's apartment over the shop. It is a simple apartment. Immediately, David smells onions and garlic and beer. Yes, he is here in this moment, he has steadied himself. He is in Patrick's apartment. The small, cluttered living room glows with the light from a broad window looking over the street. On the floor, stacks of newspapers are piled here and there like steps to nowhere. A broken light fixture hangs from the ceiling. On the sofa sits Mille Halliburton, Patrick's friend. The girls have been staying with her and her mother, she explains. She's come to collect a few clothes they forgot.

"I don't want my girls gone," says Patrick, rubbing his knuckles into his eyes.

"Just until you're back on your feet," says Mille.

Patrick shakes his head miserably, but he seems to have accepted that he is unable to care for his daughters. He wants to show David around his apartment. This is the sewing room, he says. This is my daughters' bedroom. This is Julia's and my bedroom. All are tiny rooms with warped floorboards and low plaster ceilings, barely clearing Patrick's head. Mille calls out from the kitchen that she'll make some tea. "Don't bore him, Patrick."

"My father taught me shoes," says Patrick, showing the gap between his two front teeth. "Julia was always saying that I should have done something else, so I could be a better provider. Maybe I should have." He met Julia when he was twenty-five years old, he says. At first she wanted nothing to do with him. "She had her own people." Then he asked her to go with him to an organ concert in an old church, and she went, and the sound of that organ in that church was heavenly. "It was God's music," he says. He was twenty-five years old and she was twenty-three. He has a picture of her from that time, he says, and he opens a chest and brings out the curling photograph. "Wasn't she a beauty?" Yes, David says. "She was the prettiest girl I had ever met," says Patrick, "and she loved me." When he looks at the photo, David cannot help thinking of Bethany. Can he imagine Bethany gone now? "My girls look like her," says Patrick, rubbing his face. "Especially little Mary. Susan has her eyes, but little Mary has got her spot on. I mistreated her, Mr. Kurzweil. I want you to ask her to forgive me."

"Call me David." David avoids Patrick's eyes. Poor Patrick. What can he possibly do for him?

Mille brings out the tea, and the three of them sit in the little living room while the tea kettle wheezes in the kitchen. Patrick, a big man, has sat next to Mille on the sofa, while David lowers himself into one of the two chairs. It wobbles precariously.

"Julia wanted me to replace that chair," says Patrick with a grim laugh. "But we never had the money."

Patrick, his eyes bloodshot, wants to tell a story. When he was in his twenties, he says, he had a buddy named Aidan. Aidan and he were both members of a pacifist club. They would get together with their friends and stick pins on a world globe marking all the places where wars were raging, and then they would write reprimanding letters to the leaders of those countries. They never heard back from anybody, except once they received a form letter from the presidential office of an African nation, declaring that inquiries would be made. Aidan was not a handsome man, says Patrick. His face was a blasted mess with pockmarks from childhood acne. But he had a heart of gold. He was always befriending the children from poor families in his neighborhood, taking them to the amusement park, and he sometimes convinced Patrick to go along. For some reason, Aidan took it into his head to swim the English Channel. What a wild, harebrained idea! He was only a mediocre swimmer, but he had a fierce endurance; he had once run a marathon, and he had a burning desire to do this thing. All of his friends tried to talk him out of it. His former sweetheart pleaded with him to abandon the idea. But Aidan would not be dissuaded. It was something in his head. He trained for months. He ate a diet of potatoes and beef. Then in late August, when the water was warmest, he was ready. There was nothing to be done but to accompany him to Dover. Patrick helped grease down Aidan's body, said a prayer, and then rode beside him in a small boat as he swam, watching him constantly and ready to throw him a life ring the moment he tired. About twelve miles out, a wave came and Aidan disappeared beneath the water and drowned. "I was the distance from him that I am from you," Patrick says to David. "One minute he was alive and the next he was dead. Just like that."

For a few moments, no one can speak. "That's a terrible story," says David.

Patrick rubs his knuckles into his eyes. "I can't take it anymore. It's not right."

"No, it's not right," says David.

"Aidan didn't need to be any kind of fool hero," says Patrick. "But he had this crazy idea." He looks down at the floor, then back at David. "I've had enough of this. Now it's my Julia. Forty years old. Do you think this is right?"

"No," says David.

"What sense is there in it? Tell me that, David. I'm a Christian man. I was raised religious. But I want to know what sense there is in it. I blame God for this. God needs to tell me what meaning there is in it. Or maybe God can tell you. What did Julia do wrong?"

"Nothing to deserve this."

"She didn't do anything wrong," says Patrick. "God strike me down this second if she did anything wrong. But I did. I want to tell you something." Rocking back and forth on the couch, he glances at Mille and then back at David. "Guys were always staring at her. It made me crazy. . . . Sometimes, I beat her for it." Patrick puts his face in his hands. "I want you to talk to my Julia. You see, my life is over."

"Patrick, please stop," says Mille.

Patrick goes to the kitchen sink and begins washing the shoe polish off his hands. He washes his hands, dries them, hesitates, and then washes them a second time. When he's finished, he comes back to the living room and sits in the good chair next to the window. Mille looks at him silently, worry on her face.

"I don't know how I can help you," says David. "I'd like to help you. I don't think I can talk to Julia."

"Please talk to her," says Patrick. "I know you can talk to her." He bites his lip. "When Julia finished her bath at night, I used to rub lotion on her back. It kept her skin from getting dry." He turns and gazes out of the window. "She had the most beautiful white back. Have you touched a woman's bare back, David? You must have. It's a lovely thing, isn't it."

"You seem to be forgetting that I'm here," says Mille, forcing a smile. "You're embarrassing me, and probably Mr. Kurzweil as well."

"Come on now, Mille," says Patrick. "I'm not saying anything risqué. All I'm saying is that I put lotion on my wife's back. To keep her skin moist after her bath. It was . . . so smooth and soft. It was the smoothest thing I ever touched. She had a little birthmark on her left shoulder, like a horseshoe. A little brown horseshoe." Patrick gets up from his chair, goes into his bedroom, and closes the door.

Mille sighs and places the girls' clothes in her bag. "We're going to a doctor next week," she whispers to David. "To help him get back on his feet. He's still in a state of shock."

David nods, shaken. He feels a sense of helplessness, and guilt.

"It was good of you to come, Mr. Kurzweil."

"I wish I could do something to help him," says David.

"You are helping him."

Martin could hardly spare David for a few hours, but he's been concerned about those redheaded girls, and he's relieved to hear that they're staying with Mille Halliburton. "Jenny and I should have taken those girls," Martin says to David. "But now Ms. Halliburton has them."

"Patrick is in a bad way," says David.

"He's had rotten luck," says Martin. "One thing my father said to me. It's a blessing to help the grieving families, but you see too many tragedies."

"You take it so personally," says Jenny, kissing her husband on the cheek. "You're not really made for this. You think you are, but you aren't. And you're working too hard. You should retire. A man seventy-two years old, it's time to retire."

This is a conversation that David has heard many times before. Jenny knows that her husband will never retire. But Martin indeed appears haggard. He's lost weight. His trousers bunch up around his waist, making him look even more ungathered than usual. Dark hollows form under his eyes. In the last few months, since the articles in the paper, the mortuary's business has increased to the extent that the facility cannot manage the onslaught of new cases. And Martin, who has always labored long hours, is working even harder in a futile attempt to accommodate the demand—constantly hurrying from his office to the arrangement room to the sitting parlor to the basement, hardly stopping to sit down and talk to the families as he likes to do. And, of course, the gawkers on the sidewalk in front, the closed curtains, the screenings of families, have set things on edge.

That evening, David stays late to straighten up after a viewing. Martin and Jenny have gone to bed early, and the rest of the staff have left. As David puts away chairs in the slumber room, he cannot stop thinking of Bethany, the way that she looked at him, the paleness of her face. What did she mean when she said she would stay a few days? Was that an invitation? Does she want him to call her or not?

He walks down the hallways to lock up. There, in the dark corridor, he sees a faint light flickering under the door of the arrangement room. Opening the door, he is surprised to find Ophelia. Even though illuminated by only a single candle, her stubby silhouette is unmistakable. And she's sitting in front of a little black box.

"Ophelia! What are you doing?"

Ophelia leaps up, startled. "I thought everyone was gone."

"What are you doing?" David says again, turning on the overhead light.

"You know what I'm doing," says Ophelia. "You did it. Now I'm doing it. Please don't tell Martin. Please. I'll do any favor you want."

"Ophelia. What exactly are you doing? I don't see any wires. I don't see a computer. What are you doing?"

"You don't need a computer," says Ophelia. "All you need is the box. Isabelle Poole said I could make it float in the air just by concentrating on it."

David sits down in a chair. He has no intention of mentioning any of this to Martin, but he's worried about Ophelia.

"You're not telling Martin, are you?" pleads Ophelia.

"No, of course not."

"It hasn't floated yet," says Ophelia. "I haven't been able to concentrate hard enough. Your mind has to be clear. That's what people say. Well, you know." Her eyes are shining.

"Where did you get the box?" David asks.

"From the bead shop," says Ophelia. "They've read about your big experiment with Dr. Tettlebeim. It's in the papers, you know. You are like . . . a god, or something. I can't believe I know you."

It seems a nightmare to David, becoming worse and worse and worse, spiraling downward. "Why are you doing this, Ophelia?"

"Because it feels awesome. What did it feel like to you?" David doesn't answer; he's transfixed by Ophelia's excitement, and alarmed. "To me," she continues, "it feels like my head is lifting off my shoulders, and my brain sits up in the air and can do anything it wants. Did you feel anything like that?"

What should he say to her? David wonders. She is so sincere. "Yes. I felt something like that," he says.

Ophelia runs over and hugs him. "I know that I'm going to make it float," she says. "All of my life, I've known there was something like this. There's stuff that we have no idea about. We can't be here without a reason, that's what I think. There's some force, and it goes through everything, and it can make anything happen. I don't know where the force came from, maybe from God or from Buddha or whatever, but it caused the universe and it goes through people and rocks and it's more powerful than anything. Isabelle Poole says that a lot of people can get in touch with the second world, but they just don't know it."

"That was beautifully put, Ophelia."

"You're just making fun of me," says Ophelia, sweeping her blond hair out of her eyes. "I don't have the education that you do."

"I'm not making fun of you. I want you to know that." He looks into her eyes and she nods. "But I don't think you should do this in the mortuary. Okay?"

"Okay," says Ophelia. "I keep the box at home anyway. I was about to concentrate on Robert. He hasn't written or called me once since he's left. It really upsets me."

"I know that he cares about you," says David. "He's probably just busy unpacking, don't you think?"

"I don't think he cares about me as much as I care about him." She begins to fuss with a loose thread on her blouse, then looks up at him. "Tell me the truth. Do you think I'm fat?"

"No, of course you're not fat. I think you're very pretty."

She sighs and wrinkles her mouth, as if she doesn't believe him. "Thank you."

At home, late, the telephone rings. It's Harry.

"Sorry to call so late," says Harry. "Knowing you, I figured you'd be up reading some book. What's all this wild stuff in the press about you and that supernatural society? How in the world did you get mixed up with those people?"

David explains about Ms. Gaignard. "One thing led to another."

"It's outrageous, the position they're putting you in," says Harry.

"Yeah. I'm upset about it," says David.

"You should be. Listen, if you need any legal representation on this thing, please call me. For you, it'll be free. Okay? Call me."

"Thanks, Harry."

"I mean it. How are you doing otherwise? How's your mother?"

"She's getting old."

"It's a tough time of life, isn't it. My dad can hardly hear anymore. We have to write down what we want to say to him."

"I'm sorry about that, Harry."

"We're all headed there. Are you seeing anybody?"

David hesitates, not knowing what to say. "It's a long story."

Harry chuckles. "I guess I asked the wrong question. We'll save that for another time. But listen. Please call me if you need any help with that society. That stuff is outrageous. They're dragging you through the mud."

"WHAT IS IT?" ASKS ELLEN.

"I don't know," says David, lying. Since coming to her apartment an hour ago, he's found it difficult to touch her. When he kissed her at the front door, he imagined that he was kissing Bethany and pulled back with guilt. Everything has changed.

"Something has happened," says Ellen. She stands by her bureau and gazes at the photograph of herself and her sisters. She wears only a gauzy slip and she looks fragile and beautiful and he can feel every part of her body with his eyes, but he cannot bring himself to touch her. "I know that something has happened," she says. She turns and sits on her bed, legs crossed, looking at him with her dark Asian eyes, and it seems as if a mile separates them. "There's another woman, isn't there."

"Yes."

She puts her hands to her face. In the distance, a train passes by. He listens to the whistle grow fainter and fainter.

"Is she anyone I know?"

"Bethany."

"Bethany! Is she here?"

"Yes."

"Did you sleep with her?"

"No. We had coffee. That's all."

She lets out a long breath. "So Bethany is here. I don't understand. Why would you want to be with that woman again, David? All she did was make you feel bad about yourself."

David finds himself angry at Ellen. The anger feels good and softens his guilt. "Where do you get that?"

"From you. From you. You can't see yourself. What is it about Bethany?"

David doesn't know what to say. The more he talks about Bethany, the more it will hurt Ellen. All he can do is stare at the floor.

"I don't think this is only about Bethany," says Ellen. "There's just too much going on. You've been rattled for months. You don't know what's real and what's not. All this stuff in the newspapers. You're being exploited. It hurts me to see you exploited. Why don't you stop it, David? Why don't you speak out? What are you afraid of? Show some integrity."

"Integrity! Are you saying that I don't have integrity?"

"I'm saying that you should stop letting yourself be used by those people. It's not doing anybody any good. It's not doing you any good. It's not doing us any good."

"You never believed that I saw anything at the mortuary."

"It's gone way beyond that and you know it."

"No. That's the core of it. You never believed me."

Ellen begins crying. "I care about you, David. I love you. I can give you love. And you need love. I need love. I really do. I thought you were it for me. I thought some luck was coming into my life." She wipes the tears with the back of her hand. "I don't know if Bethany ever loved you, but if she did it was a destructive kind of love. You've never been truly loved. Your father died when you were eight years old. I've never met your mother, but from what you've told me, you don't get much from her either. You're a lonely man, David."

"Do you believe what I saw at the mortuary? Yes or no?" Ellen doesn't say anything. "Yes or no?"

"I don't believe in ghosts. Is that what you want me to say? I don't believe in ghosts. But if you think that you saw a ghost, that's okay with me. I can live with that."

"But you don't believe me. You don't believe me." David leans against the wall and slumps to the floor. "Why don't you believe me?"

"I can't make myself believe something I don't believe."

He stares at Ellen across the room, and she grows smaller and smaller, like a boat rowing away from the shore. He feels as if he never met her that morning in the library, never walked with her in the park, never went to the concerts with her, never slept in her bed. How has it all slipped away? And he has slipped away from himself as well. She mentioned his father. He closes his eyes and can still feel the embrace of his father after that first triumphant ride on the bicycle, so long ago. Ellen is right. He is alone.

For several minutes he remains sitting on the floor, listening to Ellen's quiet sobbing. "I should go," he says finally.

"Yes," says Ellen. "You should go."

A long time he walks by the lake, wondering if he will ever see Ellen again. Over the years, this lake has brought him comfort and peace. He knows its indentations like he knows the shape of his hand. He knows every grassy spot on the shore where he can sit. He knows the gum tree with its hiding branches. On the opposite bank, he can see waves of light rippling over the trees, sun reflected from the undulations of the water. The water gently laps at some rocks, and the wind and the sun make bright flowing stripes glide over the surface while the color changes from dark green to azure to pale blue. The pale face of Bethany. Finally, Bethany has come back to him.

Perhaps she's been planning to come back for years, the pale of her skin, and there's Ronald Mickleweed walking toward his table. He has far too much on his mind to argue with Ronald about zeroes and ones, but there Ronald is, and he looks unhappy. His colleague from the physics department looks more unhappy. They've come, Ronald says, to discuss their alarm at the increasing press coverage of David's psychic abilities.

Even at this early hour, the heat from the kitchen stove combined with the summer weather have made the diner too warm, and the men begin sweating as soon as they sit down at the Formica table. Ronald takes off his jacket and rolls up the sleeves of his checked shirt.

With his bad lazy eye and his lopsided gait, Ronald is easily recognizable from years ago. But he's now balding, with a face grown plump and soft like a ripe pear. Seeing him now, David cannot help remembering Ronald in school. As a boy, Ronald loved to build things. He made his own glue. He delighted in explosions. David once saw him pour sulfuric acid into a ceramic bowl with other chemicals, whereupon the mixture sizzled and seethed and produced a gush of steam and a mound of black carbon. Ronald's bedroom was littered with coils of wire and electrical devices, test tubes, curved glass flasks, Bunsen burners, dangerous chemicals. On the high school math team, Ronald would get a faraway look in his eyes while the problem was still being read out and, before his opponents could begin to compute, write down a single number and draw a circle around it. Then he would let out a loud sigh and grin.

From an early age, Ronald knew that he wanted to be a scientist, and he made a straight beeline from high school to college to his doctorate in chemistry. Ronald wanted to change the world. David marveled at that kind of ambition, but he never had it himself. David didn't care about changing the world. Instead, he wanted to understand the world. And he was growing more and more confused by the day.

Of course, life threw a few messy uncertainties into Ronald's world of logic and precision. One of the uncertainties, Ronald says matter-of-factly as he squints at David, is that he's discovered a retinal disease in his good eye. "There's no cure for it," Ronald says, and shrugs his shoulders. "In another few years, I'll be blind. My wife tells me that now I won't have to watch her grow old." He laughs, but it is a sad laugh.

"What miserable luck," says David. He always liked Ronald, always admired his spirit.

Without waiting for orders, Marie brings scrambled eggs and toast. For a few moments, she hovers near the table, eager to listen in on the conversation with the professors.

"We've done a little checking on Dr. Samuel Tettlebeim," says Ronald. "Would you like to know what his doctorate is in? Psychology."

Ronald's colleague from the physics department, Professor William Grindlay, rolls his eyes. William is a tall man, dressed in blue jeans and sandals, with a wide brimmed sun hat and a set of keys jangling from his belt. He hasn't touched his eggs and pushes his plate out into the middle of the table. "I don't eat eggs," he says in a voice so soft it can scarcely be heard.

"Tettlebeim was in academia twenty years ago," continues Ronald, "but he couldn't get tenure. The scuttlebutt is that he used to be an alcoholic. Apparently he was involved with a bad accident of some kind."

"I'd bet he killed somebody drunk in a car," says William.

"We don't know exactly what happened," says Ronald. "But he dropped out of academia and went into consulting and private practice. The main thing is that his Ph.D. is in psychology."

"So what," says David. "He seemed knowledgeable to me."

Ronald nods and places his pen on the Formica table. This is a sign that he is preparing to do some calculations. "I'm sure that Dr. Tettlebeim is knowledgeable about some things," says Ronald. "But he doesn't know anything about the physical sciences. I've been corresponding with him. I asked him some basic questions, really basic stuff, and he doesn't know anything. Believe me, he's not equipped. But that's not the point. The point is that the claims he's been making are simply absurd."

"The man is a nut," says William.

Taking some papers out of his briefcase, Ronald explains that he's gathered together a list of major earthquakes, hurricanes, and economic events that occurred somewhere in the world in the last six months. What number of them would be expected to occur by chance within three days of David's "session" with the black box? he asks. With his pen, he scribbles some math on one of the napkins. "See," he says, squinting at what he has written. "The number of phenomena that Dr. Tettlebeim has claimed to be correlated with your session are no more than what would be expected from random chance. You had no effect."

No effect! David is willing to acknowledge that he had no effect on world events. But certainly he had *some* effect on the R box itself. And the R box definitely had an effect on him. There was an effect. "But what about the ones and zeroes?" "We went over that before," says Ronald. "That was a rare occurrence. If you sat down with that black box again, it wouldn't happen."

For the third time, Marie comes to the table asking if anyone wants fresh coffee. William stares at her, and she hurries away.

"I'm afraid that Samuel Tettlebeim is beginning to get personal," says Ronald. "In his last message, he said that I was 'a narrow-minded elitist.'" Ronald smiles. "I guess anyone who believes that two plus two equals four is an elitist."

"What concerns us," says William in his paper-thin voice, "is that the public believes this crap. Our faculty is concerned. Even some of our students are asking us what this is all about."

"David, we want you to denounce this stuff," says Ronald.

"What do you say, David?" says William. "We can clear up some ignorance out there. It's amazing how ignorant people are. People have no idea what's possible and what's not. We have an opportunity. Opportunities like this don't come every day."

A hundred thoughts are running through David's head, all of them distressing. With a sigh, he turns and looks out the window, where the flashing EAT sign slowly revolves on its post. The nightmare continues. But he brought it all on himself. He wishes he had never said a word about April 23. He regrets that he ever spoke to Ms. Gaignard. He regrets that he allowed Dr. Tettlebeim to conduct his experiments. Now he's paying for his mistakes. At the thought of making public denunciations, or any statements at all, his stomach turns over. He is not a public person. He is a person who likes to read and to learn and to quietly reflect on the world. "What would I have to say?"

"I don't want to tell you exactly what words to use," says Ronald.

"This thing needs to come from you. You're the man. You need to say, first, that you never saw anything supernatural in the mortuary. It could have been a daydream or a light effect or something like that. You need to say that you don't subscribe to psychic phenomena. Dr. Tettlebeim has his data, of course, but we could give you some text about the nature of probability, et cetera. That kind of thing. What do you think?"

"It makes me nervous," says David. "I need to think about it. I'm so tired of this whole thing."

"But you do agree that this is a bunch of crap, don't you?" murmurs William.

"Most of it," says David.

"What do you mean by that?"

"You guys are really pressuring me," says David.

"David, I want to tell you something," says Ronald. "A couple of days ago, I came home and found my teenage son and his friends in our basement staring at a black box. I don't know where they got it. I asked him what he was doing, and my son said he was planning to make the box spin. One of his friends had done it, he said. Made it spin with his mind. That's my son, Alex. He's been living with me for seventeen years. I've never seen him doing anything like that before. And he believes it. I don't know what else he believes."

"I need to think about this."

"I understand," says Ronald. "I know that you didn't want all this to happen. But we've got a situation now. Please, David. Do the right thing."

Ronald and William stand up from the table. David watches them as they drive off, a cloud of dust following their car until it becomes only a tiny dot in the distance and then disappears.

IN HIS APARTMENT, DAVID PACES THE KITCHEN. The clock on the wall says eight-thirty, time for him to leave for the mortuary. He continues to pace. What should he do? He's being squeezed from all sides. When he imagines himself making a public pronouncement, he gets a panicked feeling in his gut. But Ronald is right. Dr. Tettlebeim's claims are absurd. So cleverly the gentle doctor makes his insinuations, pretending to be cautious while suggesting the most outlandish results. World events! Yes, he's being used. He's being exploited. More than being exploited, he's being made to look like a fool. Harry was too polite to say it, but he thought it. Make a public denunciation, whether frightening or not. Do it. He's done other frightening things. The morning he dived off a ledge into the pond when he was fourteen, terrified and shaking. He can see the pond, distant and scary below. And only weeks ago, he confessed to his mother that he'd been lying to her for years. He can do it. He must do it. He's not jumping just because Ronald told him to jump. He's jumping because he knows he must jump. He must jump. He has integrity. *Show some integrity*, Ellen said. Well, he has integrity. He's had integrity all of his life. He'll make a denunciation. He'll stop being used. But exactly what is he going to denounce? Certainly the most extravagant claims of the so-called Society. The world events. Those claims are irresponsible. Should he also denounce the result with the zeroes and ones? Should he denounce what he saw on April 23? Those things happened, whatever the explanation. He'll figure out the explanation some other time. To denounce them would be a lie. That would also lack integrity. And what about Mr. Chee? The red splotches rising onto his forehead. The intelligent eyes, steady like a windless lake. Could Mr. Chee be deluding himself? Where is he at this moment? David wants to talk to Mr. Chee. Have they imagined it all? He certainly did not imagine the zeroes and ones. Dr. Tettlebeim has proof; he has the graph from his printer. And that feeling was so intense. But maybe it was a rare event, as Ronald said. Maybe it was simply random chance. What is the truth? Everything is so nebulous. They're pressuring him. He kicks the refrigerator hard and the bottom panel falls off. Then he kicks the panel and it goes skidding across the floor and smashes into the wall and leaves a gash. Good. He paces. Now, it's eight forty-seven. For sure he'll be late.

Slow down. One step at a time. Start with the R box. Ronald says the preponderance of zeroes was a rare event. Okay. So repeat the experiment. Yes. That's the logical thing to do. Repeat the experiment. Settle it once and for all. Get Tettlebeim's telephone number.

David calls Dr. Tettlebeim's office. A secretary says that Dr. Tettlebeim is not in yet. I'd like his home phone, says David. Dr. Tettlebeim does not give out his home phone. This is David Kurzweil. Oh yes, Mr. Kurzweil. I recognize your name. I need to speak to him immediately, says David.

"I'd like you to repeat the experiment with the R box," he says when he gets Dr. Tettlebeim on the telephone.

"Certainly," says Dr. Tettlebeim. "Why are you shouting?"

"And I'd like to have a couple of witnesses from the university."

"As you remember, we prefer not to have spectators," says Dr. Tettlebeim in his gentle voice. "It may interfere with the intentionality force."

"I insist."

"Can I ask why you want to repeat the experiment?" says Dr. Tettlebeim. "Are you skeptical of our results?"

"I'm skeptical of everything," says David. "I want to repeat the experiment."

"Of course," says Dr. Tettlebeim. "We are all interested in discovering truth."

The next day, in midafternoon, Dr. Tettlebeim arrives with his equipment. He and his assistant trudge up the steps to David's second-floor apartment carrying the sound-absorbing panels, the computer and printer, the various connecting cables, and of course the R box. Up and down, up and down, four trips in all, without any complaints. Although heavily sweating, Dr. Tettlebeim will not remove his jacket or bow tie. "A private performance," he says with a little smile. "With spectators."

Raymond watches with consternation as the men labor up the stairs. "What's going on?" he asks.

"I'm getting a new stereo system," says David.

His neighbor shakes his head. "Yeah. Whatever."

After a half hour of fiddling, Dr. Tettlebeim has the equipment installed to his satisfaction. "It's not the ideal space," he says, "but as long as you can concentrate, Mr. Kurzweil." There is a moment of concern, when the assistant thinks he forgot the Bach fugue, but they find the CD in the printer cover.

"Calibration," says Dr. Tettlebeim. His voice sounds odd. With the sound-absorbing panels installed, every sound in David's apartment has a strangeness that he's never heard before. Spoken words are immediately swallowed in the air, like light in a fog.

" 'It is an ancient Mariner, / And he stoppeth one of three . . .' "

David begins reciting from Coleridge, marveling at how each sylla-
ble is sucked into nothingness.

At that moment, there is a knocking on the front door. Ronald
and William have arrived.

Dr. Tettlebeim is visibly upset upon being introduced to Ronald.
"You didn't tell me that Professor Mickleweed would be one of the
spectators," he says to David. "I'm not sure we can proceed."

"Why?"

"He is not a person I can work with. It's a personal matter. I'm
sorry."

"What does personal have to do with it?" injects Ronald. "We're
doing a scientific experiment. The ones and zeroes will speak for
themselves." William smiles.

"It is not so simple," says Dr. Tettlebeim, talking to David and
refusing to look at Ronald. "Professor Mickleweed and I have been
exchanging messages, and I can tell that he has a closed mind. He is
negative. He could block the intentionality force."

Ronald sighs and sits down on the couch.

"I'd like to look at the random number generator inside the box
if I may," says William.

Dr. Tettlebeim hesitates. "You may," he says.

William opens the box and examines the tiny computer inside of
it. Then he puts the computer back in the box and studies the wires
leading to the printer. He opens up the printer itself, examines the
circuit boards, and closes it up. "I'd like to do a test," he says.

"We always do calibrations," says Dr. Tettlebeim. "We were in the
process of performing a calibration when you arrived."

"Then you shouldn't have any objection if I do one now," says
William. Dr. Tettlebeim nods in approval. William turns on the

black box. It makes a faint humming sound. The printer whines as it spews out its numbers. After a few minutes, William analyzes the output of the printer. "A hundred numbers per second," he says.

"Yes," says Dr. Tettlebeim.

William and Ronald look together at the output. They whisper to each other. "Binomial distribution," says William. "We can just do root N over four." Ronald does a calculation. "It appears that the machine is working properly," he says to Dr. Tettlebeim. "Your random number generator is doing what it's supposed to do."

"Did you think it wasn't?" says Dr. Tettlebeim, looking at Ronald for the first time. "Didn't you trust me?"

"We just wanted to make sure," says Ronald. "We're happy. You have a legitimate random number generator there."

"Thank you very much," says Dr. Tettlebeim's assistant, the pimpled young man, now wearing a green nylon jogging outfit. The assistant yawns and begins eating some peanuts that David left on his dining room table.

"I want to go ahead with the experiment," says David. Dr. Tettlebeim takes off his glasses and rubs his forehead, debating with himself.

"It's a scientific experiment," says Ronald.

"I'm concerned that you will interfere with the results," says Dr. Tettlebeim.

"I'll tune him out," says David. "I want to do the experiment."

Dr. Tettlebeim shakes his head. "All right. These are not optimum conditions, I want to say that in advance." He puts his glasses back on. "I would like everyone please to sit down. We need stillness. We need quiet. There should be only the music."

"Music?" asks William.

Dr. Tettlebeim's assistant starts the Bach fugue.

David sits in front of the box and concentrates. At first he is distracted by the people in the room. Dr. Tettlebeim stands by the printer, Ronald and William sit on the couch, the assistant makes rustling sounds from the kitchen. Someone coughs. The relentless shuttle of the fugue. The box. David concentrates on the box. Bethany. No, he must not think of Bethany now. The box. Project your mind on the box.

Someone is shaking his shoulder. "It's over," says Ronald. "We've got thirty thousand numbers. There's no effect." Dr. Tettlebeim examines the graph without speaking. "The excess is well within one standard deviation," says Ronald. "Do you agree?"

Dr. Tettlebeim looks again at the numbers. "Yes," he says. His face shows no emotion.

William stands up from the couch and strides to the door. "It was a pleasure meeting you," he says to Dr. Tettlebeim, sarcasm in his voice. He turns to David. "It's time for you to step up to the plate, good sir. We'll be in touch."

"I'd like to do the experiment one more time," says Dr. Tettlebeim. "I believe Mr. Kurzweil may have had trouble concentrating."

"Right," says William. "Now come the excuses." William's face has turned red, but his voice never rises above a whisper. "Keep the data you want, throw out the data you don't want. You know something, I don't care what you believe. Believe in whatever you want. Believe in goblins and fairies if you want. But don't promote your garbage to the public. The public is ignorant. The public is vulnerable. Our students are vulnerable." Dr. Tettlebeim has turned away from William and looks at David with something like sadness in his eyes. "And if I can," William continues, "I'm going to put you out of business. I'm going to shut you and your organization down. But right now, you're not wasting another minute of my time. I've left my laboratory to come here for this travesty. Let's go, Ronald."

"Let him do another experiment," says Ronald.

"What for?" says William. "What would that accomplish?" He looks at his watch.

"Just let him," says Ronald. "It's only another ten minutes. Let's leave no room for doubt. Let's finish this with a clear conscience."

"He's just going to give another excuse," says William. "The temperature in the room wasn't right, or David wasn't sitting the correct way in his chair."

"I'd like to do one more experiment," says David.

"Thank you," says Dr. Tettlebeim.

William throws up his hands, his keys jingling at his waist. "Okay. Okay. Ten minutes." He goes back to the couch.

Again, David sits in front of the box. The fugue begins. He stares at the box. He stares, and the black box seems to grow and shrink with the music. He imagines the insides of the box, the tiny computer whirling out its zeroes and ones, creating the numbers from some hidden electrical pulse, like the vein throbbing on his neck. He concentrates on the box. His body tingles. Concentrate on the box.

"That's enough," says Ronald. He walks to the printer and squints at the graph. After a few moments, a quizzical look comes over his face. He scratches his balding head. He takes out his pen. Dr. Tettlebeim examines the graph and compares it to his printed probability tables.

"So what is it?" says William.

"About one and a half standard deviations," says Ronald.

"What does that mean?" asks David.

"Let me see it," says William. He takes the printout from Ronald and studies it, twisting his mouth.

"What are the results?" says David.

"I'm afraid this time it's not so clear cut," says Ronald. "There's about a fifteen percent probability that a random number generator would give a preponderance of zeroes as big as what you got."

"And an eighty-five percent probability that it wouldn't," says Dr. Tettlebeim, with a slight smile on his lips. "Mr. Kurzweil has done it again. He's controlled the R box with his mind. It's the power of the intentionality force."

"We can't draw any conclusions from this one experiment," says Ronald.

"This is all ridiculous," says William, still holding the output of the printer. "I can't believe we're having this conversation. There's no such thing as an intentionality force. Ronald, why are you entertaining this crap?"

"I'm not entertaining anything," says Ronald. "We did two runs. One of them was within a standard deviation, one of them wasn't."

Dr. Tettlebeim and his assistant begin packing up their equipment.

"So I had no effect on the box in the first experiment, and I did in the second?" asks David. "Is that what you're saying?"

"Yes," says Dr. Tettlebeim. "That's what the results show."

"I wouldn't quite say that," says Ronald. "I'd say that the second experiment was a somewhat improbable event. Not extremely improbable but somewhat improbable. If we did the experiment many times and combined the results, we'd conclude that David had no effect on the box."

"Why are you so sure?" asks Dr. Tettlebeim.

"Because it's a random number generator," says Ronald.

Dr. Tettlebeim nods without comment, then continues folding up the acoustic panels.

"He smells of cologne," says William. "He's worse than an ignorant person. Much worse."

DAVID SITS ALONE IN THE SLUMBER ROOM. No longer is it his haven of silence. Even with the door closed, he can hear Martha's voice telling callers that he can no longer come to the telephone.

What can he say to the callers? What can he say to the members of the Society? Already he's issued a denial of any ability to control world events. But the narrow wording of his denial has only enhanced their belief in his powers. What can he say now? He is far too confused. The new experiments have clarified nothing. Around and around he goes on his globe of confusion. He is dizzy with possibilities. With the drapes now always drawn, day cannot be distinguished from night. Here, and elsewhere in the mortuary, there is no longer dawn or noon or dusk or night. The light holds in its liquid constancy, spilling out evenly from the porcelain lamps. These lamps are old. Martin's grandfather purchased them abroad, as well as the fraying beige Oriental rug on the floor, the crystal decanters on the mantel above the fireplace, the semicircle of chairs with embroidered seats—all now chipped or in tatters, illuminated only by artificial light. What happened here that dusk afternoon? How can he ever find out? Whatever it was never happened again. Does something that occurs only once truly exist? His birth occurred only once.

Although he cannot describe it in words, he remembers the sight as if it were only moments ago, the fleeting thing at the edge of his eye. For an instant, he lifted the veil. Was it another world? Was it the dim infinity before he was born? Why was he able to affect the R box? That he didn't imagine. There were witnesses. And if he did not imagine the zeroes and ones, perhaps he did not imagine whatever he saw on April 23. And even if he did imagine it. The imagination is part of the world, Jason Chee said. Is imagination part of this world? Or part of another? Even the theorem of Pythagoras now seems in doubt. His eyes circle the room. Once this intimate space flowed over his body with quiet and calm. Now the stares of the gawkers and passersby. The invasions. Ophelia and Jenny, even Andrew the driver, cannot stop talking about Dr. Tettlebeim's experiments, the strange machines and equipment right in their home. What time is it? Martin needs him. The mortuary is drowning. Louis, the young man hired to replace Robert, keeps asking everyone to repeat his instructions. Martin can no longer keep up. He looks toward Jenny with his milky eyes, knowing that he cannot turn people away.

Ronald is on the telephone. The latest results with the black box are about to be published in several newspapers, Ronald says. He's got early copies. Tettlebeim must have talked to reporters. There are photos of him and William, "distinguished scientists from the university," claiming them as witnesses. But you were witnesses, says David. Don't you understand? shouts Ronald. This is all preposterous. William and I never endorsed your psychic abilities. We never endorsed the Society for the Second World. This new junk in the press makes it appear that we're sponsors. It makes us look like supporters. The public certainly thinks so. We're getting calls, lots of calls. People want us to hold a symposium on the paranormal. At the university. Can you believe it! The department chairs are getting calls and the deans are getting calls and the president. People believe this bunk. And now we've been presented as supporters. It's illegal,

I'll tell you that. It's slander and misrepresentation. Those jerks have gone too far. The university is hiring more attorneys. We're going to sue them back to the Stone Age. People here are enraged. And they're enraged at me too. The dean of science hauled me and William into his office. This is what happens. You try to straighten out something, and it only gets worse. I can't believe we had the bad luck to get a rare event on that second run. I just can't believe it. The reporters don't know anything. All they want is a good story.

Ronald's voice is cracking.

I'm sorry, says David. I should never have asked you to be a witness. I apologize for that. I thought we were going to settle things, but it didn't turn out that way.

There's a long pause on the other end of the line. I don't blame you, David. Don't blame yourself either. You made an honest mistake. Now we're all in this. I just wanted to give you a heads-up because you have a relationship with those people. It's war now.

I'm so sick of this, says David. I wish I'd never said anything. Tell me the truth, says Ronald. Do you believe you saw something supernatural in the mortuary? I do, says David. I'm embarrassed to say that to you, Ronald. I know it doesn't make any sense. I don't have any proof. But I can't talk myself out of it. I wish I could talk myself out of it. If you saw something supernatural, what would you do?

There's a pause. Let's define our terms, says Ronald. When I say *supernatural*, I mean something that has no scientific explanation. Something that lies outside science. Yes, says David. All right, says Ronald. What would I do if I saw something supernatural? First of all, I'd try to find a logical explanation. You have to remember that some stuff, in some circumstances, appears supernatural when it isn't. A solar eclipse appears supernatural unless you happen to know some astronomy. If I went to a remote tribe in New Guinea and demonstrated my laptop, it would freak them out. Okay, says David. Suppose you looked hard for a logical explanation but couldn't find one. Then what? Then, says Ronald, I would *assume* that there was some logical explanation that I just wasn't able to find for some reason. Just because we can't find a logical, scientific explanation doesn't mean that one doesn't exist. So, says David, you wouldn't accept that a supernatural event had occurred even if you saw it. Is that what you're saying? Yes, says Ronald. I guess that's what I'm saying. And I want to add that I've never seen anything that would convince me otherwise. Does that mean, asks David, that you might possibly be convinced otherwise? Could *anything* convince you that something supernatural might exist? With a great deal of evidence, I could be convinced, says Ronald. But it would take a lot of evidence. If many different phenomena showed that there were strange things going on with no known explanation, then I would of course accept that. I respect evidence. But . . . if there were many different phenomena that showed something strange, I would consider that as evidence for a new kind of physical force. Not something supernatural, but a force that we didn't yet understand. A physical force, not a supernatural force. The force of magnetism must have seemed pretty magical and strange to the first humans who experienced it. So, says David, you're saying that there are *no* circumstances in which you'd believe in the supernatural, even if you had evidence. I don't believe in the supernatural, says Ronald. I'm sorry if I've disappointed you. I believe that everything in the physical world can be explained by science. You said physical world, says David. What about the nonphysical world? I don't believe in a nonphysical world, says Ronald. What about love? asks

David. Oh, love is very much a physical thing, says Ronald. I realize that it's very complicated, and I'm sure it can't be traced to individual neurons and hormones, but I think it's very much a physiological sensation that takes place in the brain. Don't you feel something magical when you're in love? asks David. I do, I certainly do, says Ronald. But I think that feeling of magic is a hardwired psychological response. It's a chemical thing in the brain. It's a flow of chemicals and electrical currents, and it developed over millions of years in the process of evolution to aid in the procreation of the species. What about God? asks David. Ronald snorts a dry laugh. You're really trying to back me into a corner, aren't you. Look, I've got to get back to my lab. I've got to meet with the stupid attorneys. I just wanted to let you know the new developments. One more minute, says David. Okay, says Ronald. What about God. God is an interesting case. I'll certainly agree that God, as people conceive God, would have to be supernatural. Yes, God would be supernatural. First of all, there's no scientific evidence for God. So that's my first answer. But let's assume that God exists. As long as God doesn't intervene after He or She released the grand pendulum, then there's no problem, as I see it. No interventions or miracles, no problem. That leaves us, for all practical purposes, with a physical world. Does that make sense to you? Yes, it does, says David. So how are you feeling about all of this right now? asks Ronald. Confused, David says. That's not so bad, says Ronald. People are often confused right before they make a discovery.

Alone again with his books, turning the pages of his confusion. From Albert Einstein: *The most beautiful experience we can have is the mysterious. It is the fundamental emotion which stands at the cradle of true art and true science.*

In a slim volume, he reads the death poem of Tosui Unkei:

Seventy years and more
I have tasted life to its utmost.
The stench of urine sticks to my bones.
What matter all these?
Ho! Where is the place I return to?
Above the peak
the moonlight whitens
A clear wind blows.

AS HE RAISES THE DELICATE STAMP to the light, its colors vibrate and gleam like enamel. Misty blue mountains rise in the distance. In the foreground, a quiet lake, a tree-covered hill, white boulders beside a straw-colored path. All in exquisite miniature, a tiny painting of a stamp.

"It's one of my favorites," says Martin, holding the stamp with his forceps like a jeweler holds a diamond. "They were printed for only a year, I think. A small country. Malamar."

"Can I see it?" David asks, and puts down his wineglass. Martin passes the forceps. With a magnifying glass, David peers at the stamp. He follows its microscopic terrain with his eyes, follows it until the little jagged edges disappear and the stamp swells and fills up the room and he falls into the scene. He hovers. He walks along the straw-colored path. "It's a work of art," he says. "It should be hung in a museum."

"Yes," says Martin. "A museum of miniatures. I'm happy that you see what I see." He carefully returns the stamp to its plastic container, then sinks down in his leather chair near the television. Letting his house slippers fall from his feet, he rubs his bare toes on the jute rug. "I find such peace with these stamps." He sighs. "It's been chaos around here, hasn't it. Please don't think I'm angry at you for it, David. There's nothing to be done. What really concerns me are the families. I'm not giving the time that I should to the families. That family in here yesterday with the husband who could barely stand up—you remember—and I spent only ten minutes with them. I felt terrible. And Louis isn't working out. I don't know what we should do about Louis." He looks over at David as if waiting for a confirmation of his assessment, or advice. "I'm glad you could come for dinner. Keep an old man company. I don't like to eat alone. It seems that Jenny is out every week at one of her bird lectures. She tells me it's only once a month. Tuesdays. Mondays and Wednesdays she's got her TV shows. Anyway. I'm glad you could come."

"I'm glad you invited me," David says, yawning. It's nearly midnight. He is tired and sluggish and drunk. With effort, he walks to the littered dinner table and pours the last drops of wine into his glass. Then he sits across from Martin, pushing aside the standing brass lamp between them. Its pale-lemon light just barely reaches the corners of the room, which looks more like a stamp dealer's shop than a home. It is always surprising to David that Jenny allows such clutter, but then again she leaves her bird books strewn about as well, one of their compromises with each other. Outside a back window, David can see the dark silhouette of the overturned horse carriage.

"I've got some apple pie in the fridge," says Martin, leaning his head back in his chair.

"Thanks," says David. "But I'm stuffed."

"What about some goat cheese? Jenny's brother sent us some goat cheese from wherever he lives."

"No, thanks. I can't eat another bite."

"How about some cookies? I got some chocolate pecan cookies."

"Thank you, but no."

"All right," Martin says, and sighs. "I'm not much of a cook. I can heat up what Jenny makes, but that's about it. I can cook beef Stroganoff. You do any cooking?"

"I'm pretty bad," says David. "I eat all my meals at a diner."

Martin laughs and scratches his white stubble. "I can't remember the last time I ate at a restaurant. I don't like going out. But you know that about me. I'm sorry that you've had to witness a couple of my . . . episodes."

"Nothing to apologize for."

"Jenny says I have a phobia. Maybe I do." He looks at David with his milky eyes, and again he seems to be asking for something. "It's dangerous out there," says Martin. "I read the papers. I see the news. Maybe I do have a phobia. But I think it's deserved."

"Don't you ever want to go out walking? In the park, or beside the lake? Don't you miss going out?"

"I have everything I need here," says Martin.

Never before has Martin spoken of his phobia. In fact, David always wondered how he regarded it. Now he speaks of it matter-of-factly, as if it were a minor inconvenience. So many juxtapositions. With the grieving families, Martin feels completely comfortable. He can sit in the slumber room with two dozen strangers.

It must be the wine causing Martin to talk in this way. Neither of them is a big drinker, yet they've finished off a bottle of Merlot to go with the meatloaf and salad and sweet potatoes.

Martin looks at his watch. "I don't know why Jenny hasn't come home yet. She never seems to mind the hour." Tomorrow she'll have to be at home, Martin says, because it's her television program on the great painters. Tomorrow night it will be Daumier. Last week it was Picasso. Martin says that he doesn't have time to watch television anymore. He's losing weight, he's noticed. In another few weeks, he'll have to hire new staff. Robert is gone, Louis is incompetent, and the business has practically doubled. It's like a hotel with three people in every bed, Martin says. He doesn't have time to interview people. Jenny will do the interviews. She's smarter than he is, Martin says, and he recounts her management training once again and how they met when she was running a pastry business. It was a friend's business, and Jenny had been hired only on a temporary basis, but she had the place running like a new car within three months. She could probably manage the funeral home by herself, he says, but she doesn't want to damage his male pride.

Martin's speech is getting slower and slower, with more spaces between words, and he closes his eyes. For a few minutes, they sit without talking. David listens to the faucet dripping in the kitchen, to Martin's breathing.

"What do you think you might have done if you hadn't gone into the funeral home business?" says David, breaking the silence.

"I never thought about doing anything else. You grow up with it all around you in the family, and that's all there is."

"But what if you had to do something else?"

"I don't know. It's hard for me to imagine doing anything else. Maybe teaching. I like young people. How about you? I know you worked at a bank."

"I might want to be a writer. I like reading."

"Well, that would be a fine thing. A writer. I can imagine you as a writer. You could still do it, you know. You're still young."

"Maybe. You'd be a wonderful teacher," says David. "You already are. You're a master."

"Not me," says Martin. "My father was the master. My father took the grieving families into his flesh, like they were his own. You should have seen him. You know what he used to say?" Martin opens his eyes, his face puffy from the alcohol, and looks at David. "He used to say that part of the grief was that each member of the family was mourning his own mortality. My father understood that." Martin takes the last swallow of his wine. "You have a talent in this business, David. I've seen you with the families. You have a talent." His eyes glisten in the dim light. Are there tears? David looks away, embarrassed. "I always wanted a son," says Martin. "Jenny did too. We couldn't have children. Something wrong on my side, the doctor said. Jenny didn't want to adopt." He shifts in his chair to get more comfortable and gazes sleepily across the room at a window with its drawn shades. "You and Ellen should get married and have kids. It's not too late. . . . Pardon me for sticking my nose into your business." Martin is drunk.

"It's complicated," says David. He pauses, thinking about whether he should open up completely. "There's someone else."

"Ah."

And he tells Martin about Bethany, something he's wanted to do for a long time. This seems like the moment, with both of them loose from the wine and Martin so sweet. "I can't believe she came back," says David.

"What are you going to do?"

"I don't know," says David. "What do you think I should do?"

"Well, she is married," says Martin. "There's that." He leans his head back and closes his eyes again.

"Yes, I know. But she's not happily married."

For a few moments, silence. Martin seems to be thinking, or sleeping. "How do you feel about Ellen?" he murmurs.

"Ellen and I . . . I thought I was in love with her. But after I saw Bethany, I couldn't touch her. Doesn't that mean something?"

"I suppose," says Martin, his eyes still closed. "Have you burned your bridges with Ellen?"

"I might have," says David. "She was pretty upset when I told her about Bethany."

"Of course she would be. I like Ellen. She has character, she's smart. . . . I can tell that she cares about you. . . . Not bad-looking either. . . I never met Bethany, of course."

"I think I should call Bethany. She's still in town."

"Maybe that would be . . . a good idea."

Martin is almost asleep. Slowly, David stretches out on the sofa and he feels the soft cushion against his head and he listens to Martin's breathing and then his own. One by one, he hears his shoes drop to the floor. Something dry and burning. It is his throat. He needs a drink of water, but the kitchen is miles away. The room spins. With his eyes closed, he feels better. The sofa envelops and holds him, like Bethany, her body. Martin's breathing. The drip of the faucet. Far away, footsteps, whispering. *So many juxtapositions.* He sees Martin in the church surrounded by people and floundering. Now, cast up on a wooden pier, Martin gasps for air, mouth opening and closing, eyes bulging, gills twitching. Why aren't you calm? he asks Martin. I came from the sea, says Martin, and his eyes bulge and twist. Save me. David reaches for Martin and finds himself suddenly submerged, green salty sheets billowy and thick. It happened so suddenly. Something tears. First, ordinary life—then, in a flash, the extraordinary. Juxtapositions. People lie on the embalming table. They are side by side, in rows, one vacant face after another. What are they thinking? Surely they are thinking, because only minutes ago they were walking down hallways and writing at desks and breathing and eating. He recognizes a bank teller, the grocer, one of his schoolteachers. In a few minutes, they will get up and return to their jobs. He puts his ear next to their mouths and asks them to speak. Talk to me. What are you thinking? Where are you? He bends down to the mouths, waiting for sounds. Someone is whispering. *All of this beautiful life. To have it end would be such a waste.* It is Mrs. Chee. He sees her lying on the table, smiling at him. Her body sinewy and brown and long. She is so still, but she smiles. We are just resting, she whispers. Because it cannot end like this. Have you received Bethany's letter? Certainly, he thinks. Then you know, she says, that the world can change in an instant. You can't see the world underneath, the world that is about to be. And then it unfolds. She changes into a butterfly and flies out of an open window. More whispering. Someone walks across the room, Jenny in her bathrobe. He opens the letter. *I'd like to visit you.* Bethany has come back. In the abandoned railroad car, she takes off her clothes and rubs her body with white flour. She is a field of fresh snow.

Can you meet me at my apartment building on Saturday afternoon? he asks. In the lounge. It looks like the sitting room of a house. Yes, she says. I've been wondering . . .

When she arrives, she reaches out as if to shake his hand, then seems to change her mind and kisses him on the cheek. She is as tall as he, and their eyes meet on the same level. With a tentative expression, she steps back. "So," she says, "you wanted to talk?"

"I wanted to see you. We can talk or not talk."

She stands in the lounge wearing a sleeveless cotton dress that fits close to her body, her face and bare arms moist from the heat. She glances around the room and frowns. "This is where you've been living for eight years? Can't you move into a nicer place?"

"It's comfortable enough," David says. "The rent is low."

She nods. "I shouldn't have said that." She fans herself with a brochure from some perfume shop. "I'd forgotten how hot it is here this time of year. It's hard to move in this heat."

"You used to like the heat. You used to bake in the sun for hours without a hat or anything."

"You're misremembering. I never liked the heat."

He's puzzled by what she says. Doesn't she remember? Perhaps when she left him she destroyed all the details of their life—the leaves falling in her hair as they walked, the mornings he sat listening to her play the piano, the way that he tickled her feet, their cat, Tiger, which she couldn't bear to replace after it was hit by a car, the poems he read to her in the bath, the Sunday evenings when they unplugged the phone and lay in bed watching old movies until falling asleep, the time that she flew into a rage because she couldn't convert centigrade to Fahrenheit on the new thermometer. And, yes, the hot summer days when she draped herself across the lawn chair in her underwear, or not even that. All of these scenes flash through his mind in an instant.

He gazes at her, perfection, and he wants to make love to her. He will show her his passion, and then she will be his again. Afterward, they'll take a cold shower. The water will feel cool on their skin. "Let's go up to my apartment. It's just on the second floor. I kept one or two things from the old house."

She gives him a look. "I don't think that's such a good idea."

"Why not?"

"You know why not."

"Why did you come back, Bethany?"

She puckers her lips. "I'm not sure. I thought something was different with you. Something . . . maybe interesting." She pauses. "That sounds terrible, doesn't it."

"No."

"Because," she says, "nothing interesting has happened to me."

Eight years of her life in a sentence. He wonders if she's been unconsciously wanting to come back to him all of those years, unconsciously regretting that she ever left. "Let's have some coffee in the diner," he says. She nods and puts on her sunglasses.

As soon as they enter the diner, David recalls that the tenants are having a going-away party for Gunther the cook. Saturday afternoon! He completely forgot. The tables have been pushed to the wall. In the middle of the room, Gunther is singing, tears streaming from his eyes, while George accompanies him on the accordion. Two dozen people stand about swaying with beer mugs and chips.

David turns to Bethany, apologetic. "I forgot."

"It's beastly hot in here," she complains in a low voice. "I'd rather go somewhere else." They turn to leave.

"David," Gunther yells, and stops singing. "Come in with your pretty lady. You have brought her for me, yes?"

"He's brought her for thee, an apple from a tree," sings George in an awful voice.

"Play, sweetie, don't sing," says Sally, George's wife.

Now David can see that it's too late to leave. Freddie is stumbling forward, offering them a beer in each hand. David introduces Bethany. One by one, the men and women say hello to Bethany. None of them know her past relationship to David, but they do know Ellen, and he can see the surprise and curiosity in their faces. Then they return to their dancing and singing. Everyone is sweaty in the heat. Some of the men have stripped to their undershirts.

Marie, wearing the red polka-dot dress of a German beer hostess, goes from one person to the next refilling mugs. As she walks, the beer sloshes in her pitcher and spills on the floor.

"Marie, you shouldn't be serving," says George. "You're off today. Enjoy yourself."

"I am enjoying myself," says Marie. "As much as possible." She turns to Gunther. "Don't leave us, Gunther."

Gunther begins singing again, a song in German. His long blond hair, which he keeps up in a baseball hat when he's cooking, hangs limply in his face. The accordion bellows and swings like in a carnival, a merry-go-round in the diner.

Some of the couples are dancing. Henry, who has no one to dance with, introduces himself and tells a long story about the cook they had before Gunther, a young man who used to smuggle sirloin steaks out of the restaurant for his family. His brother married a vegetarian, whereupon he began asking Ms. Jacobs, the diner owner, to buy mountains of tofu, and he smuggled that out as well. Eventually, he was caught because none of the tenants ever ate tofu. Henry laughs at his story until he's red in the face and then leaves to tell someone else.

"Do you want to dance?" asks David.

"No," says Bethany. "Can we just sit? God, it's hot in here. I can't believe this place doesn't have air-conditioning." The perspiration glistens on her face and her arms. To David, she is even more beautiful perspiring.

Marie sits down with them. Leaning forward to be heard over the music, she says to Bethany, "I love these guys." Gunther has been like a brother to her, she says, and now he's leaving to care for an aging parent. "We told him to bring his father here. We'd take good care of him. But Gunther says that his father has a young girlfriend, and she doesn't want to move. You'd think young people would be more flexible."

"Why can't the young girlfriend take care of Gunther's father?" asks Bethany.

"Good question," says Marie. "I don't know what we'll do without Gunther. He has a heart. You can hear it in his singing. Just listen." She looks over at Gunther, a sad smile on her face. "Are you from around here?" she asks Bethany.

"No," says Bethany.

"Visiting, then?"

"Yes." Bethany turns and gazes out of the window.

Marie waits for a few moments, hoping to get more out of Bethany. "David is special, you know. He's been chosen."

"Please, Marie," says David. "Don't say that."

"It's true," Marie says. She looks again at Bethany as if sizing her up, excuses herself, and returns to the counter to serve another pitcher of beer.

"She's obviously very fond of you," says Bethany. "She said you've been chosen. Have you?"

"How would I know," says David.

"But you think something unusual happened to you," says Bethany.

"Yes."

"You saw something strange." David nods. "What was it?"

"I can't describe it."

"Try," says Bethany. "I really want to know."

David takes a long swallow of beer. "All right." He pauses. "It was a thing near a dead body. A vapor. But more than a vapor. It seemed alive. It had . . . intelligence. It looked at me. It seemed to come out of the body. Or maybe it went into the body."

Bethany is listening intently as she fans herself. A vapor. Intelligence. She repeats his words. She stares at him. "And what about the other stuff? What was it? The numbers from a box. What about that?"

"I don't know about that," says David. "There's a difference of opinion." She is leaning very close to him, so that he can see the beads of sweat on her upper lip. "Sometimes," he says, "I think I'm on the brink of something. It feels like I'm about to . . . understand something, see something. I feel that my head is lifting off my shoulders. I feel like I'm looking at myself from somewhere else, outside of the world. And then it dissolves."

"Your voice sounds different when you talk about that," says Bethany. She sweeps her matted hair back. "I'm boiling. I've got to drink something. But I don't want beer. Can I have a lemonade?"

David walks over and talks to Marie and comes back. "Marie says they don't have lemonade. You can have a Coca-Cola."

"I don't want a Coca-Cola," says Bethany. "What I want is a lemonade." She sighs and looks out the window again. "I guess I'll have water."

She drinks the water and David begins rubbing her bare arms with a wet napkin dipped in the water and she allows him to do it.

"Let's go to my apartment," he says. Without looking at him, she nods.

In David's apartment, he kisses her full on the mouth. She doesn't pull away. Instead, she slightly opens her lips and leans into him with her eyes closed. Yes, he thinks, she has come back to him. He knows that now. For eight years, he has waited for this moment. He feels her against him, every precious part of her body, he feels her breasts touching him through her dress, her belly and thighs, he feels his heart pounding, his face burning, his penis stiffening, his legs growing weak, the room floats and drifts and he leads her to the couch, strange and new as if he's never seen it before, they sink into the strange cushiony boat, and they're still kissing, he will kiss her forever, their mouths locked together forever, she has come back to him as he knew that she would, his goddess, the couch floating, the smell of her hair, the white of her, and he kisses her neck, runs his tongue down her neck and her shoulders, and her sweat tastes like honey, he wants all of her in his mouth at once, his blood is rushing through his body, he can hear it, and he runs his tongue over her bare stomach, the undersides of her breasts, her nipples. What is that look on her face? Is it pleasure? Bethany, Bethany, somehow they've taken off their clothes, and her skin feels so good against his skin, and he runs his tongue over her belly and between her legs and into her deep place the wetness, the tender folds inside of her, and he hears her moaning, the room bucks and floats, I want you inside of me, she says, and she grasps his swollen penis and guides him into her, and he hurls himself over the waterfall, down and down. She waits at the bottom.

Something brushes his forehead. Where is he? Her fingertips. How long was he sleeping? Ten minutes? An hour?

Across the room, Bethany sits in a chair, dressed. She is putting a lipstick into her purse. He gazes at her hands.

"Why did you put your clothes back on?" he asks.

"I can't stay, David. I'm leaving. I'm sorry. I'm so sorry."

"What is it?"

She hesitates. She looks distraught and confused. "I was hoping . . . I don't know what I was hoping for."

His eyes focus on her fingers holding the strap of her purse. "Bethany. We can be together again."

"We can't."

"But you don't have a happy marriage."

"No, I don't." She stands up. "Charles and I deserve each other."

"I don't understand."

"Misery loves company. Charles isn't going anywhere, and neither am I. You know what a marriage is? It's either a housekeeping arrangement or a power struggle. I thought it was something else when we were first married, but that's what it is."

Bethany's words don't make sentences. They are just sounds, which he doesn't understand, and he tries to hear, tries to think, and he looks at her and notices that she doesn't seem so pale in this light with her fresh makeup. She looms like a bright building.

"You shouldn't have written," he says. "It would have been better if you'd never written." He gets up from the couch and puts his trousers on, and they face each other. "You're playing with me."

"I'm not playing with you, David. Maybe I shouldn't have written." She pauses. "I'm . . . I'm a mess."

"Yeah," he says, looking hard at her. "You are. Don't ever write me again. Don't call me again. I don't want to think about you ever again."

She nods and leaves. Did he see tears in her eyes? She was here just seconds ago, and now she is gone.

After a few moments, he begins collecting the rest of his clothes. He'll go out. He's hungry. *The world can change in an instant. You can't see the world underneath.* Didn't Mrs. Chee say those words? Or did he dream them?

You can't see the world underneath. But he has seen the world underneath. For a moment.

Monday morning. He can't remember what happened to Sunday. Now, as he looks out his bedroom window, a cottony summer haze fills the air. Across the street, he sees children kicking a red ball back and forth, houses, mailboxes, garbage cans, a glass bottle in the grass, a laundry line with damp clothes draped over it. Everything hovering and blurred in the haze.

At the mortuary, Martin is downstairs putting makeup on Madame Deschanel. This job would normally be performed by Ophelia, who inherited it from Robert, but Ophelia is chasing down a death certificate. And Louis, who would normally be chasing down the death certificate, has abruptly quit with a snippy note left in the sitting parlor. For the next several days, at the expense of his other duties, David will be posting job advertisements and screening applications. The mortuary is drowning.

"I saw Bethany again," David says to Martin.

"Ah," says Martin as he combs Madame Deschanel's thin and dyed hair. "What happened?"

"It didn't go well."

"Is that her opinion or yours?"

"Hers. I thought it was going well. But ... she didn't find whatever it was she was looking for."

With his fingers, Martin rubs a white moisturizing cream on Madame Deschanel's wrinkled face, then a skin-colored liquid. He waits while it dries. "I'm listening," he says. "I can listen while I work."

David describes the afternoon with Bethany.

"Did she seem the same as you remembered her?" asks Martin.

"I think so. Eight years is a long time."

Martin nods. Then he places a photograph of Madame Deschanel next to the table and studies it. He begins putting blue eye shadow on the eyelids.

"She's at least twenty years younger in the photograph," says David.

"Yes," says Martin, "but that's what the family wants. That's what she wanted too. She left instructions. She picked out the photograph herself, I've been told. I said to the family that you can't make an eighty-year-old woman look like she's sixty, but I'll do my best."

Gazing back and forth between the photograph and the face, Martin brushes pink blush onto Madame Deschanel's cheeks. He chooses from dozens of eye shadows, face colorings, and lipsticks on a tray.

"You know," says David, "on Saturday, Bethany really wasn't what I remembered. I don't remember her being so negative. Nothing pleased her."

"And you don't remember her being like that when you were married?"

"I remember her being bored," says David. "But not so negative. She seemed irritated with everything."

"Memory is a strange thing," says Martin. "In my experience, it's unreliable. We remember what we want to remember. Look at Madame Deschanel here. She wants to appear the way she was at age sixty. I don't blame her."

"It's always cool down here, isn't it," says David.

"Yes, it is," says Martin. "I like it especially in the hot weather."

David unrolls his sleeves and sits down in a plastic chair next to the table. For a few moments, he watches Martin work. "However Bethany was before," says David, "she's unhappy now. I don't think she's capable of being happy."

Martin shakes his head. "I'm touched that you told me about her." Martin is applying a glossy rose-pink lipstick to Madame Deschanel's lips, carefully comparing to the photograph. He turns and looks at David with his worn, milky eyes. "How would you feel about coming to our place for dinner with Ellen? It's just a thought. Jenny can call and invite her."

"Ellen doesn't want to see me again. I doubt she would come."

"You don't know until you try."

Just before dawn, the telephone rings. Could it be Ellen? A wave of guilt, and hope, passes through his body. It's Patrick McConoghy. I've got to talk to you, says Patrick. Do you know what time it is? says David. I do know, says Patrick. I've been waiting to call since three. I've had this dream. Please. Okay, says David. I'll come to your building, says Patrick. I'll be there in fifteen minutes.

David barely has time to splash some cold water on his face, brush his teeth, and get dressed. When he goes downstairs, Patrick is already waiting at the front door. Patrick's red hair is uncombed and wild, his face is covered with red stubble, and his eyes are bloodshot. He reaches out his big hand and shakes David's hand. "My apologies," he blurts out.

They sit on one of the sofas in the lounge, sweeping aside newspapers and crossword puzzles and ashtrays filled with cigarette butts.

"Well, then," says Patrick. "Julia came to me in a dream." He pauses. "She looked good. She looked like she did before she got sick."

Outside, the night is just beginning to lift. To the east, a layer of purple and apricot stretches across the horizon. An automobile faintly coughs in the distance.

"She told me she loved me," Patrick says.

"That's wonderful," says David. Tears come to his eyes. He reaches over and touches Patrick's broad shoulder.

"I had to tell you," says Patrick.

David nods, unable to speak.

"I want to thank you," says Patrick. "You brought my Julia back to me. Thank you."

"You shouldn't thank me," says David. "I didn't have anything to do with it."

"I believe you did," says Patrick. Patrick looks down and notices that his checked shirt is unbuttoned and begins buttoning it up. He tucks the shirt into his blue jeans.

"Do you want some coffee?" asks David. "I can brew us some coffee."

"No, thanks," says Patrick. "I've got to get back and get cleaned up and open the shop."

"I'm glad that you called me," says David.

"You come into the shop," says Patrick. "I'll work on your shoes for free, anytime."

"I'll do that," says David. "I'm glad that Julia spoke to you."

"Yeah," says Patrick. "I've been in hell. I've been so lonely. When I lost Julia, I lost my girls too. I know that you don't have any children. You don't know what it's like to have them and then lose them. But maybe that's happened to you with a woman. It's worse with children because they are your blood. You feel that a part of your body has been cut out of you, and you're crawling on the ground." He rubs his knuckles in his eyes. "But I think I can get back on my feet now. I'm going to get my girls back." Patrick stands up, a big man. Awkwardly, he gives David a hug. Then he leaves.

David remains sitting on the sofa. Slowly, the room fills up with daylight. David thinks of Mr. Chee and how much he would like to hear about Patrick's dream, and he pictures the little redheaded McConoghy girls sitting with Patrick in the mortuary and Julia McConoghy lying still on the embalming table, the only time he ever saw her, and he thinks about how unpredictable everything is. The world branches and branches and branches.

At six o'clock, Raymond wanders down the stairs in his pajamas and begins to work on one of the crossword puzzles. "I've never seen you down here at this hour," Raymond says to David. "You an insomniac too? I thought I was the only one in the building."

"No, I sleep," says David. "I just came down to say hello to somebody, early."

"You're lucky," says Raymond. "I don't sleep more than two hours a night. I feel like shit all the time. I guess everybody's got their thing, don't they." He looks again at the puzzle. "You got any ideas about a six-letter word meaning 'right away'? Fifth letter is a *p*."

David shrugs his shoulders.

"It doesn't matter," says Raymond. "I just do it to pass the time until breakfast. You're lucky you don't have that problem."

———

As he arrives at the mortuary that morning, hurrying toward the back entrance, a freckled young mother with a baby strapped to her back walks up to him. "You're David Kurzweil, aren't you," she says. "I've been coming here every few days waiting to meet you." "You shouldn't have done that," says David. "Oh, I haven't minded one bit," says the woman. "I've been waiting to give you something," and she hands David a manuscript, the loose pages held together by a yellow ribbon. "These are poems I've written about the meaning of life," she says. "I hope that you'll read them. I realize it's pushy of me, but we all have to express ourselves, don't we, and it's all so mysterious. Is that what it's about, Mr. Kurzweil, the mysteries? Maybe we're not supposed to know." Someone jostles David from behind, and he almost falls down. He drops the manuscript, picks it up, brushes off the dust. A man wearing a white shirt and white tie presses a Bible into David's hands. "Have you seen into the Divine Mind?" he asks. "I don't think so," says David. "Tell us what you have seen," says the man. "I have to go," says David, and he struggles to break free, clutching the manuscript of poems and the Bible. "Please, Mr. Kurzel," says a red-faced man. "I need to contact my father. Deceased seven years. Please help me." "I can't," says David, walking away as quickly as he can. "You have the power," says the man. "You have a duty." The red-faced man is following right behind David, panting. "You have a duty," he says, and puts a rough hand on David's shoulder. "Let me go," says David. "Help me speak to my father," says the man, and he tightens his grip. David swings around and he sees the man's face six inches away, his cheeks blood-red, his mouth screwed up, his eyes full of frustration and hope mixed together, and David pushes him hard and runs toward the mortuary door, dropping everything on the ground, and dashes inside the door and slams it shut.

"The telephone has been ringing off the hook," Martha complains, and gives David a list of messages, all numbered and taken down in her meticulous, back-slanted handwriting. Three from the university, without details but asking him to call back as soon as possible. Two from news organizations wanting interviews. And two from Ms. Gaignard, saying that the Society has been contacted by unfriendly lawyers and would like David's help right away. "We have our own lawyers, of course."

That afternoon, after promising Martin that he will work through the night to make up the lost time, David goes to an "urgent meeting" at the university. It is his first visit to the university for many years, since his student days, and he has trouble finding his way. In the place of his old dormitory is a new edifice for cultural studies. Across the courtyard, the student union has been enlarged with a glass-and-steel walkway, not to good effect, as far as David is concerned. Bicycles lean against its side walls.

After consulting a map, David walks up four flights of stairs of the most likely building, finds only locked doors, and returns to the central courtyard. The great clock tower points to four o'clock, the time of the meeting. "I'm looking for the Salinas Room," he asks a curly-haired student wearing headphones and sitting cross-legged on the grass. "I can't hear you," says the student. David repeats his question, shouting. "It's in the McMillan building," the student says, and flings his hand toward a Gothic building of copper-colored stone. In the McMillan building, David again climbs four flights of stairs and comes upon a long, empty corridor. He walks from one end to the other without finding anything called the Salinas Room. By now, it's quarter past four. He descends to the third floor, knocks on a half dozen doors, and eventually finds a sleepy secretary in one of the offices. "You want the Salinas Room?" she says, looking up from her paperback novel. "What's doing in the Salinas Room? You're the third person this afternoon who's asked for the Salinas Room." David has an urge to flee the building at once and skip the meeting, which will surely be dismal and dull. But the secretary is chattering nonstop and leading him on, taking him back up to the fourth floor, to one of the rooms he already passed. There, in tiny gold letters, a sign says SALINAS ROOM. "Mr. Salinas must have been a little man," David says. The secretary shrugs her shoulders without laughing and trundles back down the long corridor.

AS SOON AS HE OPENS THE DOOR, David feels as though he's entered a backroom political caucus. A dozen people sit around a long mahogany table, hunched over and talking in low voices. The air is warm and thick, and the room is illuminated by a single window and a crystal chandelier. On the dark wood walls are portrait paintings in heavy frames, possibly past presidents and deans.

"Come in, David," says Ronald Mickleweed, with a welcoming but concerned look on his face. Ronald introduces David around the table. For a few moments, David feels everyone looking at him as if he were a strange bug brought into a museum. Then, apparently satisfied with their preliminary assessment, they sit back in their chairs and turn toward President Buckingham. The president is a plump man in his fifties with bushy eyebrows, a bulbous nose, and spectacles that dangle around his neck on a black cord. David vaguely remembers something he read about President Buckingham, a man who came from a small village and later changed his name from Budzko to Buckingham, a man who learned six languages on his own. The president projects confidence and optimism.

"We much appreciate your coming, David," says the president. "We wouldn't have bothered you like this, but I'm afraid that you're inextricably tied up in this mess, certainly as far as the Society for the Second World is concerned." One of the assistant attorneys removes a yellow notepad from her monogrammed briefcase and begins taking notes. Ronald has told them about David, says the president, and they've read some of the background information. As David can imagine, they've been very concerned about their linkage to this Society. The long and the short of it, says the president, is that they cannot bring legal action against these people, as much as they'd like to. The president goes on to explain that the published statements of the Society, when examined closely, do not actually say that professors Mickleweed and Grindlay endorse the claims of the Society. The implication is there, of course, but an implication does not provide grounds for a suit. "Am I summarizing the case correctly, Sheila?" The chief counsel nods and whispers something to one of her assistants.

"Those people should be put in jail," William Grindlay says.

"I agree with that," says Professor Arthur Petit, dean of science. Professor Petit is vast, almost spherical. He wears an open sports shirt without a tie and, like Ronald Mickleweed, gives the impression of a man seldom wrong. "This is the price we pay for free speech. We have to eat a lot of garbage."

"What we would like, we can't always do," says Sheila Pillbeam, chief counsel.

"That is true," the president says with an unhappy laugh. At any rate, to bring David up to date, they've been discussing the matter for some time, and they feel that they must respond to this Society. There's a nodding of heads. The faculty and the university have been associated against their wishes with an organization that pays no attention to scientific evidence and makes unfounded and dangerous claims about important issues. Basically, says the president, this Society is intellectually dishonest. The university stands for intellectual honesty. The president pauses and looks around the table. "Do we all agree with what I've said?"

"I agree up to the point where we decide to respond," says Professor Mildenstein of the economics department. "When you respond, all you do is give legitimacy to these people. That's what they want. Better to let them wither on the vine."

"But they're not withering on the vine," says Ronald, squinting with his good eye at Professor Mildenstein. "Their membership is growing. Half the population believes in the supernatural."

"Wait a precious minute," says Professor Elaine Gilchrist, dean of humanities, a brown-haired woman with sunken cheeks and penetrating eyes. "We're not challenging the supernatural wholesale here. We're contesting some particular claims that involve our faculty."

"Of course we're challenging the supernatural," says William Grindlay, rolling his eyes.

"Personally, I wouldn't be comfortable with that statement," says Professor Gilchrist, "nor would many of my faculty. The supernatural has many facets, some of them subtle, and there is a wide range of views. We're a university, after all, and we encourage a range of opinions."

"What in the world are you talking about, Elaine?" says Professor Petit.

For starters, says Professor Gilchrist, she's talking about the whole of religion. Professor Petit may not be religious himself, she says, but she assures him that many of the faculty are. She's talking about divine inspiration, which, as everyone knows, is the root of a great deal of art and literature. In fact, she's talking about inspiration of all kinds. The metaphysical experience, to use Emily Dickinson's expression. She's talking about Jung's archetypes, and about Kant's transcendent reality. She's talking about the cultural power of totems and icons and talismans. "There's a lot more to the super-natural than ghosts and spoon bending."

"I never knew this about you," says Professor Petit. "All of these years. I'm astounded."

"All I'm saying is that there are subtleties and nuances," says Professor Gilchrist. "We can't lump everything together."

"Well said, Elaine," says the shriveled Professor Jacubois of anthropology, thumping the floor with his cane. "Magisterial."

"I can't believe this conversation," says William. "I've got a headache. I think I'm going to let a little blood to cure it. Does anyone mind?"

"Let's be civil to one another," says the president.

Please, says Ronald. We've got brilliant people sitting around this table. We should be able to put our heads together. How's this for a statement: We are contesting any claim of the Society that contradicts scientific data. Does everyone agree to that?

Heads bob.

"You okay with all this, David?" asks Ronald.

David nods his approval as well. The meeting is not as dull as he thought it would be. Nevertheless, he has trouble focusing on all the remarks, and he finds his mind drifting back to Bethany. All those years they lived together are becoming a fog in his mind. Could it be that he misremembers? The poems he read to her in the bath? The mornings he sat listening to her play the piano? Surely they had a piano. He pictures it in his mind, sturdy and made of light brown wood, with a busted music stand that kept falling down. What exactly did she play? He cannot remember. And, it now occurs to him, if he cannot remember what she played, perhaps she didn't play anything at all. Or, if she did, perhaps he never sat listening to her on sunny Saturday mornings, as he remembers. And what about the thousands of their other days and nights together? They sit at the breakfast table, sections of a newspaper scattered about, a blue glow in the air from the blue-colored walls, her putting cubes of sugar into her coffee with her fingers. Has he misremembered that as well? How can he be certain of anything that occurred in the past? He cannot be certain of thoughts. His thoughts, her thoughts. Even if every minute of their twelve years together had been recorded on a video camera, with oceans of gigabytes, that camera could not show thoughts. Hasn't he built a universe of thoughts? Unrecorded, except in his mind. Untested and untestable. Even recently, when they made love in his apartment. Did it actually happen? How can he prove that it happened? Already, the image of that moment is beginning to fade. Soon, it too will slip into the fog. Already, her bitterness and unhappiness are softening, becoming part of the faint circle of her, a circle that grows smaller and smaller. The only thing he knows for sure is what happens this instant, this razor blade of the present. But immediately the present is past. What were those twelve years with Bethany? A glance? A thought? Which world is true, the world of faulty memory or the world of the fleeting present—also faulty because it disappears as soon as it begins? The day that he went wobbling across the front yard on a two-wheeler for the first time—he sees the clouds in the sky, he sees his father waiting for him at the bottom of the hill. Then, in his father's strong arms. You rode like a prince, his father said to him. Did he imagine that? Someone is talking. David looks up, into the face of the president.

"Which brings us back to our response," says the president. "Any ideas?"

As distasteful as it is, says Professor Petit, we are going to have to stage a public demonstration, a test of some of the claims of the Society.

Ronald agrees. We'll have to make sure the demonstration is decisive.

There is general agreement around the table.

"Is there any downside to this plan?" says the president, turning to Ms. Pillbeam.

Ms. Pillbeam appears to be a woman in her forties. She wears a close-fitting blouse that emphasizes the curve of her breasts, yet she carries herself with a certain ruthless masculinity, as if to say that she's well aware she's risen to the top in a man's world and she can do battle with all comers. "You're making yourself vulnerable," says Ms. Pillbeam. You'll have everyone watching, she says. The public. The press. If the demonstration doesn't produce the results you want, you'll look foolish.

"The results we want?" says Ronald. We're doing a scientific test, he says. The facts are the facts. Any results are by definition the results we want. Unless we get a string of horribly bad luck. These people in the Society are opposed to the facts.

"I'd be very careful," says Ms. Pillbeam, looking not at Ronald but at President Buckingham. You should meet with some representatives of the Society beforehand, she says, and work out the conditions and ground rules of the demonstration. You want everyone agreeing in advance exactly what's going to be done, how it's going to be done, and what results will show what. "You don't want any surprises." Ms. Pillbeam's assistants look at her with admiration.

Very sensible, says the president. We'll form a little subcommittee. Ronald. Elaine. Arthur. Please get in touch with those people and discuss the arrangements. The president turns to David and thanks him for coming to their powwow. "I imagine that you'll be part of any demonstration. You seem to be in the middle here." The president pauses and smiles. "I understand that you and Ronald were classmates. Ronald speaks highly of you. He says that you were always a thinker."

"Ronald was the whiz kid."

"I can believe that," says the president, beginning to put away his papers. We are still counting on his winning us a Nobel. He winks at Ronald. There's one other thing I want to ask you, says the president. Since you're here. The president hesitates, as if not sure he wants to ask the question. "Do you believe that you affected the . . . what do they call it? . . . the R box, with your mind?"

William hisses.

"I've already talked to David about this," says Ronald.

"But here we all are," says the president. He looks intently at David. "I respect whatever you believe. I'd just like to know."

"Yes," says David. "I believe that I affected the R box with my mind. Dr. Tettlebeim has the results. There are recorded results."

"It doesn't matter what he thinks," says William. "I don't mean to insult you, David, but it really doesn't matter what you think. It doesn't matter what I think or what Ronald thinks or what any of us think. What matters are the experimental results."

"Well, I for one want to know what David thinks," says the president. He puts on his spectacles and peers at David as if his face were a line of newspaper print.

"So do I," says Professor Gilchrist.

"And the other thing," says the president. "The thing that you saw at the mortuary. What about that? I've read only secondhand accounts. Can you tell us about that?"

"It's hard to describe."

"Try. Please."

"We shouldn't push David if he doesn't want to talk about it," says Professor Jacubois.

"Did you see anything unusual?" asks the president, ignoring Professor Jacubois. "Anything . . . you know. Or is the press just making this up?"

"I saw something," says David.

The president moves forward in his seat toward David. "You did?"

"Yes."

Professor Petit and Professor Mildenstein look at each other and shake their heads as if David is a sad case. David sees them out of the corner of his eye, pretends that he doesn't see them.

"You *believe* that you saw something," says the president, placing a slight but unmistakable emphasis on the word.

David feels a rush of hot blood in his face and a tightening of his stomach muscles. "Yes."

"That's interesting," the president says, and continues staring at David for a few moments. Then he looks away. "Well," he says, standing up, "I think we've accomplished something this afternoon." We appreciate David taking the time, says the president. Ms. Lanier, the president's personal assistant, also rises.

"You don't believe me, do you," says David.

The president has taken two steps toward the door, Ms. Lanier following close on his heels with a cell phone already out of her purse. "I acknowledge your beliefs," says the president.

"I'm not asking that," says David. "I'm asking if you think that I saw something unusual at the mortuary."

The president pauses. He glances at Ms. Pillbeam. "How could I know what you saw?" says the president. "I wasn't there."

"But I was," says David. "And I'm telling you that I saw something unusual. It was like a vapor. It came out of a dead body. For five seconds. It looked at me." Everyone in the room has become silent. "That's what I saw at the mortuary, on April twenty-third."

"That's certainly something unusual," says the president.

"Do you believe me?" asks David.

"I believe our meeting is finished," says Ms. Pillbeam.

"No, it's not finished," says David. He is standing now.

"I believe that you think you saw something unusual," says the president. "What more can I say? I wasn't there." He turns to the other faculty, as if to get their support for his reasonable position.

"You haul me into this urgent meeting of yours," says David, "to help with your demonstration or whatever it is, protecting your intellectual honesty, and you think I'm a nutcase all along. You don't respect me at all. You think I'm a nutcase. You're mocking me. And you're using me."

"I'm sorry that you feel that way," says President Buckingham.

"I want to apologize to you, David," says Ronald.

Ms. Pillbeam begins saying something, but David doesn't wait to hear what it is. He strides past the president and out the door, down the long, empty corridor, and he runs down the four flights of steps, taking pleasure in the thrashing of his legs and the pounding of the stone steps against his feet, the shock as he hits each landing. Outside, in the courtyard, he is surprised to see light, grass, sky.

STANDING JUST OUTSIDE THE DOORWAY of the sitting parlor, he sees Mrs. Lupo, her three children, her son-in-law, and her daughter-in-law, all waiting to speak to him. Now he can't remember their names. He would ask Martin, but Martin is interviewing job applicants. Mrs. Lupo wears a wide-brimmed blue hat, which sets off her black dress and shoes. Her legs rock back and forth under the coffee table, and she has picked up the latest bird magazine. Two of her children, in their forties, dab at their eyes with Kleenex. Should he walk into the room?

There's Ophelia in the hallway. Do you know their names? he whispers. Nope, says Ophelia. Just start gabbing. They'll tell you their names. What's that thing you're wearing around your neck? he asks Ophelia. It's a crystal, she says. Crystal energy. Crystal energy? Yeah, she says. I've given up on the black box. I never could get it to float. People have been telling me about crystal energy. You should try it.

He walks past the sitting room again. What is that phrase Martin says to the grieving families? *Let the evening come.* But first, he should listen to them. Always listen, Martin says. They will tell you what they need.

One of the sons wants to see the slumber room. Mr. Lupo hasn't been brought there yet, David explains. Can you show us the slumber room anyway? asks the son. All of us would like to see it. Because of what happened. We thought maybe . . . The son looks at

David. His face is pockmarked, like Aidan's, and David pictures Aidan as he slides under the wave. Patrick reaches out from his boat, but it is too late. Aidan sinks below the surface. His face becomes a dim ocher stone and disappears. And now Julia has appeared to Patrick in a dream. How unpredictable it all is. He should have said that to President Buckingham.

IT IS A CLASSROOM IN ONE of the old buildings of the university, with wooden chairs and desks, a scuffed wooden floor, a blackboard, a chart of subatomic particles on the wall, portraits of Faraday, Darwin, Madame Curie. It is a room David remembers from his student days.

To avoid conversation, he has come at the last minute, hurrying through the hallways and corridors. He looks around quickly, trying not to make eye contact with anyone. A dozen people, he should think. After much insisting by the Society that the attendance be minimized "so as not to interfere with the intentionality force," the joint demonstration committee has invited only four members of the university, four members of the Society, and one newspaper reporter. In addition, a couple of graduate students from the physics department have arrived with odd-looking antennae to probe for "unexpected" electromagnetic emissions. Evidently having some fun with the occasion, the students have worn extra-long white lab coats, which drag on the floor as they pace the perimeter of the room with their equipment. Sitting in the front row is Sheila Pillbeam, watching everything like a hawk.

"Good. David is here," says Ronald. "I hope you're up to this, David."

"I had a light lunch," says David, with a touch of sarcasm. But he likes Ronald and holds his gaze for a few moments and smiles, trying to reassure him of his friendly intentions. Poor Ronald Mickleweed. A brilliant and decent man, who has been challenged and defamed and sucked into this quagmire only because he was kind enough to answer David's questions. For the occasion, Ronald has worn a jacket and tie, but David can see that he is uncomfortable as he fidgets with the computer and tries to loosen his collar. Ronald would be far happier in his laboratory, making synthetic compounds or whatever he does there. And in two years, he'll be blind. David feels a wave of sympathy flooding over him. He wishes he could do something to relieve Ronald, to please him, but events are now beyond his control. Is he mistaken, or is everyone staring at him, as they did in the Salinas Room? He takes a deep breath to steady himself and can smell that familiar odor of chalk dust and musty old wood—the classroom must be a century old. And there, outside the window, is the grand clock tower of the university, like an old soldier. A warm breeze flows through the open window. How strange to be here, as if walking in a dream.

"Mr. Kurzweil has arrived."

A rotund little wheezing man, the reporter waddles over to David and asks to interview him. No interviews, please, says David. His words are always distorted.

The reporter wrinkles up his face. "No interviews? What's the point, Mr. Kurzweil? Well, at least tell me one thing. Do you feel like a guinea pig?" He stares at David with fascination, his stubby fingers holding a pen to his notebook.

A guinea pig! Is that what he is? "I'm here for myself," says David. "I'm not here for anyone else."

The reporter nods and copies down David's words. He remains standing near the front of the room with his notebook out, wheezing and sweating and studying each person in the room. Then he takes a small camera from his pocket and photographs the R box, which is mounted on a lab table next to the blackboard. On the blackboard itself is a tangled vine of an equation, next to which are the words DO NOT ERASE, OR ELSE.

"This is quite the scene," says the reporter, smiling mischievously.

"Would you like to examine the R box?" Ronald asks Dr. Tettlebeim.

"I've already examined it," says Dr. Tettlebeim, who is wearing a checked suit and vest despite the warm weather, with a yellow carnation in his lapel. He takes off his spectacles and scowls at Ronald. "It's very similar to the ones we use."

"But you approve of it?"

"You seem anxious, Professor Mickleweed."

"I'm only anxious to make sure that there will be no disagreements about procedural matters."

The reporter is scribbling at high speed, taking delight in the repartee between the principal antagonists. Then he puts down his notebook and motions for David and Professor Mickleweed and Dr. Tettlebeim to pose together for a picture.

"I'd rather not be in a picture," says David.

"You haven't been very cooperative, Mr. Kurzweil," says the reporter. "I'm just doing my job. I have a responsibility to my readers."

"Well, I don't want my picture taken," says David.

"Be a good sport," says Dr. Tettlebeim, putting his arm around David and gently pulling him in. "You've got to be in the picture. Theresa wants you in the picture."

The reporter's flash goes off. Giving David an apologetic look, he puts away his camera.

Now the graduate students approach David, their white lab coats dragging on the floor. They pass their wires and coils over David as if he were a magnet lying on the lab table. They do the same with Dr. Tettlebeim.

"You won't find any electromagnetic emissions from either of us," says Dr. Tettlebeim. "The intentionality force does not operate in this dimension."

One of the students struggles to stifle a laugh. "We're looking for tricks," says the other student.

"Magicians and frauds do tricks," Dr. Tettlebeim says softly.

"This is a wonderful opportunity for the Society," Ms. Gaignard says to David. The two of them have sat down together in the cramped desks. Despite all that has happened, David still feels a warmth toward her. She's dressed as she was the first day he met her, with a smart tapered jacket over a white blouse, immaculate. A tiny gold SSW pin gleams on her collar. Touching David lightly on the shoulder, she whispers to him. "These people think they know everything. It's such a waste, isn't it. All that education. We probably went to some of the same schools. You would think they wouldn't have such closed minds." She pauses, waiting for him to respond. "What do you want out of this, David? I know what everyone else wants."

He doesn't know what he wants. But he feels that a heavy pendulum has been set swinging, and he cannot stand in its way. Since April 23, a momentum has picked him up and carried him along to wherever it is going. Some kind of fissure opened up that late afternoon, some discontinuity. Something changed in him. Is that why people are staring at him? This morning, Ellen called to wish him good luck. That's all she said. He wanted to speak to her, to plead with her, but she hung up. Good luck with what? he wondered. With what does he need good luck?

"I want my life back," he says to Ms. Gaignard.

"I don't think you want your life back. In any case, you can't get your life back. You're in another place now. Just remember this. All these people here, that's not what it's about. It's a personal experience."

"Don't you think all of us are making fools of ourselves?" says David.

"Possibly," says Theresa Gaignard with a smile. "But it's a great day for the Society. We're getting a hearing from people who . . . well, you know. I try to pretend that it doesn't matter, but it does. My husband is here, the first time he's traveled with me for years." She points to the back of the room, where a diminutive man sits reading a newspaper. David notices that there are tears in her eyes. "I know that he supports me, but . . . now he's finally here. We've been married for nineteen years."

David is about to say something to her—she has opened herself up to him and he wants her to know he has listened—when he is summoned.

"Mr. Kurzweil, it's beginning."

He takes his place near the R box. It's a little larger than the black boxes he's seen before, shiny and metallic. It looks comical in a way, with its gray cable trailing off to the computer like the long tail of a rodent. In a sudden flash, he remembers sitting in this room as a student decades ago, early in the morning, far too early, when an earthquake shook the building. While the students fled to the exits, the professor continued to write equations on the blackboard.

Bach's "Well Tempered Clavier" begins chopping the air.

David attempts to concentrate on the box. He hears someone cough. People shuffle their feet. How can he possibly concentrate under these conditions? And this time the fugue is making him nervous. Why is he doing this? They are all making fools of themselves. He stares at the box, and he feels his heart beating. Perhaps there is no intentionality force. But there is himself. And he has a secret. He's been searching for something. That is his secret. It is a pearl that he holds close to his heart. Even when he was a boy, he was searching for something. The searching itself creates a crack in the wall. Someone is coughing again. No, a wheeze. The wheezing reporter, no doubt. It's a sound that starts out as low thunder, becomes an automobile putting on its brakes, and ends like the high squeal of a boiling teakettle. David imagines an orchestra of wheezers, each with a different musical pitch and rhythm. There are high-note wheezers and low-note wheezers. There are fast wheezers and slow wheezers. Symphonies for wheezes would be written. The conductor of such an orchestra would be a great wheezing man himself, standing high on his platform and pointing his baton at each wheezer when it was his turn.

"The period is finished," says Ronald. He walks to the computer printer. David can see Ronald's hands shaking. For a few moments Ronald studies the results. "Nothing," he says. Dr. Tettlebeim frowns and looks at the printout himself. This must be a momentous occasion for Dr. Tettlebeim, David thinks; all that he believes in is being scrutinized and judged at this moment. His hands also are shaking, although he seems to control his demeanor, his blue eyes hold steady. But his hands shake, the slight visible tremor from the seething that must be inside of him.

"Dr. Tettlebeim, do you agree with Professor Mickleweed's assessment of the results?" asks the reporter.

"Yes and no," says Dr. Tettlebeim. He takes off his spectacles. "We are looking for patterns, not just relative numbers of zeroes and ones. The intentionality force sometimes produces patterns. I want to display the numbers in a matrix of columns and rows." How composed he is, despite the seething inside of him.

"That's ridiculous," says Ronald. "There are too many possibilities." He looks over at Arthur Petit, who throws up his hands in frustration.

"Let's try rows repeating every one hundred numbers and every two hundred numbers," murmurs Dr. Tettlebeim. "Just those two displays. That's not a large number of possibilities, is it, Professor Mickleweed? Is two a large number?"

"What's going on?" asks the reporter.

"Why are we talking about this?" moans Professor Petit. "The test has been done."

"We'll do Dr. Tettlebeim's two displays," says Ronald, "and finish this thing." Ronald types something into the computer, and the printer begins chattering again. Between pages, it pauses and gulps, as if taking a breath. Page by page, Ronald squints at the output. "No patterns that I see," he says. "But this whole exercise is arbitrary." He hands the paper to Dr. Tettlebeim, who studies it without expression. Ronald passes the printout around the room.

"I don't see any patterns," says Professor Petit. "Just a hodge-podge of zeroes and ones, what you'd expect from a random number generator." Professor Petit slaps the printout down on Professor Gilchrist's desk. "Do you see a pattern, Elaine?"

"You act like I'm on the other side," Professor Gilchrist says. She flips through the pages. "I don't understand any of this. I never did well in science."

The reporter ponders the printout, shaking his head in confusion.

"That's the one hundred by three hundred," says Ronald. "Now, we'll do the two hundred by one hundred and fifty. Then we'll be done." Ronald types, and the printer clucks.

Dr. Tettlebeim picks up the new ouput and puts on his spectacles. He places the four pages in a square. For a few moments, his eyes rove over the picture. Then a smile creeps to his lips. "Yes," he says. "There it is."

"It's a random fluctuation," says Ronald, looking at the picture.

"No, it's not," says Dr. Tettlebeim. "It's the intentionality force."

"Show me," says David, and Dr. Tettlebeim points to a region toward the bottom right of the rectangle of numbers. There, amid a random sea of zeroes and ones, is a jagged circle, its perimeter formed of ones, its interior nearly all zeroes. Not a perfect circle, but a pretty good circle, clear enough to stand out from the erratic jumble around it. Oddly, David feels a little triumph. Not that he was concentrating on anything other than the reporter's wheezing, but he'd rather have an effect than no effect at all. Yet it all seems so remote to him, so far from that feeling of power and magic that sometimes comes over him.

"There's been no adequate control experiment," says Professor Petit. "Nothing has been proved here." He turns and looks at Sheila Pillbeam as a guilty child looks at a parent. Ms. Pillbeam has taken out her cell phone and is whispering into it.

"It's a random fluctuation," says Ronald. He puts his hand on the arm of the reporter to get his attention.

"I have no idea what a random fluctuation is," says the reporter, "but I sure do see a circle."

"We have received a message from the second world," says Dr. Tettlebeim. "But what does it mean?"

"Well, that's really something," says the reporter, smiling and writing everything down. "Professor Mickleweed, do you know what it means? You're the scientist."

"It doesn't mean shit, pardon the French, because there's no message to begin with," shouts Ronald. "This circle is a chance occurrence. It's an accident. It's like finding a face in the clouds." To David, it seems strange to hear Ronald shouting, something that should never happen, like an equation that contradicts itself.

"Professor Mickleweed, you should accept evidence when it is placed in front of your eyes," says Ms. Gaignard. "Joseph, come look at this."

"Mr. Kurzweil, would you like to comment?"

David sits down and closes his eyes.

And what would he say if he did offer a comment to the obnoxious reporter who just now snapped his picture when he asked him not to? Whatever he says, the reporter will twist it into a story to titillate his readers. The truth is that he was concentrating on a symphony of wheezes, not on the box. That's what he should tell him. Let them think what they want. He can indeed affect the box—he's pretty sure of that now—but the effect is not so trivial as to appear in an odd sequence of zeroes and ones. He feels powerful, although he doesn't understand the nature of his power, and he looks up to speak to the reporter about the symphony of wheezes, but he's no longer there. The wheezer has gone. So has Ronald. Dr. Tettlebeim is gone. Ms. Gaignard and her husband are gone. In fact, the classroom is empty. On the floor, beneath his feet, is the curled-up gray tail of the R box.

In the hallway outside the classroom, he sees a man sweeping the floor. The man has long hair gathered into a ponytail, dark glasses, a sleeveless black T-shirt. While sweeping, he smokes a cigarette.

"It was a hot one today," the man says to David. He offers David a cigarette. With a wave of his hand, David declines. The man exhales through his curled lips, flicks some ashes on the floor, and sweeps the ashes up in his dustpan.

"Did you see a bunch of people coming out of this room just now?" David asks.

"Folks come and go down this hallway all the time," says the janitor.

"There would have been about a dozen people," says David.

"What do they look like?" says the janitor.

"I can't tell you what they look like," David says in frustration. "A few people wore jackets and ties. There were several professors. A newspaper reporter with cameras and notebooks. A couple of students with long white lab coats. A dozen people. You couldn't have missed them."

The janitor gives David a quizzical look and smiles, showing yellow smoker's teeth. He's one of those people who have learned how to talk while keeping a cigarette clamped between their lips. He couldn't be more than forty years old. Seeming in no hurry, he moves slowly down the corridor with his broom and dustpan, sweeping in long sideways strokes.

"A dozen people, you say," remarks the janitor. "They all came out at once?"

"I don't know if they all came at once," says David. "They were all in that room a few minutes ago, and now they're all gone. They must have come out within a minute or two of one another."

"Maybe I did see some people in the hall," says the janitor. "I don't know about the white lab coats and the cameras and whatnot. People are coming through here all the time, on their way somewhere, to the restrooms down the hall, or down to the courtyard, or who knows where. It makes it hard to clean up, you know."

"When did you see them?" David asks.

"When did I see them? That would be hard to say." The janitor takes another long drag from his cigarette. "You know, it's not easy to find a place where you can smoke these days."

The light is getting dim. David looks down the corridor and cannot see the end of it.

"I've got an idea," says the janitor. "Why don't we just wait here for a few minutes. In my experience, you have a meeting like you were describing, somebody always forgets something, a book or a coat or whatnot, and they come back to the room to pick up what they forgot."

David hesitates and looks at his watch. He needs to return to the mortuary.

"I can see you're in a rush," says the janitor. "Let's sit here for fifteen minutes. I'll bet that somebody shows up. I've got some folding chairs in the closet over there."

David follows the janitor to the closet across the hall, where he pulls out a couple of striped lawn chairs, and they sit down.

"You a professor here?" asks the janitor, taking another cigarette out of his pocket.

"No," says David. "I work in a mortuary."

"Wow. Dead people. No problem, man."

"Do you work by yourself?"

"Yep. I like it that way. People talk your ear off. Yak yak. I like it quiet. You married?"

"Divorced."

"Yeah, I've been there."

David looks at his watch. Six minutes have gone by. It's crazy, sitting here waiting for somebody to come back. But everyone disappeared so suddenly. The obnoxious reporter asked him a question, and then everyone was gone. Somehow, he must have dozed off for a few minutes.

"Somebody will come back for something," says the janitor.

"This is a good way to find out who hangs out in the building. I used to work at an automobile shop, but this is better. So you work in a mortuary. Have you ever wondered what it would feel like to be dead?"

"No." This kind of talk could go on forever, David thinks. The guy is probably starving for conversation. David looks at his watch again. Fifteen minutes have gone by, and they haven't seen a single person or heard a sound.

"Somebody will turn up," says the janitor.

"Yeah," says David. He walks down the corridor toward the window at the end and goes to the next floor, passing only dark offices with locked doors. He listens for telephone conversations, voices. No one is in the building.

"The R box made a circle," says David, "but I'm not sure I had anything to do with it."

"That's all they need," says Ellen in a hoarse voice. "What time is it?"

"Two."

"Most people are asleep at this hour."

"I'm sorry that I woke you up."

"A circle. What do you mean?"

"A picture of a circle made out of ones and zeroes. There should have been just a jumble. Nothing. The university people—Ronald Mickleweed, et cetera—say the circle was an accident. The total number of zeroes and ones came out the same."

"I see . . ."

"I didn't think you'd ever talk to me again."

"I didn't either."

"Bethany is gone. That's finished."

"You won't ever be finished with Bethany."

"Yes, I will. We're finished."

"It's too late to talk about this."

"What are you wearing?"

"You know what I'm wearing."

"Have you thrown out my clothes?"

"No."

"I figured by now you would have thrown them out."

"I thought they might be good for something. Dish towels or cleaning rags."

"Can I see you again?"

"I'll have to think about that. I'm too tired to talk now."

"Okay. Good night."

"Good night."

"I COULDN'T HELP NOTICING THAT all the curtains are closed," says Laura Fiorini, one of the new people Martin has hired.

"Yes," says Jenny. "We've had a few people hanging around the building and trying to see in the windows. You get used to it."

Ms. Fiorini nods and smiles. David likes her. She's a smart young woman two years out of college. She wears her brown hair in a bun with a beret and hardly any makeup, and she looks people straight in the eye when she's talking to them. She'll be good with the families. Even Ophelia, who David thought would resent any new female employees, has warmed up to Laura Fiorini.

They're touring the facilities—Martin, Jenny, David, and Laura.

"There was a fire here forty years ago," Martin tells Laura. "Put your nose to the wall. Do you smell the burnt wood?"

"I remember that odor," says Laura. "My cousin's house burned down, and it smelled like that."

"There's a lot of history here," says Martin.

"Yes, love," says Jenny, "and you are one of the oldest relics."

"I don't feel old," says Martin. "Actually, I feel young." In fact, it seems to David that Martin has been looking better lately. His face has color again, and his trousers are straining against his belly as they used to. Evidently, some of the worry is gone now that he's hired two new people. Still, he constantly frets about not spending enough time with the families.

"Ah," says Martin as the strains of "Claire de Lune" float through the hallway.

"I thought we were going to play the Vivaldi this morning," says Jenny.

"We can play the Vivaldi later," says Martin. "I don't find the piece as calming as you do."

In the slumber room, the chairs have been arranged in the usual semicircle, in preparation for a viewing later that day. With the draperies closed, the room is quite dark when they enter. Martin turns on the porcelain lamps.

David slumps down in one of the chairs. After a late night working on follow-up letters, everything is a blur. The public demonstration with the R box seems a lifetime ago. Even the flood of newspaper articles and fevered "Letters to the Editor," with all parties claiming victory and maligning each other, have dried up in a sludge of confusion. He leans his head back and listens to "Claire de Lune" while Martin explains to Laura Fiorini what happens in the slumber room, the procedures and rules for visitors. When his great-grandfather started the business one hundred years ago, Martin says, this room was where they did everything except the embalming. At this moment, a heavy perfume wafts through the room and combines with the hot air to make a sweet, suffocating blanket. The overhead fan merely recirculates the hot air. Laura Fiorini has taken off her jacket and is dabbing her forehead with a handkerchief.

"I guess you know many of the families, living here as long as you have," says Ms. Fiorini.

"Oh yes," says Jenny.

"It's not uncommon to work with three or four generations of the same family," says Martin. "Just last week, we buried Lisa Bernacke. Before that, we buried her father and aunt. And before that, her grandfather Mr. Tate. I wasn't personally involved with Mr. Tate, of course, but my father was. It's all in our records. We might even have buried Mr. Tate's mother. I can't remember." Martin gazes off, as if listening to the music. Like waves, the notes flow up and down the scale, the gentle undulating waves of the notes. "The families know us," Martin says, still gazing off.

"That's very special," says Ms. Fiorini. "To have that kind of long relationship. They must trust you."

"That's what we want," says Martin. "Trust and respect. That's what it's all about."

So many times now, David has heard those words. His eyelids are so heavy, but he must not fall asleep, the room shimmers with the music, the waves of sound, he must not fall asleep, and he remembers the first time he was in this room, how he struggled to stay awake, with the single white orchid on the coffee table—no, that was the sitting parlor next door. He'll say something to Laura. Is she married? he wonders; she's such a pretty young woman, and centered. She knows what she wants. At this age, he had not yet married Bethany. How quickly the years have trickled by. He must say something to stay awake. "Martin is a master at soothing the families," he says, listening to his own words. "You should see him in action."

"I'm looking forward to that," says Laura.

She's just right, David thinks. How will she get on with Ophelia? They are so different. Ophelia is combustible, spontaneous, emotional, while Laura seems careful and measured. Thinking of Ophelia, he smiles.

"I don't know why it's always so much hotter in this room," says Jenny. "Do you know, love?"

"It's always been that way. It must be the orientation."

"I wish we didn't have to keep the windows and curtains closed." Martin grimaces.

"Martin tells me that you were in nursing school for a while," says Jenny.

"Yes," says Laura. "Since I was a little girl, I wanted to be a nurse. I guess I loved the idea of taking care of people. But when the time came, I changed my mind. It's not the people. It's the hospitals. There's something about hospitals I don't like. I can't exactly say what it is."

"I don't like them either," says David. Every time he's taken his mother to the hospital, he's hated the long white walls, the smell of antiseptic, the bad music piped into every room like a forced feeding.

"Hospitals these days are factories," says Martin. "They're big and impersonal."

"Yes, that's it," says Laura. "That's it."

"Let's go to a cooler room."

They pass quickly through the casket room and the arrangement room. Martha appears in the hallway with a note in her hand. Ophelia is evidently having some kind of trouble with the Birkhoff certificate, reports Martha, oblivious to Laura Fiorini. Has the service already been set? asks Martin. Wednesday at four p.m., says Martha. Martin shakes his head, thinking.

"I don't want to interfere with your work," says Laura. "You can take me through another day."

"It's no problem," says Martin. "I'll just call Ophelia to see what's what. It'll take five minutes." They walk into the sitting parlor. "You can wait here, or Jenny and David can take you through the rest of the building now. Whichever you prefer."

"I'll be happy to show Laura around," says David.

There's a loud bang followed by the sound of the front door being shoved open. Martha rushes toward the reception area.

"Who could that be?"

"I want to speak to David Kurzweil," a man shouts in the reception area.

"Leave at once" comes Martha's voice.

"I'm here to see Mr. Kurzweil," the intruder shouts again.

They hear scuffling.

"Where is he?" The man's voice again.

"I'm calling the police," shouts Martha.

They hear heavy footsteps. Suddenly a man appears at the doorway of the sitting parlor. His clothes are disarranged and he has a red welt across his face. His eyes dart about the room.

"Get out," Jenny shouts.

Everything has happened so quickly, no one has moved. They are all statues.

David feels the man's eyes fasten on him. A recognition crosses the intruder's face. "You," the man shouts. For a second, he hesitates. Then he lunges toward David. In doing so, he collides hard with Martin. As David watches, Martin's legs fold up and he buckles at the waist and goes down and his head strikes the corner of the coffee table with a loud crack and Martin is on the floor of the sitting parlor with a pool of blood forming around his head. Somewhere, Jenny is screaming. David rushes to Martin and turns him over. His face is a mask. This can't be. Martin. Call an ambulance. David looks down and his hands are red with blood. *Crack.* The sound over and over. The intruder has dropped to his knees. I didn't mean to, he cries. What have I done? What have I done? The intruder has put his mouth on Martin's mouth, trying to breathe air into him. And Jenny is on the floor, pushing the intruder away, weeping. Martin. Martin. Now Martin's eyes are fixed and dilated.

ROBERT PULLS OUT THE CHOKE and starts the engine. With a nautical skill no one knew he possessed, he eases the boat out from the slip, hovers for a few moments as if saluting the mourners gathered on the dock, and then heads out toward the middle of the lake. A breeze shuffles his hair. He looks much older. He doesn't look well. He looks, David thinks, with the blue-green water flowing out behind him, like some dried-up gray reed hanging out from the shore. Perhaps he has suffered loneliness during his time away. Or perhaps it is the terrible loss they are all now suffering.

Exactly where should they scatter the ashes? They will just feel it, Jenny says. Ophelia, her head shaved in mourning, holds the small urn hard against her chest. She stands stiffly in the bow of the boat, facing forward like a wooden figurehead.

Looking back, David can see the white froth of the wake. He can see houses on the far shore, their windows glinting with white dabs of sun. He can see the mourners on the dock. Old Louise Abernathy stands there in her black dress and black hat, the same outfit she wore for her husband's funeral. Just a few minutes ago, she was saying that Martin was one of the last of a generation of gentlemen. That was the word she used. Men who had a "natural sense of kindness and nobility, a sense of their place in life." David wonders whether Mrs. Abernathy would say the same of his father. Yes, she would, he decides, if she knew him. Now he has lost his father a second time. He looks back at Mrs. Abernathy, standing erect and fierce on the dock. Sarah Abernathy is there as well. Working his way through the crowd, a man has reached Sarah and is talking to her. In the rear, small and almost hidden, Ellen stands and waits. The dock buckles slightly on its green, algae-covered posts. So that's what it looks like from here, David thinks, the dock that he's walked past for years.

David regrets that more people could not get into the boat. But there was room only for himself, Jenny, Jenny's sister, Susan, and brother, Terrence, Robert as captain, Ophelia, and Martin's sister, Abby, whom David had not met before today. Since they left the dock, no one has said a word. The engine sputters and drones, and the water falls away from the plunging hull with a soft lapping sound. Despite the rocking of the boat, Jenny is reading a book of some kind. Looking at her now, David can see that it is the little book of poems by William Blake. Her tears have stopped, and she concentrates on the poem she is reading, unconscious of the others in the boat, seemingly unconscious of the occasion itself. She was never as sentimental as Martin; that was always her strength. And now, holding tightly to the little beige book, with the wind blowing her hair about, she will move on with her life. She will miss Martin dearly, and she will never love anyone as she has loved him, but she will move on, just as the boat is now plowing steadily ahead toward the center of the lake. Already, she has sold the funeral home to Bertram Bigelow—in a single day, lock, stock, and barrel—with enough money to pay off the debts and retain a modest retirement fund for herself. Suddenly closing her book, she retrieves a scarf from her purse and ties it firmly around her hair. She will take care of herself, David thinks.

David looks back toward the dock. It has grown smaller, a

brownish-green twig in the distance. The mourning party is still there, also shrinking in size. Beyond is the shore, a curved line of houses and shops, and beyond that, to the east, must be David's apartment building with its dozens of small rooms. He imagines all of those men he has lived with for years but hardly known, walking about in their rooms, walking down the hallways and stairs, using the toilets and showers. All now compressed to a dot on the horizon, growing smaller and smaller, until it is all a tiny red point in his mind, which swings this way and that with the rocking of the boat.

The wind flutters and gusts and makes a thousand little dimples on the skin of the lake. On the shore, trees bend over like tired old women.

"Let me know when it's time," says Robert, breaking the silence. "We'll have to point downwind. We don't want Martin's ashes to blow back into the boat."

"You really are a sailor," says Jenny. "I never knew."

"He is," says Abby.

Abby has already announced that she hates water and hates boats, so her compliment to Robert has all the more thrust. She has Martin's nose and his eyes. With a suddenness, David remembers the look on Martin's face as he went down, the confusion and then a kind of resignation, as if he knew that his time was up even if due to a horrible mistake—that look of surrender to some greater power, the look of a zebra or wildebeest caught in the jaws of a lion and knowing it is useless to struggle. Somehow, David thinks, there is a gruesome logic in Martin's end, killed by the outsiders he so feared. But that doesn't make it right or fair or less horrible. The sadness wells up in him again, making his face burn, and he senses that a hole has been punched in the sky and will never be filled. Mrs. Abernathy called Martin a gentleman, for his kindness and nobility, but she failed to mention something else—his tenderness. Why isn't a man allowed to be tender? David wonders, tears in his eyes. But Martin was tender, and David felt it every moment, and the tenderness enveloped him and gave him a home. What a good father Martin would have been. Something wrong on my side, he said that night in his apartment, both of them drunk. Jenny didn't want to adopt, he added. The sadness he must have hidden inside of himself. Perhaps that was the secret of his compassion and tenderness. David should have said more to him that night after the wine, he should have comforted him, he should have said out loud what they were both thinking: that he would be Martin's son. Why didn't he say it? Why didn't he? He was right there, the two of them sitting not more than ten feet apart, Martin leaning back in his leather chair and rubbing his toes on the jute rug and drinking the last sips of wine from his glass. His hands. Despite the stubbiness of his fingers, his hands had a fineness. The way that Martin touched each of his stamps, the way that he once put his arm around Robert, the way that he rested his hand on David's shoulder. Kindness and nobility were only a part. He didn't know how much he was loved, Jenny said as they sat in the apartment with the letters and notes and food from friends. How does anyone know something like that? David asked. He lived in his father's shadow, said Jenny. He never thought that he measured up to his father. He never thought he was as capable as his father. Martin never talked about it. But I knew how he felt. You should have seen his father, Lawrence Shaw. When Lawrence walked into a room, he filled it up. He had a presence. He was only an inch taller than Martin, yet he seemed a foot taller. But he didn't have Martin's heart. He didn't have Martin's . . . Jenny began weeping. It was all my fault, David said. That crazed man was looking for me. No, said Jenny. It was an accident. No one was to blame. It was me that man was after, said David. I should have gone to the reception area to meet him when he came in. Then nothing would have happened to Martin. It was an accident, said Jenny. Then she stood up from the couch and looked around the room, looked at the pies and salads on the dining table. I've been happy here, she said. But I don't want to live here one more day. I feel like I'm on fire. You take the place, David. Martin wanted you to. I couldn't, said David. Jenny nodded. She was wearing a black widow's shawl, which looked misplaced on her. Her eyes were red, like his.

Susan asks for a life jacket and adds that she's feeling seasick. Opening the locker under the seat, David finds a dozen orange life jackets and parcels them out. He helps Susan fasten hers, but no one else wants one.

While Susan fumbles with her jacket, Robert slows the motor, but they are still moving briskly through the water, with each gust of wind shoving the hull like a fist and the wake falling behind them in a seething white V.

"Are we there yet?" asks Susan.

There? Where is there? When will they know? Martin specified only that his ashes be scattered "in the middle of the lake." David still marvels at Martin's instructions to Jenny, evidently spoken years ago, that he not be buried in the family plot but instead be cremated and scattered in the lake. Finally, Martin will mingle with the world.

Jenny stands up, holds herself steady against the gunwale of the boat, and looks about. "Here," she says at last.

"Here?"

"Yes." Jenny stares at the water and begins weeping. After a few moments, she dries her eyes with her scarf and gathers herself. "Here," she repeats.

Robert slows the engine to an idle and does a circle. They are somewhere in the middle. In the distance, the dock is now a thin line, almost invisible. David peers through binoculars and can barely make out the smudge of something on the dock. In the wind and the waves, the boat pitches and rolls. Susan moans in her discomfort.

"We would have to have a windy day," says Abby.

"It's the way it should be," says Ophelia. She turns around from her perch at the bow, strange with her bald head, and stands ready to scatter the ashes.

Yes, David thinks, admiring Ophelia. For Martin's death seems to have given her a solidity. Ophelia has been a wandering soul, bored with her life, unfulfilled in her romances, and now she seems to have gained something. Something has been clarified. Martin's death has rung in her ears like a struck bell, collected her and pointed her to the future. David always felt that she had a strength. There she stands, the steadiest person on the boat, clutching Martin close to her chest, ready to scatter him over the waters. She has scarcely spoken to Robert, David has noticed. Robert, for whom she pined so long. With her new confidence, Ophelia doesn't need Robert. She doesn't even glance at Robert, but she knows that he is looking at her, and she quietly exalts in her new strength. Yes, it is the way it should be.

The moment has come. Robert swings the boat around in one last circle and turns the stern to the wind.

"Maybe you should read the poem now," says Terrence.

Jenny nods and takes out the Blake book. Holding the boat's gunwale with one hand, the gusty wind flapping the scarf on her head like a flag, she begins reading.

Little Fly,
Thy summer's play
My thoughtless hand
Has brush'd away.

Am not I
A fly like thee?
Or art not thou
A man like me?

Her voice wavers once in the middle, but she finishes. She will move on with her life, David thinks. She was the one who believed him from the beginning. She never doubted him. And when he wept the day Martin died, when he said it was all his fault, she said no. No one was to blame.

"Ophelia," she says, finished with the poem.

Ophelia turns around, taller than David has ever seen her, and empties the urn. Martin's ashes fly out and away. Some get hurled straight down to the water and float gray and powdery for a moment before disappearing, while others get lifted up by the wind and sail off in the air, high above the lake.

FOR THE FIRST TIME IN MONTHS, Martha opens the draperies, and the light comes pouring in, almost with a pressure, erasing the clogged shadows as if sweeping dust from the corners of a long vacant room. "I've been wanting to do that," says Martha, teary-eyed. Moving slowly, she goes to each window and lets in the light. "It's all wrong," she says, and wipes her eyes with a handkerchief. "I can't believe what's happened." She looks around the bare room. There's a strangeness to it now.

"You don't need to stay," says David.

"No, I won't stay. We all have to be out by noon, Mr. Bigelow said."

"Yes. Ellen and I will stay just a few minutes more."

"Well, then. Good-bye."

"Good-bye, Martha."

"Is that the woman who was such a beast?" Ellen asks after they hear the front door close.

"I thought so at the time," says David.

"So this is the slumber room," says Ellen, sitting beside him. "I'm glad that I'm finally seeing it. I'm glad that you brought me here today. I guess we won't be able to come again."

"No."

Some pink gladioli lie on the one table, left over from a recent service. David turns around in his chair and gazes out the window. The world never stops, he thinks. Outside, the leaves of trees flutter, two men and a woman walk along the sidewalk in oblivion, the air brims and glows. The world branches and branches. The world swerves unpredictably. He turns back to the room, and to Ellen. He understands that she would like to say something to comfort him, but he also understands that she knows him well enough to be silent. They have come closer together. She sits beside him, holding his hand.

His eyes move about the room. It is almost empty. The beautiful old porcelain lamps and the crystal decanters, the tables and the fraying Oriental rug, have all been taken away. Jenny will sell most of it or give it to charity. For some reason, the chairs have been left behind, the embroidered chairs purchased by Martin's grandfather long ago. David's eyes follow along the semicircle of chairs and then move to the center of the circle, the imaginary pivot. The space is both empty and full. The air there seems to have a thickness and bulk. Squinting, he has the sensation of seeing the air there, a dull fluid, suspended at the center of the circle. This is where it began. The center of the circle. What happened here that dim afternoon? He stares at the pivot, and he wants to feel it and see it again, but now the image that burned through him for months will not return. Even in his mind, it will not return. He looks down at Ellen's hand holding his hand. He studies the shapes of her fingers, he studies the lines running and splitting, the map of a country. It is all in the details, he thinks, the world underneath. It shimmers and waits. It is right there.

Beyond the window, a woman is calling her child. He can hear her voice, now louder, now fainter. The radio blares from a passing car. The world never stops.

With a sigh, Ellen lets go of his hand, and her own hand falls to her side. She turns to him. The world is branching again. What would she say to him? He remembers the damp smell of her hair that night they went to hear Schubert, the blend of lily and fresh rain. He remembers how she wouldn't get out of her seat, she was so full of passion. I feel like he sees into my heart, she said. Perhaps that is what she would say. See into my heart. Is that a way through?

The air is denser there. He strains to see something, to see again what he saw then. It was so fleeting, so quick. Is something true if it happens only once? If it is experienced only by one person at one time? The seconds and years stretch to infinity, but a thing might be felt only at one moment. It might always be there, the world underneath and the miracle, but felt only in brief, fleeting stabs. Another voice from the street. Suddenly, he feels very tired, despite the early hour, and leans back in his chair. There will always be that line between them, Ellen and him. But here she is beside him. Outside the glass window, a cloud skates over the sun, the light dims with a rush, the light blooms again. Yes, he thinks, it is like that. Did Ellen notice? In just a brief moment, something happened. Did Ellen notice? He wants to tell her. This instant, this light falling, this table, this chair, it is all more than it seems. But how can he put the thing into words.

how much time did you
waste on This?

ACKNOWLEDGMENTS

A deep gratitude to Charlie and Susan Dee of Dee Funeral Home for many meetings and discussions. To John Zaffis of the Paranormal Research Society of New England. To LaRose Coffey, high school teacher of long ago, for her insightful comments on the developing manuscript. To Lucile Burt and Janet Silver for their good critiques in the final stages. To my literary agent and friend, Jane Gelfman, for her continuing encouragement over the years. To my excellent and encouraging editor and friend, Dan Frank. And finally, with love and appreciation, to my wife, Jean, and daughters, Elyse and Kara.

Alan Lightman is the author of four previous novels, two collections of essays, and several books on science. His novel *Einstein's Dreams* (1993) was an international bestseller, and his novel *The Diagnois* (2000) was a finalist for the National Book Award. His writing has appeared in *The New York Review of Books, The New Yorker, The Atlantic Monthly, Harper's, Nature,* and many other publications. A Ph.D. in physics, he has taught astronomy and physics at Harvard and MIT and is currently adjunct professor of humanities at MIT.

A NOTE ON THE TYPE

This book was set in Albertina, the best known of the typefaces designed by Chris Brand (b. 1921 in Utrecht, The Netherlands). Issued by The Monotype Corporation in 1965, Albertina was one of the first text fonts made solely for photocomposition. It was first used to catalog the work of Stanley Morison and was exhibited in Brussels at the Albertina Library in 1966.

Composed by Creative Graphics,
Allentown, Pennsylvania

Printed and bound by R. R. Donnelley,
Harrisonburg, Virginia

Designed by M. Kristen Bearse